α
BOTTLE OF RUM

ALSO BY STEVE GOBLE

The Bloody Black Flag

The Devil's Wind

A BOTTLE OF RUM

A Spider John Mystery

STEVE GOBLE

SEVENTH
STREET
BOOKS®

Published 2019 by Seventh Street Books·

Cover design by Jennifer Do
Cover illustrations © Shutterstock
Cover design © Start Science Fiction

This is a work of fiction. Characters, organizations, products, locales, and events portrayed in this novel either are products of the author's imagination or are used fictitiously.

Inquiries should be addressed to
Start Science Fiction
101 Hudson Street
37th Floor, Suite 3705
Jersey City, New Jersey 07302
PHONE: 212-431-5455
WWW.SEVENTHSTREETBOOKS.COM

10 9 8 7 6 5 4 3 2 1

978-1-64506-003-1 (paperback) | 978-1-64506-009-3 (ebook)

Printed in the United States of America

This one is for Tom Williams,
even though he suggested calling this book
"Beyond the Lowering Sun," for some damned reason

I

AUGUST 1723

"Pirating wasn't so bad, Spider John," Odin said, his voice hushed as he lifted a small wooden horse from the board. "Maybe we could go back to that. Remember? We could walk about on the deck in the fresh air, instead of sulking in the shadows and hurrying from one doorway or alley to the next, like fucking rats hiding from a cat."

He plunked the knight—a nicely carved bit of wood Spider hoped to replicate one day if they ever got a chance to stop running for their lives—onto the board. "Ha!"

They sat in the darkest corner of the common room, drinking and playing chess as though they had never been cutthroats on the Spanish Main, as though the king's men were not seeking them, as though the gallows would never claim them. For a few moments, Spider John Rush had even felt a bit defiant, sitting here drinking among landsmen. But they were, after all, staying to the shadows and keeping their heads low to hide their faces. And Spider still took care to keep his maimed left hand, missing the small finger, away from spying eyes. He himself tended to notice small details, and he did not need anyone remembering encountering a buccaneer, shorter than average, missing a finger, and traveling with a frightening one-eyed son of a bitch.

That would not do at all.

They were still pirates, even though they were trying to flee that life. If they were caught, the Admiralty would not care about their current intentions or declarations of remorse. The Admiralty would judge them by the bloody things they'd done in the past and listen to

7

some preacher read from the Bible while the executioner looped nooses over their cursed heads.

"Aye," Spider answered, muttering in equally quiet tones and waving away a bit of curling candle smoke that stung his eyes. "We were as free as the fish in the sea, you and me and all the other lads, except the fish could swim right into any civilized port they chose and we could not. And we were only free until we ran out of food, or fresh water, or we needed a new mast or new sail, or a few new hands to replace the poor souls that lost their lives the last time we ran out of such things. Then we went and found someone who had what we needed, and we took it from them—and sometimes we took a lot more."

Spider inhaled deeply from his pipe and blew a great cloud into Odin's ugly face. The old man blinked his one remaining eye, and Spider continued. "And then we went back into hiding on the Spanish Main and drank heavy in hopes we'd forget what we'd done. And now we sit here, hiding our faces from anyone who might be on the hunt for an ugly mariner and his much smarter and handsomer shipmate."

He sucked at the pipe again. "Not so free, I reckon. Not free at all."

"Aye," Odin muttered. "It was a rough life, I grant you that, but we had fresh air and sun. Do we have the better of it now, Spider John? Are any of the fellows in here waiting for us to leave, so they can follow us and rob us? Has the lady back in the kitchen sent for the authorities, because she thinks maybe we are suspicious gents?"

"She is a fine woman, Odin, truly," Spider said. "She'll not turn us in, though we look rough and talk rough. She's dealt with us fairly, I say. I doubt I can say the same for her husband, though. He's the type might sell us to the Admiralty, proof or no."

Spider understood his friend's feeling. He did not feel free sitting in a Lymington tavern, either. Luck and circumstances had landed them here, not thought and planning. He always felt more at ease at sea, where he could see enemies coming across the waves and prepare, and where he always had a crew of men on his side who had no more wish to die than he had. Strength in numbers, old Bent Thomas had always preached.

Here, it was just Spider and Odin. Here, a sneaky bastard with a dirk could easily step from an alley and slit his throat. That's why he'd taken the seat against the wall, and that's why his right hand dropped to his belt every thirty heartbeats or so, to make sure he could find his knife at the first sign of trouble.

The shipmates ignored the noises around them—although Spider remained alert for the sounds of press gangs outside—and they were careful not to meet anyone's gaze. That was easy enough, until the tavern owner bellowed from the table he shared with a tall ruffian Spider had seen here a time or two before. All eyes raised when Thomas Bonnymeade bellowed at a scraggly gent who approached, hat in hand, and asked a question.

"Agatha, for the love of God, come tell this man the price of a pint and a sausage pie! I am engaged here!"

It was an impressive roar, the only real talent Spider had ever seen the man display in their short time here at the Crosskeys.

The man who'd interrupted Bonnymeade and his mean-looking friend stepped back and bowed, then turned around to look for the owner's wife.

Bonnymeade and the ruffian went back to their quiet discussion as Spider watched them. Bonnymeade scratched mutton-chop whiskers and breathed like a fat seal giving birth. The other man had the darting eyes of a thief, and the odor of a stable clung to him.

Spider looked up from the chessboard, drank the last swig of rum in his small leather flask, and glared at the tavern keeper. He had already developed an intense dislike of the lazy proprietor.

"Scallywag has not done a lick of work since we arrived," Spider whispered to his companion.

"Well, he's got his wife to do it all. Ha!" Odin's one eye went wide, and he leaned his ugly, ancient face out over the board. In the dancing candle-flicker the crusty scars left by the long-ago blast that had claimed Odin's right eye gleamed a fiery red. Spider, despite the growing friendship between himself and this old man and shipmate, shuddered. When looking at Odin, Spider could not help but think of witches. That thought always stirred up memories of his dead Gram, hung near Salem after a witchcraft trial, and of his dead friend, Ezra, whose own family had been tarnished with a reputation for devil dealing. Odin himself had never made any witch claims, of course— the old bastard had never revealed any family history or even his real name to Spider—but the scarred face, limp and thinning gray-white hair, and long thin fingers conjured witch thoughts in Spider's mind.

Odin hemmed and hawed for a moment, then pointed at the knight he had dropped on a central square. "Have you noticed my little horse, Spider John, all ready to gallop and stomp your puny king? Pay attention to the game. We've wagered a bottle of rum, remember, and I am powerfully thirsty."

"Neither of us can pay for a bottle of rum, Odin."

The slam of a door caught Spider's attention. Predictably, Thomas Bonnymeade's hollering had brought his wife scurrying from the kitchen, a platter of beef and bread in her hands. "Who is it, then? Oh, sir, hello. Have a seat if you please, and I will be back in just a moment. And you'll have a jack of ale for your wait, on the house."

Her husband glared at her, but Mrs. Bonnymeade ignored him. The entire time she spoke, she kept moving toward a corner table where three men rolled dice. They suspended their game briefly when they caught the aroma of roast beef. Spider caught it, too, and his belly rumbled a bit.

The newcomer found an empty table and sat alone as Mrs. Bonnymeade placed the platter before the dice players. "Here you go, gentlemen, hot as can be." Then she hastened to arrange a meal for the new customer, instructing the girl in the kitchen, while her husband continued his conversation with his surly companion.

"Bastard sits and talks to comers and goers all day, while she cooks and cleans and does everything else," Spider said.

"Aye," Odin said. "And are you not hoping to get back to your own lovely woman in Nantucket and make her do the same for you? Ha!"

"I am not so lazy," Spider said. "But I'll duck out of washing the clothes, by thunder!"

Odin laughed. "Bonnymeade reminds me of some cap'ns I have known, loving to bark but not sullying their hands with any labor. Are you going to play or ought I just topple your goddamned king now?"

Spider's gaze returned to the board. He had been studying its construction of oak and maple more than the game itself, with the eye of a ship's carpenter. He hoped to create a box and board Odin could keep and carry, and so his attention had been on the carved pieces and the box the set had been housed in, with its elegant little drawer for all the pieces and the ornate royal figures carved into its top. Spider had no doubt he could replicate the box and the drawer, but he envied the artistry of the master carver who had engraved the figures into the lid, and the steady hand that had brought the black and white figures arrayed on the board to life. One day, when he wasn't running from the law or dodging cutlasses and musket balls, he'd produce such treasures himself, while Em brought him jugs of small beer and Little Johnny asked him to impart such skills to him.

One day.

Spider shook those thoughts off and focused on the game. His lack of attention to tactics had put him in a sore spot. He reached for the rum, remembered his flask was empty, and growled. "I think you cheat, Odin."

"I think you let your mind wander," Odin said, grinning. "You always have too much in your thoughts, Spider John. It all gets tossed about, flotsam drifting across your brain."

"Aye." Spider tried to focus on the game. Half a minute later, he glanced up as Thomas Bonnymeade's companion left the tavern, allowing some of the night's chill to enter as he passed through the door, and the fat innkeeper finally moved away from his table, fingers drumming on his rotund belly. The man headed upstairs without a word to his wife, who brought Spider and Odin some cheese and bread.

"Mister Davies and Mister Hughes," she said, addressing them by the false names they'd given her rather than the names they'd sailed under as pirates, "this is for you, and I am sorry it took so long." She placed the platter on the table, then fixed the scarf that kept her gray hair under control. "I hope you enjoy this. The beef is all gone, I'm afraid, but we've another roast on the spit if you can wait."

She picked up Odin's empty jack. "Another ale for you, sir?" She glanced at Spider. "And did I see you dribble the last from your flask?"

"Aye," Spider said. "But you know we can't pay."

"Codswallop," she said, laughing. "Mister Davies, you did such a fine job on those stairs, they don't even creak under my man's weight. You spoke true, Mister Hughes, when you said your friend was a master carpenter. Food and board is yours until you find a berth somewhere, don't you worry. I'll return with ale and rum in a blink."

Spider watched her go. She was a large woman, but she expertly dodged between tables and guests and the fiddler who played softly, more for his own enjoyment than anyone else's. Spider looked around the common room; the door to the kitchen hung a bit crooked, and more than one table wobbled badly. He could easily make some repairs to repay her kindness to wandering sailing men, if only he could afford to tarry here.

"Caw! Caw!"

Spider jumped at the sound, rising completely from his seat, and covered his face with his arms. He spun quickly, peering between his forearms for the crow or parrot or macaw that had cried out. He looked into the rafters, at every window, and on every table, but saw no bird—no sharp beaks, no scratchy talons, no dead soulless eyes.

Odin's quiet laughter caught Spider's attention.

"Odin, you seal-humping bastard."

"Ha!"

"You cried out like a bird!"

Odin's shoulders quaked. "I could not help it! If you're not going to play chess, I must have my fun some other way. Ha!"

"I wish you would fly away, old crow." Spider sat, scowling. His hatred—nay, fear—of birds was a constant amusement for his shipmate. Spider himself knew the terror to be unwarranted—he had never actually seen a bird do anything to harm a man, woman, or child—but that did not make the fear vanish.

If the other drinkers had noticed the prank, they gave no indication. Spider sat and glared at Odin.

Mrs. Bonnymeade hustled by, placing a fresh jack of ale before Odin and a small wooden cup sloshing with rum before Spider. He caught the aroma, sharp and spicy, and licked his lips.

"There you be, gentlemen." Then Mrs. Bonnymeade crossed the room and climbed the newly mended stairs.

Spider took a bite of cheese and a drink of rum, then returned his attention to the game. Odin's only remaining knight had neatly forked Spider's king and queen. Spider glowered at Odin and shook his head. "I am not going to make you a board of your own after all, you goddamned whore-licking old pirate."

Odin chuckled. "Maybe I'll steal this board. It brings me luck."

Spider moved his king to safety then watched as Odin cackled and took Spider's queen from the board. "She's mine, all mine! I plan to steal all your women, Spider, even the wench in Nantucket! Ha! You can keep the boy, though!"

They played on, although Spider's heart was not in it and he stood no real chance of winning. He was about to resign the game when a cry erupted from above.

"Murder!"

It was Mrs. Bonnymeade's voice. As the word echoed down the dim stairwell, the second syllable stretched into an anguished wail. Other sounds died: the drone of a hornpipe scratched out on the badly tuned fiddle, the rattle of dice on oak tables, the animated laughter of slightly drunken men. Spider risked one quick peek from behind the wooden cup and was relieved to see that all eyes were looking up the stairs and toward that mournful cry, and not at him. Then he lowered his gaze so that the wide brim of his much-abused hat would hide his face from any curious onlookers who might happen to glance his way. He moved the candlestick a few inches further away, too.

"Do not, Spider John . . ." Odin said, adjusting his own hat.

"Do not what, Odin?"

The old man's reply was a ghostly whisper. "Do not scratch your damned itch to always figure out what goes on. Do not poke your ugly beak into this, do not rush to the lady's side, do not get us involved in this." Odin swirled his ale in its jack before taking a swig. "Remember the plan. It was your own plan after all, aye? Lay low. Pay attention to gabbing sailors, maybe head to Plymouth if we must, to find a ship bound for the colonies. Join up, pretend we're honest men . . ."

"We are honest men."

"Well. We've not been so for long, have we? But the plan, we set sail for Nantucket, find your woman and your boy. Remember?"

Spider gritted his teeth but said nothing. How long since he'd seen Emma and Little Johnny? Years and years. He reached to his chest and tapped the pendant hanging on a leather strip beneath his grimy shirt. He'd carved it for Em, and one day he'd place it in her hand.

Other men rose from their tables and moved slowly toward the staircase, at times blocking the light from the hearth so that shadows and bright firelight alternatively leapt and crawled across the common room. Men stared into one another's faces, asked fool questions and waited to see if someone would take command and rush up the stairs, where the horrible moaning had given way to great gasping sobs.

"Is that Missus Bonnymeade?"

"Aye! Should we help her?"

"Maybe she is drunk? I saw her quaff some wine."

Spider winced and looked at his friend.

Odin scowled and shook his head, slowly.

"I know," Spider said. "You are wise, Odin. It would be foolish to rush up there. But she has been kind to us."

"She is the one wailing, so she isn't dead."

"Aye, but . . ."

"But," Odin said, gritting his teeth. "It is nothing to do with us. All our crimes are in the past and far from here. This is not for us to fret over."

Odin was correct, of course. Spider knew it. It would not do to be recognized as pirates—former pirates, Spider reminded himself— especially when the word "murder" had been uttered. He was a stranger here in Lymington, but the town was big enough that it certainly had night watchmen, and there was a garrison nearby, so His Majesty's Naval officers could come mucking about. Whatever had happened upstairs was certain to draw official attention. He listened again for the sounds of an approaching press gang.

Spider did not want that, by thunder. They'd survived too many brushes with fate already; it was foolish to court more.

He and Odin had survived a trap sprung by pirates, and been marooned on a Caribbean isle. They had dodged many questions aboard the Brighton-bound schooner that had rescued them. They had artfully navigated the uncertain moments when some of *Redemption*'s survivors had told their rescuers a bit too much regarding how Spider and Odin and their young friend Hob—*may God save that foolish young wayward bugger*—had cleverly outwitted and fought off Ned Low's piratical brigands.

"Why, one might think John and his friends had spent considerable time among pirates," the dour Reverend Down had said, perhaps intending to stir up trouble, perhaps not. Either way, Spider had felt constant gazes on his back from that moment on and had noticed a distinct chill thereafter from the captain and crew.

Odin had confessed to the same concerns as they huddled in the cargo hold, wondering what the hell to do.

So once they knew *Fiddler's Dram*, their salvation ship, was bearing down on the Isle of Wight, Spider and Odin had stolen a boat and gone over the gunwale under cover of darkness the moment they judged land was close enough for an escape. They had had no time for farewells to the other *Redemption* castaways, and they certainly had no intention of waiting around to answer questions from the Royal Navy's fine fellows, by thunder. Fate had given them a chance to run, and they would not waste it.

It had been a longer row into the Solent than they had expected, with Wight's bulky shadow looming south of them and the ominous Hurst Castle and its array of big guns poised to the north, and a trickier coastline than either had expected, but eventually they found a small, suitable cove and tucked the boat away. Then, choosing to go east only because they saw the lights of a town, they had found their way by night along muddy roads to Lymington, a town neither of them knew.

Now, they sat in the Crosskeys, where half-drunk men sought some sort of courage in one another's faces while a woman sobbed upstairs. She forced the word out again. "Murder!"

The anguish in Mrs. Bonnymeade's voice clawed at Spider's heart.

"Goddamn it, fuck and bugger all," Spider muttered, his besieged black king forgotten. "Will no one help her?"

"Do not do it," Odin warned, quietly. "We are wanted, you and me, and this is none of our worry. Once these nice fellows remember they have balls, they'll go up . . . and we can slip away in the night and finds some other place to hide, some place without murders. Someone will be summoned here, no doubt, to settle this murder business, and you and I should be getting drunk somewhere else far away then, unless you do something stupid."

Odin pointed to Spider's cup, as if to remind him how much he liked a good quaff. "Worrying over other people's problems is for preachers and judges, not for pirates."

"Do not utter that word, Odin, but aye," Spider said. He got up and started up the stairs anyway, ignoring the excellent rum.

"Damned fool," Odin growled, before snatching up Spider's cup and chugging its contents. Then he yelled. "You are doing this to stop me winning a bottle of rum!"

Take care, Odin, Spider thought. *Bellowing might draw notice to your ugly face.* He did not turn to answer the man, though, for that might draw unwanted attention as well. He did, however, make a fist of his left hand to hide the fact of his missing finger, just in case anyone was on the lookout for a short, long-haired seaman maimed in such a way.

Spider rushed upward and soon heard his friend clambering up the steps behind him, stairs Spider had repaired just two days ago at Mrs. Bonnymeade's request.

Spider gained the second story, listened in the stairwell, then shot up another flight. Once there, he determined the wild sobs were coming from the end of the hall. He dashed that way.

Spider reached the room Mrs. Bonnymeade shared with her useless husband. He peered in through the open doorway and instantly knew Thomas Bonnymeade was not going to do any work, ever.

The man was lying on the floor, on his back, with a wood-handled knife jutting up from his neck. His horrified wife knelt in a growing pool of blood, sobbing wildly.

Odin glanced over Spider's shoulder. "Lazy sot, he was. I do not blame her a goddamned bit," he whispered.

"She didn't kill him," Spider snarled, rushing forward to put an arm around the terrified woman. "What happened, ma'am?" Behind him, he could hear the other men coming up the stairs, their footsteps pounding like drums in the narrow stairwell.

Mrs. Bonnymeade waved her hands over her dead husband, trying to talk but issuing only incoherent gasps. Spider, no stranger to violence, looked at the dead man with a dispassionate eye. The man was on his back, staring at the ceiling, and had only the one wound as far as Spider could discern. Someone had stabbed him in the neck, probably in an arc from below. Blood welled up around the knife's walnut handle and flowed freely from the wound.

"Fuck and bugger," Spider whispered, staring again at the knife. It was designed for throwing, not carving or working, and it had letters scratched into the handle. *Jesus*, Spider thought. *I know this knife.*

Spider pulled the weapon from the fat man's neck, shook blood from it and turned to the Widow Bonnymeade. "Did you see the killer?"

Mrs. Bonnymeade shook her head, then nodded, then shook it again and continued to make sounds only God could possibly understand. Spider examined the room and saw drops of blood on the floor between the corpse and the window, a few red smears among them. The splotches were the prints of a small boot, left by the killer after stepping in blood.

Good God, Spider thought. *Did a child kill this man?*

The gory trail led to the open window, where Spider noticed a wicked gash on the sill. He leapt toward it and gave it a closer look, after tearing himself away from Mrs. Bonnymeade's clutching hands.

That's a new scrape or I'm no carpenter.

Spider had seen many a fresh wound left by a grappling hook on a gunwale, and he'd seen bad wood give way under a hook as well. That is what appeared to have happened here. The killer had come in by the window, and likely escaped the same way. Whether the sill had given way before the killer reached the street or when the hook had been pulled away, there was no telling. Spider could see no one below the window.

"Bonnymeade went up from the common room not long ago, Spider, remember? Not a quarter of an hour past."

"Aye, Odin," Spider answered. "The murderer can't have gone far."

A quick glance out the window and to the right, toward the night-shrouded river that led down to the Solent, told him nothing, but when he looked to the left a lucky bit of light from a mounted torch showed him a running man vanishing between two darkened buildings. The fellow seemed hobbled, as though limping. Spider figured the hook had torn away the wood as the man descended, resulting in a hurt leg.

And I am about to try this without a goddamned rope.

Spider turned to Odin, who gawked at the bloody knife in Spider's hand. The gents from the common room appeared in the doorway at that very moment and stood there with mouths wide open.

"The killer went this way," Spider said to Odin. "I am going after him."

"What? Why the bloody fuck would you be doing that?" Odin's lone eye widened as far as the crusty scabbed skin would allow, and his expression was practically a shout to tell Spider how goddamned stupid that plan was.

"I'll answer later," Spider said, wiping the knife quickly on his breeches before tucking it into his belt. He sat on the sill and measured the distance to the outstretched post holding the Crosskeys' sign. It was to his right and below, jutting out like a bowsprit over the dirt road and the horse hitches.

It would not be an easy leap, but if he could gain that he could lower himself almost to the ground with a firm grasp on the swinging sign itself. He figured the post to be sturdy enough, and he was not a big man anyway. He steeled himself for the maneuver, cursing himself for taking so long to muster the courage. The killer was getting away, and Spider had some serious questions.

As a ship's carpenter by trade, Spider had spent years climbing rat-lines, walking across yardarms and clambering among the rigging high above a moving deck. *This won't be so hard, damn you, and you've got to do it. And if you fall, it won't kill you. Probably.*

He crouched on the sill, held his breath, and pushed off. He made it to the post easily enough, landing upon it in a crouch, but his hat flew from his head and he nearly lost his balance and toppled. His attempt to regain control left him straddled on the goddamned thing as though he was riding a horse, and it was only good fortune that let his arse take the brunt of that instead of his sack. But he did not fall.

He swung a leg over the beam and took a firm grasp on the edges of the sign—painted with two large keys crossed like dueling swords—and scrambled down, scraping his nose slightly on the rough wood. He ignored the splinter that stabbed into his calloused right hand and dropped the last few feet, quickly catching his balance after stepping on the killer's abandoned grapple and rope. Then he snatched up his hat and took off in pursuit of the man he'd seen.

Behind him, he heard cries of alarm, the ringing of bells, and a salvo of curses from Odin.

Spider dashed headlong after his prey, frantic. He did not have time to explain to Odin what spurred him onward. He did not give a damn for that fat lobcock Mr. Bonnymeade, who berated his kind wife nightly and drank almost as much rum as the Crosskeys sold. But Spider had to find out how this knife—this particular knife—had come to be in the bastard's neck.

For Spider had made this knife. He'd made it for Hob.

2

Running by the light of posted torches on a cloudy English night is no easy task, and Spider stumbled more than once—and leapt over a horse trough he'd almost missed seeing in the dark—before reaching the alley where he'd seen a man disappear. He crowded against the wall and winced as acrid chemical scents mingled with the more prominent odors of horses and manure and the sea. He was unable to read the sign above the heavy oak door, but he recognized the mortar-and-pestle symbol of an apothecary's shop.

Spider listened at the mouth of the alley. He had no flintlock, and no cutlass, but he had a knife that had already killed once this night along with his own precious throwing knife, the one he'd used as a model for Hob's knife. He also had experience. He'd never wanted to be a pirate, but that life had been forced upon him years ago and he'd learned to do the bloody work required to survive. So he held his breath, listened—and heard what sounded like someone working clumsily at a lock.

He peeked around the corner. A shadowy figure hunched over a door, probably a back entrance to the apothecary's shop. Metallic tinks and clinks echoed off the walls, punctuated by softly muttered curses. The voice did not sound like Hob's, to Spider's relief. The young fool was impetuous enough to have sailed off to go pirating with Anne Bonny, and liked the thrill of action, but surely he had not become a cold-blooded killer of fat taverners since Spider had seen him last. But if this cutthroat in the alley could lead Spider to Hob . . .

A glance back toward the Crosskeys told Spider a crowd had gathered in the road. Torches flickered in the street, and shouts rang out in the night. They were gathering to find the tavern keeper's killer, and no doubt some had mentioned they'd seen Spider John escape through the man's window, bloody blade in his hand.

Fuck.

The torches began moving toward him, and Spider calculated. Run away now, and he might not have to answer pesky questions—but he might also never learn how the knife he'd made for his young wayward friend had been used to commit a cowardly murder. And that meant he might never find Hob and drag the fool away from his dreams of pirate glory.

Spider decided.

He entered the alley, treading as softly as he could, until he figured he was close enough to his prey to reach him before the distracted fellow could draw a dirk or pistol. The man, uncommonly short, looked up and growled. "Damn and blast!"

The man reached into his coat, and Spider threw a knife—his own, not Hob's. The knife sailed over the short man's head as he aimed his pistol. But Spider got to his target before the man could fire, and he drove the cutthroat's head into the wall and tripped him backward onto his arse. The flintlock thunked on the cobblestones below. Spider stooped to scoop it up. He assumed it was already loaded and primed for action, so he pulled back the hammer and aimed at the man's shadowed face.

"You and I are going to talk," Spider said quietly. His left hand felt for the lock on the door, and found a skeleton key still inserted there. It took him only a moment to open the door even though he fixed his attention on the man on the ground.

"Rise," he told his captive, "and get inside. I might not hand you over to the authorities, but those people fast approaching most certainly will. If you answer my questions, you may go free."

"John?" The man rose, groggily, holding his head. "John Coombs? Damn and blast!"

"Fuck and bugger," Spider said, recognizing another false name he'd used in the past, as well as the voice of a detested former shipmate. "Little Bob Higgins, you black-hearted, buffle-headed son of an ugly whore!"

Spider grabbed the man by the collar and flung him through the door as the gleam of torches brightened the alley entrance.

3

*I*nside, Spider closed the door and shoved Little Bob backward in the darkness until something blocked the way. It was a shelf, apparently, and it nearly toppled. A beaker or flask plunged and shattered on Little Bob's head, spraying Spider's face and chest with sticky fluid and bits of glass.

"Damn and blast!"

Spider aimed the barrel of the flintlock at Little Bob's curse and poked it like a spear. It had been an act of guesswork, as they struggled with one another in the darkness and Little Bob stood less than four feet tall. But Spider's aim had been true, and Little Bob stopped cursing, his mouth full of gun barrel.

"I don't suppose I'll miss from this range, do you?" Spider blinked fluid from his eyes. "Now you hush, and I'll hush, and we'll let the nice mob go look elsewhere for the murderer. Then you and I will have a talk."

Little Bob said nothing, but the motion of his nodding head confirmed for Spider that the gun was still in his captive's mouth.

Minutes passed as the shouts outside diminished and the ruckus they'd made in breaking into the shop drew no attention from deeper within. Spider wished he had a light, but one hand was busy holding the considerably smaller Little Bob Higgins against the shelf, while the other gripped the pistol.

So they conversed in darkness.

"Where is Hob?"

Little Bob made incomprehensible sounds, and Spider withdrew the weapon with a hard yank that scraped teeth and elicited an oath from Little Bob. "My fucking tongue, John, Jesus!"

"You've no right to call on the Lord," Spider said. "Nor have I." He repeated his question once the gun was jabbing Bob's neck beneath his bearded chin. "Where is Hob?"

"I know not," Little Bob answered. "I swear."

"You had his knife."

"What knife?"

"Do not play games, you shit-sucking worm," Spider growled. "You are useless to me unless you can answer my questions, and I never liked you anyway. So talk, or die here. Your choice."

Little Bob slumped against the shelf. "I have no notion of what you mean, John, none at all."

"You murdered Tom Bonnymeade, and you did it with the knife I gave Hob. I know he sailed off with that damned Bonny woman, and last I knew you were chained up in the orlop of *Redemption*, which she stole from us, so you sailed off with her, too. Now here you are murdering a lazy fat man with Hob's knife. Explain, or I shall gladly pull the trigger and rid the world of you."

"If I talk, will you set me free? Shipmates, we were, though not friends. Worth something, aye?"

Spider's knee caught Bob's stomach, hard. "Just answer me."

Once Bob stopped heaving, he talked.

"Well, then, John, Cap'n Bonny divided her small fleet and sent some of us off to do some smuggling ashore. Tobacco and rum and molasses, you see, pilfered from enterprises here and there. We was to sell it, make future arrangements, perhaps recruit some hands if we could find some stout lads."

"You brought smuggled goods ashore here, and Hob came with you?"

"Aye," Bob answered. "He didn't want to leave her, Cap'n Bonny, I dare say, but I think she tired of the whelp and she sent him along. Like a puppy, he was. We put in not far from here, small cove, sweet quiet spot. Cap'n had sent a pair of gentlemen ahead to make arrangements, and we was to meet up. Some fellow she'd worked with before, we heard."

Spider did not care about a smuggling operation. "Is Hob nearby?"

"John, I did not murder anyone."

Spider did not care about that, either. He tightened his grasp on Little Bob's shirt. Though not a large man, Spider was quite strong, and he nearly lifted his adversary off his feet. "Your crimes are of no concern to me. Where is Hob?"

"We were double-crossed, John. Set upon. Damn and blast, a horror it was! Smoke and flashes, not gun flashes, more like little bombs they chucked at us. It was like long nines judging by the light and the booms. Like a cannon going off against your ears. Those not killed were blind from light and smoke, and coughing. Then we were rushed, outmanned. Swords and guns, then, it was, but us choking on smoke and still blind. We had no chance."

"What are you talking about?"

"They killed some of us, aye, most of us, but rounded some men up and took them. Three or four. I was small enough to hide, you see, and so escaped their notice."

"Cowardly enough to hide, you mean. They took Hob?"

"Aye, and others. But Hob was one of the men taken. I am sure of that. I saw him lifted into a wagon."

"Dead?"

"No, he was kicking but they had the better of him and was tying him up."

"Who took them? Why?"

He never heard an answer. In the darkness, Spider never saw the jar arcing toward his face. But he felt the impact, heard the crash and the tinkle of breaking glass, and smelled the acrid odor. A splash of fluid stung his eyes and burned his skin as Little Bob shoved Spider backward. Spider fell. He fired the flintlock, throwing sparks, but the powder failed to ignite.

Little Bob laughed like a madman, and Spider hurled the useless gun at the sound. The weapon vanished somewhere in the darkness, rattling across the floor.

Spider heard the door slam as he rolled to his feet, wondering if it was glass shards or a chemist's foul acid that clawed so violently at his eyes.

He ran toward the door, or at least where memory told him the door was, but slipped on the wet floor. He fell like a mast hit at just the right spot by a cannoneer's ball.

4

*H*e found the door by touch-and-feel and stumbled into the alley. His boot brushed against something, and he knelt until his fingers found the familiar coarseness of his timeworn hat. He plopped it onto his head, then removed it quickly after it scraped the stinging cut on his brow.

Heedless of witnesses or watchmen, Spider felt his way along the alley wall as quickly as he could. The foul fluid blinded him and stung his flesh.

The trough!

He staggered toward the trough that had almost tripped him and took his best guess as to its location, praying it was not empty. His knee thudded into it, and Spider plunged his tormented face into the chilly water. He forced himself to open his stinging eyes in hopes of flushing whatever the hell it was burning them.

Spider pulled his head out with a gasp, shook it furiously, then took a deeper breath this time and plunged his face into the trough again. He had not yet determined whether the dousing had cleared his eyes of the foul liquid when someone grabbed his collar and jerked him upward.

His hand was on Hob's knife at his belt when he heard Odin's growl. "It is me, you filthy shabbaroon!"

Spider spat water onto his beard and coughed.

"If you be thirsty, Spider John, let's find better and stronger drink. Smells as though horses pissed in this more than they drank. Ha! Come!"

Spider, still shaking water from his eyes and unable to see, let Odin lead him down the road. "Thank you, friend. I'll owe you a bottle of rum."

"You already owe me a bottle of rum, for the game."

"We didn't finish the game."

"Oh, the game was done. We were still making moves, but the game was done. I won."

Spider laughed, coughing up trough water.

"This town sets a watchman in this neighborhood, I've learned, but I sent him and the search party in the wrong direction," Odin said. "People are fond of your blessed Missus Bonnymeade, however, so they've volunteers aplenty searching. They went all about. Some came your way."

"They think I killed her husband?"

"Some of those lobcocks thought so, aye, but your Missus Bonnymeade told them you chased after the killer. Some of them believed her, I think. Some of them think you are screwing her and the two of you killed the fat son of a whore. I told them that was a fool notion, but I don't think they believed me. And you've got the bastard's blood on your breeches, you know. And the knife."

"Well," Spider said, the stinging in his eyes subsiding somewhat. He could see dancing orange dots he assumed were torches in the distance. He tried the hat again, as proof against the chill on his wet hair, and winced as the cut stung anew.

"You weren't screwing her, were you, Spider John?"

"No!"

"Because I was a wee bit behind you getting to him, and he was dead and you beside him when I . . ."

"Jesus!"

"Well, you are damned clever sometimes and you hated Bonnymeade and seemed to like her. So, well, I thought maybe you and the woman might have schemed together . . ."

"I did not kill the man, Odin, by thunder! I am the one who wants to leave all the killing behind, aye? Remember? Former pirate!"

"Aye," Odin said. "Why did I find you trying to bathe in horse water?"

"Little Bob hit me with something, burned at my eyes."

"Little Bob! That tiny bastard? He's here? Where? I'll kill him."

"I think he killed Mister Bonnymeade," Spider said. "No, belay that. I'm certain he did, I should say. I caught up to him, dragged him into a shop, chemist's, apparently, and he clobbered me with a bottle of . . . I do not know what was in it. It stung my eyes. It feels better now, a tad. Little Bob escaped."

"Well, you've a gash on your forehead, but you won't likely die from it. Might catch illness, I suppose, but it is not deep and you won't lose a lot of blood."

"I can actually see a bit now," Spider said, freeing himself from Odin's strong grasp. He handed his friend the murder weapon. "When we are under that torch, give this blade a look."

Shouts in the distance indicated the killer had not yet been found. Spider and Odin paused beneath a pole-mounted torch and the one-eyed sailor examined the knife. "Ha! You made this for Hob, aye? Throwing knife? That's his name carved here, Hob, right?"

"Aye," Spider answered. "Or so the fellow who showed me the letters said, and Hob never said it was wrong. I made it, the handle, I mean, and I got a blacksmith to forge the blade using the French knife you gave me as a guide. Fuck. I just lost that knife."

"I stole that one, I can steal you another one," Odin said. "So . . . how's that boy's blade end up in Little Bob's hands and in Bonnymeade's fat neck?"

Spider shook water from his beard and reached beneath his hat to touch the gash in his forehead. He'd have a new scar, for certain, but the bleeding seemed to have stopped. "Let us go ask Missus Bonnymeade, Odin. I'll wager a bottle of rum . . ."

"Belay that," Odin scoffed. "You never pay up anyway, do you?"

5

"**M**ister Davies! Mister Hughes!"

Spider and Odin bowed upon hearing Mrs. Bonnymeade greet them. Several men moved to confront them but stopped rigid when they saw a knife in Odin's hand.

The widow looked aghast at Spider's scratched face and drenched shirt and grabbed a cloth from the bar. The common room drinkers, five of them, gave her leeway as she toddled to Spider and removed his hat. She began wiping his forehead. "Did you catch the blackguard, Mister Davies?"

"I had him in my grasp," Spider said, "but he slipped away. I am sorry."

Her jaw quivered as her eyes widened. "Who? Who killed my Tom?"

"A pirate and a smuggler," Spider said. "A filthy pirate."

"Why?" She wiped a tear on her sleeve. "Why?"

"I will tell you in a moment," Spider said, noting he had the full attention of several men drinking nearby.

"So brave of you chasing after the evil man so. You are a good man." Then she took a deep breath and whispered. "You would not believe what some of these fools are thinking."

"I have heard," he said. "They saw me standing near him with a dripping dirk. So they think I killed him."

"They think you and I were . . ."

"It's all talk," Spider said, eyeing the men across the room. "If we can catch the killer, we can make him tell the truth."

The men gathered around them. "These gents say they saw you with a knife while Thomas Bonnymeade was still spurting," said one tall fellow, clearly in his cups. "and then you fled." His eyes had something of a hawk's essence in them, and Spider recognized him as the man who earlier had sat with Bonnymeade, over much whispering and ale.

"And then I came back here," Spider said. "Fool thing if I killed him, aye?"

"Maybe you had a reason to come back." He glanced at Mrs. Bonnymeade.

Spider strode toward him and stared hard into his eyes. He had to look upward, being short, but Spider was accustomed to that. "You want to accuse me of killing him, do you?"

The man gulped, and stood his ground, but said nothing.

Odin moved away from Spider. *Good*, Spider thought. *These fellows will have more than one direction to watch if they truly want to start something.*

Mrs. Bonnymeade tried to douse the rising heat. "Mister Davies did not kill my husband, Bill. I know that."

"Can you be certain, Aggie?" Bill looked at her. "He's a rough-looking sort, and a stranger."

"You are not so handsome yourself, Bill," Mrs. Bonnymeade said, her voice still shaky. "And a missing finger and weathered face don't make a man a bad man. Mister Davies, and Mister Hughes, too, both were at their chess when I went upstairs not long after Tom, and they were still downstairs when I found him dead. So Mister Davies, bless him, wasn't the one who killed him. Nor was Mister Hughes." She began sobbing again, quietly.

Bill backed away but gave Spider a hard look. "Odd that trouble comes on the heels of these two, I think."

"More trouble might come if you don't get a lot smarter real soon," Spider said quietly.

"There be five of us," Bill said, his hawk's gaze narrowing, "and but two of you."

"Ha!" Odin laughed, as though Bill had told a joke.

"I can count," Spider said, taking note of which men had knives tucked into their belts. "And I am not worried."

Bill backed off, and the other gents followed him to a far table. They sat. "More small beer, Aggie, if you please."

"No, gentlemen, I'll not be serving more ale," Mrs. Bonnymeade said. "My God, my husband just dead and you want beer! Home with the lot of you, please."

They all left slowly, looking disappointed and suspicious. Spider studied their faces.

"I don't think they like you much. Ha!"

"They don't like you any more than they like me, Odin," Spider answered.

"Nobody likes me, save for you and dead Blackbeard. Ha!"

Mrs. Bonnymeade resumed mopping blood from Spider's forehead, and he winced as the cloth crossed his wound. "Those men are . . . well, ignore them. Thank you for chasing the villain. You are hurt, and all sopping. Did he flee to the river?"

Spider took the cloth from her and pressed it to his head himself, tossing his hat onto a table. "I am sorry I let him escape. Did you get a look at the killer, Missus Bonnymeade?"

"Aggie. You've a right to call me Aggie," she said. "No, I did not see him! I was in the next room. I heard a thump, or a thud, and I ran to see if Tom had fallen again. He drinks and he falls, he does. I mean, he did." Her jaw quivered. "What will I do?"

Odin sat at the table with the neglected chessboard, mumbling to himself.

"Perhaps a good sleep, Mrs. Bonnymeade," Spider suggested, "then morning light might make things clear."

"No. No sleep. I must keep myself busy. So much to do, and now no Tom. Sit, Mister Davies, sit. I'll fetch you gentlemen some ale. You've earned it." She rushed off before Spider could object, and he heard her muttering again, "so much to do, and no Tom!"

Spider sat across from Odin. "I do not recall seeing Thomas Bonnymeade do a damned thing around here but drink and talk, do you?" Spider picked up his clay pipe, next to the board.

"No, he's a fat sot, is all he is. Was." Odin pulled a leather pouch of tobacco from somewhere within his muslin shirt and handed it to Spider. The latter emptied the dottle onto the floor, filled his pipe, used a candle to fire it to life, and inhaled deeply. Once he'd blown a cloud toward the rafters, he looked at Odin.

"Little Bob escaped before I could learn anything of Hob," he said.

Odin lifted his jack, found it empty, and cursed.

"Bob said him and Hob and some others got sent off to smuggle some goods, and were waylaid." Spider inhaled again, then spoke around the pipe clamped in his teeth. Curling smoke surrounded his words. "He said Hob was taken by the crew that jumped them."

Odin shook his head. "Taken? Why?"

"I do not know."

Odin sighed. "I know you are fond of the lad. So am I. Ha! Hob's a fine fellow in a fight, bold as they come, and a funny, randy little shit. Handy at pilfering tobacco and rum for us, too, he was. Ha! But he left us marooned and ran off with that red-haired bitch Anne Bonny on his own, no fault of yours or mine if he listens to his tallywags instead of his shipmates. And he'd tasted enough pirating to know what he was going to find, Spider. I don't think you ought to go looking for him. I don't even know that he wants you to."

"Aye," Spider said. "I ought to forget him. Find us some honest work—no more piracy for you and me, by thunder!—and set sail for Nantucket." He had been trying to get back to Em and his son ever since he'd been given the choice long ago: join the pirate marauders who'd attacked *Lily* or go overboard with the rest of her crew. He'd lost count of the years since that dark day.

But he could not shake Hob from his mind. Hob had been a boy when he and Spider had met aboard *Plymouth Dream*, and all but a man by the time Spider had watched *Madeliene Robin* slip below the horizon with Hob aboard. The young fool was too full of pirate glory dreams, and too besotted with Anne Bonny, to remain as an island castaway with Spider and the rest. So he'd snuck off.

Odin was right. Hob had been responsible for his own actions and was smart enough to know the risks. And yet here Spider sat, trying to figure out a way to find the buffle-headed fool and drag him away from the pirate life.

Mrs. Bonnymeade returned with a platter. "Ale, and some more good cheese, and a flask. Whisky. I know you like your whisky, Mister Davies." She tried to sound casual, but a current of emotion flowed beneath her controlled voice.

"Thank you," Spider said. "Join us. You could use a drink, I reckon."

She sat, and Spider caught a pungent hint of port on her breath. "I have been at a bottle a bit, but, yes," she said.

"We are sorry you lost your husband," Spider told her.

She nodded silently. "I want to know why. I must know why."

They each took a swig from the flask, then Spider looked at Mrs. Bonnymeade. "I have a notion as to why. Please don't mind me asking, but I want to find your husband's killer, just as you do, so I'll ask. What did your husband do around here?"

She looked confused. "I do not know what you mean."

"He didn't fix the stairs, and they'd needed work for years. He didn't cook, nor clean, nor pour ale, nor do anything, as far as I could tell. A man came in tonight asking for ale and a sausage and your man didn't even know what to charge him. Had to ask you, he did. So . . . why do you worry about having more to do with him gone?"

"Well," she said, then paused to take another swig. "Well, there's . . . I'll have to . . . I mean . . ." She thought hard and took another drink. "I've a dead husband up there, don't I? I'll have to arrange a procession, and a funeral. I'll need to mend my black skirt, it's got a tear or two in it. Oh, so much to do . . ."

And no Tom, she'd said earlier.

"Did he do any work around here?" Spider took the flask and drank from it. He handed it to Odin, who gave him an evil stare.

"He was a businessman, not one for labor," she said. "A thinker and a planner. He arranged for kegs and food for the larders, mostly."

Spider had overheard Mrs. Bonnymeade doing those things herself.

"And Tom did a bit of brokering for some of the carters. Finding men to haul things for merchants, and salt for shipping, because he knew so many carters. A lot of them drink here, they do."

"That fool Bill. I've seen him talking with your husband. He's a carter?"

"Yes, he is. He works with Tom a lot. Worked." She sobbed. "Worked."

"Why would someone want to kill your husband?"

She shook her head. "I have no idea at all. You said it was a pirate and a smuggler."

"Aye."

She gulped. "Well, they are killers, then, aren't they? Filthy murderers?"

Spider and Odin glanced at one another. They both had sailed with killers aplenty. "Aye," Spider answered. "Dirty thieves and killers. But they don't go climbing up into tavern windows to stab a man, not unless they have a strong reason. We need to reckon what that reason is."

She stared at him.

"Aggie," Spider said, "I talked a bit with the scoundrel before he got away from me. He spoke of smuggling."

Mrs. Bonnymeade grabbed the flask and tilted it up violently.

"You said your husband did some brokering."

Her eyes widened, but she said nothing.

"A tavern is a wonderful spot for smugglers and merchants to arrange matters. Am I right, Odin?"

"Aye," the man said, begrudgingly. "But it is a better place for getting drunk and minding your own goddamned business, I'd say."

Spider ignored that. "The killer told me he was with some smugglers, and they had made arrangements to sell some goods but got waylaid. Someone attacked them as they unloaded their merchandise. And now your husband is dead, by the hand of one of those smugglers. So, was your husband a smuggler, Mrs. Bonnymeade? Or did he buy their wares? Or help make arrangements ashore?"

She stared at Spider.

"Did he betray some smugglers, and that's why they stabbed him in the throat?"

6

"Mister Davies! Are you accusing..."

"Yes," Spider said. "I know I should not speak him ill, because it pains you, but I am accusing your husband of some sort of illegal enterprise, and suspecting he ran afoul of some very wretched souls, men who live by the gun and sword and who do not take kindly to being betrayed."

Odin's lone eye rolled to glance heavenward, for he and Spider fit that very description quite well.

Mrs. Bonnymeade missed Odin's expression, and stared at Spider. "Thomas did not tell me all of his business," she said. "Nor did I ask. It was his work, the planning and arranging of things."

"You manage the Crosskeys by yourself, with a couple of young ones to help with chores." Spider took a drink and enjoyed the burn as he swallowed. "You seem smart as paint, Missus Bonnymeade. I doubt much escapes your notice."

Her lips tightened.

"We won't tell anyone," Spider said. "Whatever your husband's business, well, let's just say my friend here and me probably have done worse. But we're changing our ways. We just want to find the man who did this to your husband, and the more you tell us the better."

"You just want to catch the killer," Odin said pointedly. "Not we. You."

"I, then," Spider growled, feeling the liquor and the rising tension.

"But if I am going to track him down, I need to know some things. What did your husband have to do with smuggling?"

Mrs. Bonnymeade took another swig, a deep one. "Why are you willing to help me? Tom was not friend to many. You and I have no long friendship. You seem a decent fellow, but . . . foul men often do. So . . . why should I trust you?"

Spider, growing impatient, leaned toward her. "I'll tell you true, I have my own reasons for finding your man's killer. I've a mystery of my own I am trying to solve. The man I wrestled with, the man who killed your Tom, stabbed him with my friend's knife."

He snatched up the blade and smacked it on the table. "This knife right here. I made it for my friend. And I found it deep in your husband's neck, and that means my friend is in trouble, and that means I am going to follow any thread I can until I can get my friend out of trouble."

He turned toward Odin. "And I'll do so, by thunder, with your old bones by my side or no."

Spider slammed his pipe back into his mouth and drew deep, while Mrs. Bonnymeade took another swig of booze. Odin glared at Spider but said nothing.

Their hostess put down the liquor and wiped her mouth, then stared at the hearth for a long time. "Thomas stored merchandise," she finally said, her shoulders slumping. "Goods came in by night, into our cellars, and other men came for them after time had passed. He had arrangements with warehouses, too, and with captains who could carry goods off to other ports if need be. Thomas made his coin from both ends, them bringing in the goods and them taking them away."

"Sounds like easy coin," Spider said.

She nodded slowly. "Crosskeys has been here forever, and Tom knew everyone. He made the connections, handled the goods, and the transactions, and arranged all with the carters. We made more coin from that than from custom here."

"It seems he dealt someone wrong, though," Odin muttered. "Got himself stabbed dead."

Mrs. Bonnymeade sobbed. "He knew fair dealing was his best protection. He prided himself on that, he did. He knew he was breaking laws, you see, getting goods past the customs house and all, but he thought himself a fair man. I don't think he was cheating. I truly do not." She wept silently.

"Well," Spider said. "Someone did not like him, and it was a smuggler that killed him, that much we know for certain. So perhaps in tracking down our friend, we might be able to bring your husband's killer to justice as well."

"Spider . . ." Odin's expression was a grim warning.

"A bit free with names are we now, you old sot?"

Odin grimaced. "Aye, I stumbled, but you already called me Odin in front of her, remember? And you've already showed our cards a bit without asking me now, didn't you? 'We've done worse,' you said. Ha! That was reckless, but hell, I get tired of pretending we are not pirates anyway."

"Former pirates," Spider reminded him.

"Hell, pirates or former pirates, it's all the same to the Admiralty, I reckon. Smugglers and murderers are not people we need to associate with, aye? They tend to draw official attention, aye? We were hoping to avoid that? Being former pirates?"

Mrs. Bonnymeade watched the two men stare at one another, their faces brightening in the glow of Spider's pipe as he inhaled deeply.

"It is Hob," Spider said. "You know that."

Odin sighed. "He chose his life."

"And I'm choosing to drag him out of it."

Mrs. Bonnymeade, confused, looked back and forth. "Who is Hob?"

"The friend I mentioned," Spider said. "A young lad, convinced he's too clever and brave to ever swing on a noose. Listen, my friends and I have had some misadventures. Been caught up in some rough stuff, not of our own will but because fate likes to piss on us. We are trying to leave all that behind us, and I want to take Hob away from all that as well. Odin—Mister Hughes, I should say—and I were among some folks marooned by pirates . . ."

"Goddamned cutthroats," Odin muttered, as though he had never been a cutthroat himself. The old man grabbed the flask.

"Goddamned cutthroats, by thunder." Spider closed his eyes for a second at the memory. "Anyway, Odin and I were stranded, but our friend Hob ran off with a woman pirate . . ."

"Goddamned Anne Bonny," Odin growled.

"Goddamned Anne Bonny," Spider agreed.

"Led Hob away by his pecker, she did. Pulled on that, she did, and Hob followed right along." Odin drank deeply.

"Save me a swig, by thunder, or I'll scrape your balls with a holystone!"

Odin glared at Spider a moment, then handed over the flask. "Ha!"

"You gentlemen are frightening me." Mrs. Bonnymeade shuddered. "You are frightening me."

Spider lowered his voice. "You've nothing to fear from us. You gave us a port when we needed it and did not ask a lot of questions. And I will add this, too. If we track down this bastard who knifed your man, we will deliver justice on him, we will. We owe you that much. We'll see the bastard hanged, or we'll see him die at our own hands. That's a promise."

"Justice," she muttered quietly.

"Aye," he said, nodding solemnly. "Either the king's justice, or . . . something quicker."

"I'll ask you to tell me afterward," she said, her lips shaking. "I'll not ask you what sort of justice took place."

Spider touched her hand. "Fair, that, and perhaps wise. You are accustomed to that, aye? Not asking a lot of fool questions? Your husband was a rough fellow, and while you seem a sweet sort, I reckon you have been around other rough fellows, too. They came in here to the Crosskeys, right? To do business with your husband? He was too lazy to go do his dirty work elsewhere, liked to sit here and drink and let the money come to him."

She nodded.

"You know some names, I suppose?"

"Aye. Well, a few. Bill, for one, the fellow who accused you."

"He brings goods in, or buys them?"

"He owns a couple of wagons, and hauls things for pay. It was him and his lads that usually would go to the cove and load up whatever came ashore and bring it here to the cellars or to a couple of other places Tom arranged, and they would take messages back and forth between Tom and the smugglers, or between Tom and the merchants."

"Have you any reason to think Bill and his lads would be angry at your husband? Enough to kill him?"

She shook her head. "Lord, no. They all made good coin off the smuggling, and Tom was a lazy tub but he knew enough to keep those fellows happy."

Spider drained the whisky. "Who else did your husband do enterprises with? Are you certain he did not cheat someone?"

"I do not believe him to be that much of a fool," she answered. "Lazy, aye, but not a fool. He knew these were rough people."

Spider looked at Odin, who did not look happy. "Maybe his hand was forced, Aggie. These people do not make pleasant deals. Perhaps he didn't betray the gents out of greed but did it with a gun to his head or a knife to his throat. Whatever may be, though, Little Bob said the smuggling party was waylaid. Ambushed. Fellows armed with big guns or bombs or something, lots of flash and smoke and noise. So it was no whim or lark, but a planned attack."

"Aye," Odin said. "Still not our affair."

Spider ignored that. "Little Bob said the attackers took some men away with them. Now why would they do that? Steal the goods, aye, that I can understand. Kill witnesses, certainly. But why carry men away?"

"Perhaps they wanted to drag them off on some goddamned fool errand that would probably lead to a noose, Spider."

"I thought you liked a good fight, Odin."

"I am getting old. Ha!"

"Aye. You survived life on the account longer than anyone I've ever heard of," Spider said. "Sailed with Blackbeard, sailed with Ned Low.

Maybe you've tempted fate enough, though. I won't ask you to come with me, but I am going to find Hob if I can."

They stared at one another as Mrs. Bonnymeade's head whipped back and forth like a flag in a changing wind. Finally, Odin shrugged.

"I think Hob owes me a shilling, come to think of it. Or a bottle of rum. We always bet that stake, aye? And I've beat him at chess more than I've beat you. I might not ever see that bottle unless I go fetch it. And you'll just get yourself killed without me around to remind you to prime your pistol."

Spider smiled. "I don't have a pistol. Neither do you."

"I'll steal us a pair."

"Come with me and I really will give you a bottle, Odin." Spider slapped the table. "Well, then. Missus Bonnymeade . . ."

"Aggie."

"Aggie, then. Smugglers got waylaid, some got carried off, and one of them killed your man because of it."

"Perhaps it was a press gang, snatching up hands for the king's ships," she said.

"They do that in taverns, not lonely coves," Spider answered. "And have you heard any talk of such?"

"No," she said.

"Well, then, these men were not pressed."

Odin nodded. "They blamed Bonnymeade, thought he talked."

Spider scratched his head. "Aye, but who did he talk to? Rival smugglers, perhaps? Did your husband have competition?"

Mrs. Bonnymeade shook her head. "Tom spread the work around, he did, trying to keep all the gentlemen happy. There are different bands of them, to be sure, and a few other brokers, but Tom worked with them all."

"Then why did these fellows, and Hob with them, get dragged off into the night?" Spider set the candle to his dead pipe and fired it anew. "Who would do that? And why?"

"I don't see the sense of it," Odin said.

"Aggie, did Bill and his lads ever come back from a rendezvous in a state, maybe scared or panicked, maybe something had gone wrong?"

"Not that I saw. Tom never told me of his dealings," she said, "and I did not talk much with Bill or any of the others. I cook, I clean, I make sure the neighbor children that help me out sweep the floors and wash the pots. I do not know much about the business Tom and Bill did. Or any of the smuggling, really. Oh . . ."

Spider looked at her.

"There was an enterprise that got called off," she said. "I know because Bill was in here, drinking with boys, and they got up to leave, all of them at once. Tom bade them stay and drink a while."

"Did he say why?"

"No," she answered, "but Bill asked if they would still get paid and Tom told him they would. But I don't know more than that."

Spider's pipe glowed. "Well," he said, the clay stem clenched in his teeth and smoke curling through the gap where he'd lost a couple. "I say we go and have another talk with Bill."

"If he's been smuggling, he might have a pistol or two we could borrow," Odin said, leering. "If we're quick, we might snatch them before he splatters our brains. Ha!"

Spider pulled the pipe from his mouth. "Aggie, where can we find this bastard Bill?"

7

Spider and Odin walked briskly, with their heads down, mostly ignoring the traffic in the road around them. It was still dark, and a tad foggy, but it would not do to be recognized.

Despite it being summer, it was still chilly at this misty, early hour, and they huddled in their sea coats. They dodged chickens on the loose, ignored a cat that hissed at them, and returned the wave of a passing wagoner. Hoists creaked as crates of salt were loaded into tenders, and lads sang at their work as they hauled on ropes and made pulleys squeak.

Morning mist from the river rendered most of their surroundings ghostly, and people and buildings and ship masts seemed to rise before them from nothingness as they strode forward in the dim morning light.

Spider was glad of that, because it rendered him equally invisible to most passersby. He did not wish to be seen or remembered.

Bill Cooper, Aggie had told them, housed his mules and wagons in a barn near the river, and Aggie said he surely would be at work before sunrise, ready to cart goods between the wharfs and taverns and warehouses and coopers and smiths of Lymington. So, the former pirates had decided to go to work early, too.

He and Odin had opted for a few hours of sleep, but it had done Spider little good, and Odin noticed.

"You seem a bit of a shipwreck this morning," the old man said. "Did you sneak some more whisky?"

"I did not sleep well, Odin." Spider rubbed his eyes. "When I did sleep, I dreamed. Of Hob, back aboard *Redemption* and *Red Viper*, all blond and grinning and full of glory nonsense. I dreamed of home, too."

And when I dream of the son I've never really known, he looks like Hob.

Spider did not tell Odin that.

"Aye, Hob was full of all that, and full of piss, too."

"Why did he run off with Anne Bonny, Odin?"

"She is all curvy and willing, you might recall, and Hob is all pecker and balls. His other choice was to be marooned with us, remember?" Odin spat. "Hell, I'm not certain why we didn't run off with her, too. We could have."

"I was weary of pirating, down to my soul."

"Do pirates have souls?"

Spider shook his head. "Doubtful, at that. If we do, they belong to the devil and not to us. Anyway, we've got some work, aye?"

"Aye."

Mrs. Bonnymeade's hot breakfast of eggs and ham and crusty bread had fortified them for the confrontation ahead. Spider had Hob's throwing knife in his belt, and Odin had acquired an old chair leg he thought might serve as a decent cudgel.

"I'd feel better about this if we had a few pistols and a sword or two," Odin muttered.

"I don't think those fellows have done much fighting," Spider said. "They were willing to confront us, sure, but they didn't spread out to take advantage of their numbers, and the two with knives didn't even reach for them. And that Bill, his gaze wavered, even with the odds on his side. If we catch him alone, I think he'll collapse like a sail in the doldrums."

They did not find him alone, however. They'd agreed to walk past the barn first, to do a bit of scouting, and the wide-open door gave them a decent view inside. Bill had his mules hitched already and leaned next to them with a lantern to inspect that all was in order.

Another fellow, wide-shouldered and smoking a clay pipe, sat in the wagon seat, holding the reins and humming quietly. Spider did not recognize him.

"Smells like shit in there," Odin muttered.

"Do you suppose you smell any better?" Spider shook his head, though. The reek of mule dung was almost strong enough to knock a man over.

They moved on about fifty paces, then reversed course.

"Are you ready for action, my friend?"

"I am always ready for action, Spider."

"Beat to quarters, then."

On their return pass, Spider and Odin strode boldly into the barn. "Have you any extra work, sir?" Spider said as he approached.

"I cannot afford more hands," said Bill, kneeling by a wagon wheel with the lantern on the floor beside him. He looked up to find Spider almost upon him. "Hey, you are . . ."

"That is right," Spider said, grabbing Bill by the collar and forcing the man's back against his wagon. Behind him, Odin pulled the barn door closed, blocking the dim morning light and the possibility of witnesses.

Spider heard the other man drop from the wagon. That sound was followed by a couple of hard whacks and Odin's soft chuckle, then a loud cry and some whimpering. Spider did not even look back. He had seen his old shipmate fight too many times to have any doubt of the result.

"This lobcock seems to have broke his leg," Odin said. "And if he blubbers too loud he'll get another one broke, and maybe a busted nut sack as well. Ha!"

Bill's wide eyes turned toward Odin, and Spider scraped the man's beard with the sharp blade to regain his attention.

Spider lifted the knife high enough for Bill to see it, then placed it against the man's throat. "I'm the fellow you accused of murder last night. But I won't hold a grudge, I won't, if you behave smartly. You are going to tell me all about smuggling."

"I do not know a damned thing about smuggling," Bill replied.

The only light now came from Bill's lantern, and a couple of others hanging from hooks on the walls. Spider concentrated on his prey, knowing that Odin would search the shadows and the spaces between crates and barrels for any interlopers, and counting on it being unlikely he would find any. Bill had no reason to expect an assault this fine morning.

"I have heard that you know a bloody great deal about smuggling, Bill. My friend won't hurt your friend any more than he already has, and I won't hurt you, so long as you tell me what I want to know," Spider continued. "But if you don't, well, my friend will spill your friend's ball sack all over this floor, and I'll cut yours wide open, too. It'll make a right mess, it will."

"I am not a smuggler," Bill said quietly, shaking. "I know nothing about any smuggling."

Spider shook his head slowly. "You own mules and a cart and you spoke with Tom Bonnymeade almost every night, and he dealt with smugglers all the time so you are a goddamned smuggler, to be sure." Spider narrowed his eyes and touched the sharp edge to Bill's neck. "But I do not care about that. Truly. I want to know about the fellows who waylaid a crew not long ago. They come ashore with some booty, Anne Bonny's booty, intending to hand it over to you, and they got attacked instead. Some of those men were carried off, I'm told, and one of them that was carried off is my friend. Maybe you were there, maybe you weren't, but I am guessing such an odd story gets told over pints over and over and so, goddamn it, you know something. So you are going to tell me who ambushed them, and why, and where I can find them. Or what's left of you is going to be another story that gets told over pints."

Bill shook his head. "I know nothing . . ." The light from the lantern on the ground gave him a spectral appearance, heightened by his wide, fear-struck eyes and quivering jaw.

"Think, man, because if your damned head is empty I might as well cut it off." He pressed the knife a bit closer and moved it just enough to make a tiny incision.

Bill winced.

Spider stared hard into Bill's eyes, and watched the man's resolve slowly die.

"We had a rendezvous arranged," the carter said, "not even a fortnight ago, and a fellow paid us well to forget about it."

"What fellow, and why?"

"A stranger," Bill said. "Bonnymeade set it up, and arranged for us to talk. The man said he had personal business with the smugglers, and he paid us handsome to stay away. I got the feeling he had a score to settle, the way he said it."

Spider tightened his grip on the man's collar, and Bill started talking a lot faster.

"Anyway, he said we could come in later and collect the merchandise and he held to that, too, left it right there where we could find it. So we did not lose anything on the deal. There were bodies, though, shot and stabbed, it looked like. Might still be there. I won't go back to that cove, not a place where men died. Haunted, probably."

"What was this man's name?"

"I told you, a stranger. I do not know his name, and doubt he would have told me true anyway. That is all I know. Tom made all the arrangements, really. He talked to the stranger, told us we'd best cooperate, so we did."

"What was this fellow's business with the smugglers?"

"I do not know, I told you! He worked for someone else, though, I know that, because Tom said."

Spider tightened his grip on the knife's hilt. "Who was his leader?"

"I swear I do not know! I swear! I swear! I swear!" The man was almost crying.

Spider growled. "And what of this man, then, the one who made the deal with Bonnymeade? Tall? Short? Beard? Long hair? What did he wear?"

Bill gulped. "Well, he was missing most of his left arm, and his right leg below the knee."

It was Spider's turn to gulp. "Say that again?"

"He was missing an arm and a leg."

"This man, was he taller than you?"

"Aye," Bill answered. "By a good bit. And he hobbled about on a crutch, but he still had fight in his eyes, like he could whip anyone he pleased."

"He had an earring, I'll wager," Spider said, quietly. "On his left ear."

"Aye, a gold skull."

A gold skull.

Spider backed away but kept the knife between himself and Bill. "Did you hear that, Odin?"

"Aye, Spider." Odin spat. "It means nothing to me, though. You know the bastard?"

"Aye," Spider answered. "That has to be Half-Jim Fawkes. I sailed with him a while back, under Bent Thomas, before he went off on his own with one of Bent's sloops. Nasty sort, and clever, and tough as old Doctor Boddings' plum duff. I always wondered what happened to him, where he went."

"Well, then," Odin said. "He sounds like he might put up a better fight than Bill and his useless friend here. We might need more than knives and chair legs to deal with such as that."

"Aye," Spider answered. "I will bet these gentlemen have some weapons, since they have dealings with unsavory smugglers and pirates and the like."

Bill shook his head, but Spider chuckled. "Odin," he pointed, "yonder corner is dark. No lanterns there. Good place to store powder, I reckon."

"Aye," Odin replied, heading to the spot Spider had indicated while Spider twisted the knife in the air and Bill looked nervous. Out of the corner of his eye, Spider noticed Odin limped a bit.

The sound of a trunk being opened filled the cavernous barn. "Ha! Flintlock pistols, four of them! Wadding and powder, too, and balls aplenty. And a couple of dirks that need sharpened. But we've armed ourselves with worse."

"Get it all, friend," Spider said. He put as much menace into his expression as he could and leaned toward Bill. "Now, what shall I do with you?"

8

*O*din, carrying their newly acquired weaponry in a burlap sack, rushed upstairs to collect their meager belongings, while Spider explained to Aggie that they were leaving. He also had questions for her.

"A man missing an arm and a leg? Yes, such a man did talk with Thomas," she said, filling a traveling flask with rum. "A couple of times. I do not know why, for I was chased away when they were together. But it was business talk, I'm sure. You know," she said, "I do not think Tom liked him. I think that man maybe even scared him a little."

"Did you notice if the man had any baubles dangling from his ears?"

She nodded. "Just one, a horrid little gold head, like a skull."

"That fellow is named Half-Jim Fawkes, I am certain of it, and he likes to scare people. He and his lads took my young friend away," Spider said. "Maybe pirates have taken to running press gangs, too. Manpower is lacking these days, with all the hangings. Whatever business Fawkes is in, it is sure to be ugly. Are you certain you overheard nothing?"

She handed the flask to Spider. "Take that with you. No, I did not hear Thomas and this man Fawkes discuss anything. I can tell you Thomas was nervous afterward. But I know no details."

Spider tucked the flask into his belt. "Damn."

Aggie's eyes widened. "Bill . . . What became of him? Did you and your friend . . ." She dragged a forefinger across her throat, her eyebrows arching in question.

"We hog-tied him and tossed him into a horse stall. He will live. His mate will live too, but he has a broken knee."

"He fell," said Odin, arriving at the base of the steps with their old sea coats in his arms and two leather sacks strapped over his shoulders. "He was a clumsy lobcock. Ha!"

Spider noticed Odin was still limping.

"Did you get hurt?"

"Not bad," Odin said.

"So, no, we've done no murders, then," Spider told Mrs. Bonnymeade, "yet haste is called for. Thank you for housing us, and should I get my hands on your husband's killer, again, I'll do such justice as I can. And I'll find some way to get word to you, because I suspect we won't come this way again."

"Thank you," she said.

They headed toward the door after donning their coats, purloined from the stores of *Fiddler's Dram* before their hasty departure, only to be halted by Mrs. Bonnymeade's sudden exclamation.

"Wait!"

They turned to look at her.

"Mister Kegley! He knew the lame gentleman, that Mister Fawkes!"

"He did?" Spider glanced at Odin, who hung his head the way a man does when he finds out he'll have to do his chores after all rather than settle down with a pint.

"Yes, he did!" Mrs. Bonnymeade wrung her hands together. "I remember! He came in for an ale and some boiled potatoes and we got to talking the way we do, and, well, a man with such hideous injuries as your Mister Fawkes does not come to the Crosskeys every day, so I mentioned that and he said, he being Mister Kegley, of course, he said that he had seen such a man at his shop, not infrequently!"

"Is that so?" Spider grinned. "Where might we find your Mister Kegley?"

Odin groaned. "We attacked a couple of gents this morning, Spider John. They might be describing us to the authorities this very moment.

And some people here think you killed this woman's husband. Hell, we should grab the first ship we can find, and to hell with where it is bound!"

"Since when do you run from a fight, Odin?"

"Well, I just don't want them to hang you, Spider! Ha!"

"Aggie, where can we find Mister Kegley?"

"Why, he's the apothecary. His shop is close by, go left from the door and his shop is on the right-hand side."

Spider gulped, remembering the sting of sticky fluid in his eyes and a fight with Little Bob Higgins in the darkness. "Aye, I know where that is. I've done some business there, recently. Odin, let us go speak with this apothecary."

Odin peered out the window. "There are a couple of big gentlemen with cudgels headed this way, Spider."

"That might be the watch," Mrs. Bonnymeade said. "They carry those big sticks."

Spider bowed. "Missus Bonnymeade, Aggie, I mean, might we depart through the kitchen?"

9

"You don't get to fuss about how I smell ever again, Spider John, Ha!"

Within three heartbeats of entering the dim shop, the sharp mix of chemical scents prompted a new sting in Spider's eyes, and he relived for a moment the battle with Little Bob that had sent him rushing to douse his head in the horse trough. He'd never smelled anything like it, not even after sharing forecastle space with men who had not bathed in months. He'd never smelled anything like this even in the rat realm of the orlop.

Spider wiped his eyes on his coat sleeve and approached a table in the corner, where a bald gentleman in his middle years crumbled dried, aromatic plants into a clay jar by the light of a candle. The stained table held numerous pots, small knives, a heap of yellow flowers, a scale, some measuring weights, a well-made cabinet with many small drawers that Spider much admired, and a mouse in a wooden cage.

"One moment, please," the apothecary muttered without turning around to look at them. He placed a miniscule weight upon one side of the scale, then slowly scooped the contents of his cup onto the other side until he achieved something close to balance. "One moment, please," he repeated, as though he had not already said it once. He spoke slowly, and distractedly.

A wig hung on a peg nearby. The man picked it up, started to place it upon his bald head, sniffed it, winced, and placed it back on the peg.

Spider looked around the shop, trying to decide which of the several stenches filling the room was the worst. Dried herbs of many varieties hung from the ceiling. A small sack hanging on a nail in the wall smelled suspiciously of dung. Open jars on shelves held fluids of every hue, and flies hovered over a crate of bones and hooves in one corner. A small bucket beneath the table seemed to be filled with urine, judging from the color and stench.

The smoke from the apothecary's candle fought its way through all that and gathered beneath the wide brim of Spider's hat, seeping into his eyes and nostrils. Spider doffed the hat and waved it to clear the air.

"There," the apothecary said, finally turning to face them. "Well, new fellows, I see! William Kegley, apothecary, at your services." His gaze never seemed to really fix upon one point, and his eyes were oddly unfocused. Spider wondered if the man was drunk, but of all the odors swimming about in that small room, alcohol was not among them. Spider would have bet heavily on his nose's ability to detect a tot of rum or whisky or small beer, even in the midst of all the competing scents.

"Is it something for those watery eyes, lad?" Kegley pointed to the scale on his table. "I am, at this very moment, preparing a concoction of fennel, which is a marvel for treating the affliction of poor eyesight, and it may serve to improve your condition, as well. I have more fennel and can easily prepare some for you, for a modest cost."

The druggist then noticed Odin's horribly scarred face and gasped audibly. "Is this why you've come? The wounds look old, but old wounds can bring new pains. Has there been seeping?"

"My scars are beyond help, I'd say. Ha!"

"Poor soul," Kegley whispered. "Whatever happened to you?"

"Cannon," Odin said. "Years ago. I nearly lost my head."

Kegley uttered a mostly silent prayer, then turned back to Spider. The druggist's eyes widened when he saw the gash on Spider's forehead. "Now that wound is not from years ago. Within a day, I should say, or I have never seen a wound. Does it pain you, sir? I could prepare a cataplasm of my own recipe. Rose oil, poppy seeds—white poppy seeds, I should say—and barley meal, with just a touch of the cow urine for its cleansing qualities, and a couple of other ingredients I should not mention, those being of my own devising. I assure you, though, it is marvelous in countering the pain, when applied directly while still warm."

Spider winced. "Thank you, sir, but no, healing is not what we need," he said, while Odin went to examine shelves holding rows of candles and bottles of fluids. Spider pointed to the oily smoke arising from Mr. Kegley's candle. "That's the cause for my stung eyes, I think," he said, blinking, "and leaving your shop will cure it, I reckon. My friend and I wish to ask you questions, and we can pay a small sum for your time."

Odin gave Spider a hard glance and placed a hand protectively over his coin purse.

Mr. Kegley rose, and seemed rather wobbly. "I have absorbed a great many facts regarding health over the years, to be sure, and I am confident you'll find no one in Lymington with more experience in such matters, I assure you. I will be happy to help." It took him twice as long to say that as Spider deemed strictly necessary. The man began humming softly and turning slowly, as if seeking something.

A cat, previously unseen, stepped across Odin's boots. The old man knelt and scratched it. Spider moved away and held his nose against the feline odor.

"Well, it is not medicine or healing we seek, but an old acquaintance," Spider replied. "An old shipmate, I should say. Poor soul badly used on the sea, missing most of his left arm and a bit of a leg. Hobbles about on a crutch quite well, though, and a peg, for all that. We've heard he is a customer here in your shop."

Mr. Kegley's smile, formed at the first mention of payment, quickly dimmed. "I assume you speak of Mister Fawkes?"

"Aye," Spider said. "Jim Fawkes, his name. Sailed with him years ago, I did."

The apothecary stepped back and turned to his table. He picked up a small knife and a small dish, then proceeded to scrape the dried plant crumbs off the scale. "What, may I ask, is your business with Mister Fawkes?" When Kegley turned to face them again, Spider noted he retained the knife.

"We owe him some money," Spider lied, as casually as possible. "We may have a chance to make right with him soon, my friend and I, that is, if we know how to find him. We hoped you could tell us where that may be."

"I see," Kegley said. "He is your friend, then?"

Spider could see the man was trying to navigate uncertain waters. "I do not think friend is quite the right word," Spider said. "We sailed together, shipmates, and I feel I owe him somewhat, but not out of friendship. Call it Christian duty, if you need a reason."

"Mister Fawkes is an unpleasant fellow," Kegley answered, his eyes watching for Spider's reaction.

"Aye," Spider said. "A good reason for us to pay our debts and finish with him, I reckon."

"Well," Kegley said, coughing. "He comes here on occasion, and usually in the company of ruffians." He looked hard at Odin and Spider, who certainly looked like ruffians themselves.

"We won't be put off by that," Spider said. "We won't have trouble with those gents, in any case, as we mean to enrich Mister Fawkes a bit and then we will be on our way. What business has he with an apothecary? He was a common seaman when last we knew of him. Do his old wounds cause him pain?"

"He has not been to sea for these last three or four months, at least. He has visited my shop on four occasions, each time to fulfill a transaction on behalf of a medical man and scholar. He brings a list. He never reads the list but seems to know its contents by rote, and, I should say, becomes quite menacing if I forget an item or if something is in short supply. His employer buys candles, beakers, herbs, opium, unguents, poultices and the like, in fair quantities. Indeed, his trade is of considerable value to me."

Spider rubbed his bearded chin. "Who is he?

"He is a scholar, as I said. Ambrose Oakes. He has established a hospital, of sorts, in his home at Pryor Pond, a home for the treatment of, well . . . I suppose one should say for the treatment of madness."

"Madness?" Spider looked at Odin, then back at the apothecary.

"Yes," Kegley said. "He operates a madhouse. He houses these poor souls and provides for their treatment. I don't know if the aim is to cure them entirely, for that's a rather vain hope, I should think, but perhaps he intends merely to keep them quiet and safe." As he spoke, his gaze trailed a buzzing fly and his expression was one of fascination, as though that fly was the most amazing thing God had ever created.

"I have not met the man, Oakes, you should understand, and gather this only from his letters and from what Mister Fawkes and his fellows have told me, or what they have said amongst themselves as I procured the sundries purchased." He pointed toward the sack of dung, where the fly had settled. "Have you ever tried to count all the colors in a fly's wing? Glorious!"

Spider rolled his eyes and turned to Odin. "What business would Half-Jim have in this?" He spoke in hushed tones. "And why would they take Hob captive, and other men, too?"

"I do not know," Odin muttered, "and I do not wish to know, Spider John. We've sailed with enough madmen, you and me." The one-eyed rigger strode toward the window. "We've tarried here too long, as well. You'll remember our business of this morning? Best we get aboard a ship, and set sail."

"Not so soon." Spider returned his attention to the druggist. "Where is this madhouse? We are bound there to find Jim, and could deliver something for you, if you wish, as we go to see Fawkes." *That would be a good way to gain entry*, he thought.

"Pryor Pond is north of here, near Battramsley. The home was empty many years, but Oakes moved in, oh, a year past? Perhaps more? An inheritance, I have heard. It is not terribly far. Manor house, an old one, on the right-hand side of the road. Surrounded by a low stone wall, with pillars beside the gate. Near the south corner of the property there is a wide pond, so you'll know you have the right place when you see that. I've seen it, you see, because I get called out for births or whenever some poor soul cutting trees hacks off a finger, and so I travel a bit. I have nothing at the moment to send to Mister Oakes, however, as Mister Fawkes picks up ample supplies when he comes. I don't expect another visit from Mister Fawkes anytime soon. Is that the largest fly you ever did see?"

Spider pondered for a moment. "Perhaps, then, you could write this Oakes a letter, thank him for his business, or some such," Spider said. "We could take that along with us."

"Well," Kegley considered, eyes widening. "His business is quite valuable to me. I suppose it would not be amiss to express thanks for his patronage!"

"We've no time for that, Spider," Odin growled. "I see men rushing about. I think our friends from this morning might have been found."

"Damn!" Spider rushed to the window and saw that Odin had spoken the truth. Men were running toward Bill Cooper's barn, and though they were distant, their shouts were growing louder. It would take them a little while to reach the barn, if that was their destination, but it still would not do for Spider and Odin to tarry.

Spider fished a few dull coins—his last—from his leather pouch and handed them to the apothecary without counting them. "For your help, and for perhaps keeping quiet."

Kegley looked confused. "Good Lord, are you the brigands who broke through my rear door last night?"

"We're pirates! Ha!" Odin ran out the door, cackling.

"Goddamn crazy son of a whore!" Spider followed Odin out and quickly caught up to him. They headed north, away from the barn where they'd assaulted Bill and his friend. Once they'd ducked into a side street, Spider punched Odin on the arm. "When we find this scholar's madhouse, I will just hand you over to him!"

10

Once Lymington's buildings and spires were out of sight behind them, Spider and Odin sat on an ancient, fallen oak to divide their small arsenal between them. They doffed their coats, as the effort of running and walking had warmed them considerably and the sun had chased away all the cooling mist.

Odin handed over two of the four flintlock pistols they'd taken from Bill. Along with those, they had six knives between them, although only the one from Hob was truly suitable for throwing. Spider dearly missed the French blade he'd received from Odin. It had been the best he'd ever had.

"We probably can leave these here," Spider said, pointing to the coats. "Inland, summer, we won't be needing them."

"Well, this is a good coat and yours is good, too," Odin said. "I hate to part with one, considering all the times I wanted one and didn't have it. Who knows when we can steal another one?"

"Aye," Spider said. "We can carry them. I suppose it would be foolish to part with good coats."

They inspected the pistols, made certain the flints were secure, and loaded them with powder, balls, and wadding. Odin had filched a bandolier as well. He kept that and beamed with joy once he had a brace of flintlocks strapped against his chest.

Spider tucked one gun into his belt, behind his back, and placed the other within easy reach inside his leather pouch. His share of the knives all went into his belt.

Then he realized they would be walking about with guns and knives showing. "Jesus, Odin, we're armed for battle, but we aren't on a sloop deck now, are we? Do landsmen carry weapons like these?"

"Maybe we're hunting deer."

Spider scoffed at that. "And without coats on to hide all this weaponry, we look like right criminals." He stood, pulled the tail of his shirt free from his breeches and arranged things to hide the gun and blades in his belt. Then he pointed at Odin's bandolier. "How will you hide that?"

"If anyone asks, I will wave a gun in his face and he'll pay attention to that, and not my weapon belt."

"Maybe you can carry the coat in front of you, hide the guns behind that."

"You fret over silly things, Spider John. We haven't seen anyone on the road yet."

"Just heed my words if we do. Aye?"

"Aye."

"Shall we go on?"

As they walked northward, Spider's eyes occasionally peered into the canopy of oak and ash leaves on each side of the road, wondering what sorts of birds were making the unholy racket.

"They won't come peck your eyes out, Spider."

"You are an expert with sails and rigging, Odin. You don't know a goddamned thing about birds."

Forest occasionally gave way to open fields blanketed with heather, but not often enough to prevent Spider from constantly expecting ambush from the trees. Being on land always made Spider nervous. He tried to distract himself from bird chatter by forming a plan.

"I think maybe we take you to this Oakes and tell him you are crazed," Spider said. "You are, I reckon."

"Ha!"

"Is your leg pained? You walk oddly."

"I am fine. I took a whack in the barn. That fellow was bigger and stronger than he looked, and he had a stick, a stouter one than the goddamned chair leg I attacked him with. My leg will heal, though. I've suffered worse."

Spider nodded, and glanced at his friend's ugly, scared face. "Aye."

Odin certainly had taken his share of knocks in his long life on the Spanish Main. The old man knew his business, too, so Spider trusted him to be the judge of his own leg.

"Think, Odin. We'll need to get close, to get inside. We being a couple of rough fellows coming about, they'll turn us away, probably. But if we have a purpose, like we'd have got if the apothecary had written a letter, well, that's not so suspicious."

"I don't mean to get locked up anywhere, nor drink whatever foul brew this Oakes buys from that smelly shop. I say we just go in, grab Hob, and fight our way out."

"I am sure Half-Jim and his band won't mind that at all," Spider said. "We'll just have a nice little country dance, share a drink or two, or maybe a nice civil fucking tea, and just quietly take Hob on out with us. Did you bring a fiddle? No, Odin, we'll need to see what we see, and make a real plan. I've seen Half-Jim fight, and I've a good notion of the kind of men who'd follow him. I don't want him fighting me."

"He is less an arm and a leg, Spider, or so you've said."

"And he is still more man than many. Trust me in this."

"So, we're making plans, then? Ha! So much thinking! Give me a gunwale to leap over and some throats to slit before my own neck gets a red necklace, by God!"

Spider shook his head and took a quick look behind them to assure himself they were not being followed. He had no doubt the attack on Bill Cooper and his friend had added to the intensity of the manhunt for Tom Bonnymeade's killer, and doubted the apothecary would keep his mouth shut. Spider had not given him much coin.

"What I need is a pipe." He drew the instrument from the band of his hat and began fishing about in his pouch. He filled the clay bowl with tobacco—exhausting his supply in the process—and then sought and found a spare flint. He set his pouch on the road, stepped away from it to prevent any wayward spark from hitting the gun inside it, and used the flint and a knife to bring the pipe to fiery life.

"There now," he said, retrieving his bag and coat, tucking the latter over the former. "I shall be able to think." He inhaled deeply and lofted a huge plume of smoke toward the birds in the trees. "Birds hate pipe smoke, I reckon."

"No, they love it," Odin said, carrying his coat over his shoulder. "Blackbeard, he once tied up a man to a tree and lit great piles of tobacco around him. Big black crows came quick, a whole fucking flock. Sniffed up all that smoke and it riled them up, like buccaneers swooping onto a fat Dutch trader. They ate the poor bastard a peck at a time. He lived through half of that. I can still hear him wailing. Ha!"

Spider shook his head slowly. "I fret a great deal about you, Odin." Spider sighed. "I do not believe you ever met Blackbeard, you lying one-eyed son of a bitch." Nonetheless, Spider kept an eye out for hovering crows.

Half an hour passed before they encountered anything but trees and heather and the occasional rabbit. Then a lone rider rounded a bend ahead, coming slowly toward them. He had a musket resting across the saddle in front of him, but he did not lift it, nor did he spur his mount to increase its pace. He did notice them, though, and kept his eyes on them as he slowly approached.

The distance was about fifty yards, Spider judged.

"One of Half-Jim's men, do you reckon?"

"I do not know," Spider answered. "He could be. Hold your coat against your chest, hide the damned guns."

"Nobody holds a coat that way, Spider, unless they are hiding guns or a knife."

"Jesus, Odin. Aye, then. Try to look friendly."

He tugged Odin's sleeve, and they both moved off the road on the east side. "Keep your hands away from your guns," Spider whispered. "He might be a highwayman, or he might think we are highwaymen. Best not to provoke him."

Odin spat. "Or maybe best to kill him before he kills us. We are pirates, remember?" The old man made no aggressive move, however.

"Former pirates." Spider emptied his spent pipe and tucked it into the band of his hat.

The rider stopped alongside them, still not raising his gun. His dark eyes revealed no intention; his expression might as well have been a wooden mask. It was a practiced look, Spider decided, and this man was no stranger to action. He was no stranger to booze, either. Spider caught the aroma of whisky on the man's breath.

He stayed atop the roan mare and nodded. "Well met, gents. Where do you travel?" As he spoke, the man peered into the woods to either side of the road, but his eyes never left Spider and Odin for more than a heartbeat. Spider noted a cutlass sheathed on the man's saddle, and the hilt of a knife projecting from his boot.

"Battramsley," Spider lied. "We've come from Lymington. Good beer at the Crosskeys, and plentiful food, when you get to Lymington."

"I thank you." He sounded friendly, but Spider was not convinced. The stranger's eyes still sought signs of ambush. "What business takes you to Battramsley?"

"Business of our own, I reckon, not yours," Spider answered.

"Fair enough," the man said. He stared at them, pondering, and eventually spurred his mount to continue. "I would not tarry on this road over long, friends," he said over his shoulder. "There have been troublemakers of late, no doubt robbers and thieves. Property holders get nervous, take up arms, watch the road. Wise travelers would hurry on to their destination without lingering."

"Very well," Spider nodded. "We wish you safe travels." He resumed his northward trek, Odin beside him.

After they were beyond the stranger's sight, Odin stopped. "Well, then, which of us is mad?"

"What do you mean, Odin?"

"I am thinking this dark-haired rider with the gun and sword goes to see your lady Aggie and quaffs that beer you sang sweetly about. Suppose he talks of us in front of anyone looking for the fellows who pounded on Bill and his ugly fool friend? Suppose this rider says he saw a one-eyed bastard and a little man with a missing finger walking north to Battramsley? There's been a right ugly lot of crime in Lymington of late, Spider. A murder, an apothecary robbed, Bill and his fool friend knocked about like little boats in a gale. Tongues will wag, Spider. Tongues will wag."

Spider nodded. "Perhaps you are in the right, Odin, but Missus Bonnymeade was kind to us and I wanted to repay her by sending her some business. I doubt my one good deed will be our undoing. Indeed, the preachers say our good deeds will come back to us, or some such thing."

"That is why I do not listen to preachers," Odin scoffed. "And neither should you! Leads to fool things like good deeds and turning the other cheek!"

Spider laughed. "She isn't selling as much liquor since the two of us hauled up anchor and set sail. Well, we didn't pay for most of what we drank, I reckon, but that's just another debt we owe her. And she'll need money, won't she, what with her man not dealing as he was?"

"That is all gospel." Odin shook his head. "But you should not have said anything."

Spider sighed. "Aye, perhaps. But it's done, and I do not think we'll be hurt by it. I do not suppose anyone cares enough about Bill and his friend to pursue us beyond the town's cobbled streets. And we didn't kill them, did we?"

"I broke the ugly man's leg after he near broke mine."

"So he won't chase us, then."

They stared at one another until Odin finally laughed, then Spider laughed, too.

"And the great rash of crime probably ended just as we vanished, too," Spider joked.

"God damn, Spider John! I am the crazy one, remember?"

"I never, never forget."

"Some folk might care about lazy Tom Bonnymeade getting killed, and wonder where we went," Odin said once they caught their breath. "Remember, you diddled his wife and she pretended to find him dead while you were conveniently downstairs. It's the talk of the Crosskeys."

"Aye," Spider conceded. "I am a criminal, and here I set this bastard with the gun on our trail because I wanted to help the nice lady I diddled sell some ale. I was foolish, led astray. No more good deeds, then. I shall be a right fucking bastard from this day on, Odin. I'll spit on children, kick their dogs, shoot their fathers, and fuck their mothers."

"Thank you. Ha!"

They trudged onward. Spider glanced at purple flowers and tried to remember what Nantucket or Boston looked like this time of year. He pictured Em filling a basket with heather, Johnny running about, both laughing. *Does she wait for me? What does she tell our son of his father? Do they know why I have not come home? Have they heard the pirate tales?*

Spider opened the flask Mrs. Bonnymeade had given him and took a heavy swig. Between Odin and himself, they drained it rather quickly. Spider felt the warmth on his cheeks and the slight swirl in his head and wondered if he'd drunk too much again.

Odin, perhaps noticing Spider's mood, started talking again.

"Well, maybe helping Aggie sell some beer won't hurt us. I don't suppose we'll live all that long, anyway. Our undoing likely will be when we find this Ambrose Oakes."

"Aye, perhaps."

"I still think this is a foolish mission, Spider John, and I don't know Hob is worth it."

"He is."

"Just stop being kind to strangers, and talking so much," Odin said. "We never done it on the Spanish Main, and it's a bad habit for pirates."

"Former pirates," Spider corrected him.

Odin tapped his guns and pointed to the weapons in Spider's belt. "Former pirates, you say? We are armed for battle, Spider, and ready to raise hell. All we really lack, Spider John, is a fucking ship. Ha!"

11

y the time the road paralleled a low fieldstone fence to their right Spider noticed Odin was still limping.

"Is that leg worse than you told me, old man?"

"No. I've had worse, Spider John, and you bloody well know it. Look at my goddamned face, for the devil's sake! A bump on the knee ain't to be noticed."

Spider sighed. "I reckon all this hiking is doing you no good. Do you want me to give it a look? There's plenty of wood about. I can fashion a splint for you, if need be."

"You won't be pulling my breeches down, Spider. I told you to get a woman in Lymington. Ha!"

"Stubborn old bastard," Spider said. "Well, this wall is likely the one our apothecary told us about. We won't be much longer, I suppose, and you can sit a spell. Do we want to change our plan?"

The plan, such as it was, meant walking past the gate to Ambrose Oakes' property so they could scout things out, much as they had done before their skirmish at Bill's barn. But if Odin's leg was injured, Spider would adjust.

"No," Odin said. "I like your plans, except for when they mean we must dodge lead balls or get marooned on an island or some such. Ha!" The old man spat. "I haven't clung to life this long to let a bruise on my knee slow me down, Spider. Lead on."

"Aye."

They continued their walk along the low wall, Spider intentionally slowing the pace.

"I am not crippled," Odin growled.

"We are spying on this place, remember?"

Beyond the wall, the land rose in a low hill dotted with oaks and blanketed with ankle-high grass. The house was beyond sight. Spider looked for signs of trails or tree stands that might indicate guard patrols or sentries but saw nothing of the sort. Mallards floated on a large pond between the wall and the hill.

Spider pointed. "Mark, Pryor Pond, methinks."

"Aye, most like."

They walked onward. "Think Little Bob is in with this lot?" Odin asked. "I'd love to stick a knife in Little Bob. I was hoping he'd die in chains, but I am ready to finish the job."

Indeed, the last time Odin had seen Little Bob Higgins the little shit had been locked away on *Redemption*, after waving guns about and trying to steal a boat to flee. The ship later became Anne Bonny's prize, and they'd assumed Bob had either died of starvation before being discovered locked away deep in the ship or joined up with her crew when he had the chance.

"I don't think we'll find Bob here," Spider said. "I'd like a word with the little bastard myself, but I doubt the chance. It seems to me Bob killed Bonnymeade as revenge, thinking the barkeeper sold out his smuggling crew to this Oakes, so it is not likely Little Bob is signed up here. He might be skulking about, though, meaning to kill Oakes, or Half-Jim, or just to rough up people on the road or some such. If we see him, he and I will have some words."

"If I see him, my knife will get wet."

Soon, they came to a pair of stone pillars flanking a wooden gate, which was closed but looked as though one good kick would knock it to splinters. A broad wooden beam, weathered and cracked, spanned the two pillars at the top. A couple of eyehooks beneath the beam indicated there once had been a sign hanging below the beam, but there was no sign now.

They walked past the gate. "This must be Pryor Pond. It looks just as our apothecary said," Spider muttered. "Let's continue north, see if we can spy anything beyond the wall besides trees and squirrels."

Five more minutes of reconnaissance revealed nothing new about their destination. They had not reached the northern extent of the walled property, but Odin's leg seemed to be stiffening.

"We can go on to Battramsley if you like, Odin. Perhaps there's a healer there, seeing as you were too foolish to ask the fellow this morning for a poultice or some such."

"I did not trust that man," Odin replied, grimacing. "His eyes looked like glass beads, by God, and I think all the fumes got into his head and stayed there."

"His mind and body did seem to be in a couple of different places, aye. Are you for Battramsley, then?"

"No, Spider John. I am for getting this fool quest done and then getting back on a good ship, bound for anywhere. All this walking ain't right for a sailing man."

"Aye," Spider said, eyeing the woods and peering beyond the stone wall. Truth was, Spider preferred the sea as well. You could see danger coming from a long way off on the water. Not so here, where the wall and the oaks, standing or fallen, gave ambushers plenty of cover. And he had other reasons for haste; he clutched the pendant beneath his shirt and silently asked Em to forgive him for tarrying.

"Let us go storm this fortress."

12

*O*nce they regained the gate, Spider ran a hand across its worn surface. "This is in bad shape, this gate. Lacked paint for years, plenty of rot." A gentle push revealed it was locked. "We could just bust through it, but I suspect that would be unwelcome."

"I don't care. Ha!"

Spider moved to his left and jumped up onto the wall. "Don't know why they need a gate, really, with walls you can jump over."

"Gates are fancy, Spider John."

"If you take care of them, aye," Spider said, his carpenter's disdain evident. "I am wondering if the rest of this place is in such a state." He plopped down on the other side of the wall. Odin followed, with a groan.

"If anyone shoots at us, you are moving slow, Odin."

"So I shall shoot first. Won't have a problem then, will I?"

"Maybe it won't come to that."

"Aye, maybe this good gent Oakes will just take us to Hob, say he's sorry for snatching the fool lad for whatever foul reason he did that, and send us all on our merry way with bellies full of beef and beer. Ha!"

They ambled up a dirt road, avoiding deep wagon ruts when they could, and watched the trees for signs of peril. Birds flitted between branches. Spider patted his weapons for the tenth time to be sure his hands could find them at need.

"Have you thought on what we'll say, Spider? Or do we just kick through the door and start fighting?"

"We're looking for work, we are," Spider answered. "Sailing men, looking to get off the broad sea, heard in town that Ambrose Oakes has hired such before."

"Will Half-Jim be a problem?"

"We will know soon enough," Spider said, halting. "That's him, up there. And whatever else, do not call him Half-Jim."

Spider pointed up the hill ahead of them, where a man had emerged from behind a tall oak. A wide grin flashed pale yellow, surrounded by dark beard, and a gold earring caught snatches of sunlight that fought through the canopy of trees. Tall he was, leaning on a crutch propped beneath the stump of his left arm. His right hand clutched a large flint-lock pistol. At the midpoint of the crutch, a holster contained another pistol. The man's right leg ended in a wooden stump no better maintained than the gate by the road.

"Well, I'll be damned and dangled," the man said, dipping his head slightly. Spider noticed a small knife tucked into the folds of Half-Jim's battered tricorn. "Spider John Rush! Keep your hands away from any pretty knives you've got, son. I recall how well you throw those damned things!" The man gave out a sharp whistle, and soon Spider could hear movement elsewhere among the woods.

"And I remember how well you can fight, Jim Fawkes. I did not come here looking for a fight, though."

"Why did you come?"

"Need work," Spider said. "The sea is not too friendly these days. My mate and I could use a change, as it were."

"They told a different tale on the road, Jim."

Spider glanced behind him and saw that the stranger from the road had joined the company. He casually aimed a musket at them.

"Is that right, Stingo?"

"Aye," the man said. "Told me they were for Battramsley, but kept their tongues still as to any purpose. And they are armed. So, I followed them here, at a distance, and tied my horse to a tree and snuck up once they headed onto the grounds."

"Well done, Stingo. You must be sober today."

Spider turned back to Fawkes and shrugged. "It's poor policy to talk overmuch with strangers on the road. Aye, Jim? I did not see reason to tell him any truth."

"I believe you've spent far more time on the decks of a sea raider than on any road, Spider John, but aye, silence is golden, they say. Pirates looking for a place to hide out, eh?" Half-Jim spat. "Thinking to elude the king's justice, are you?"

"Perhaps." Spider indicated his friend. "This is Odin, a shipmate. Nobody knows knots and sheets better, I'll wager, and few can best him with a sword or pistol."

"Is that true?" Fawkes looked Odin over, and seemed unimpressed.

Spider continued. "And you know my skills with wood and"— he nodded toward the weapon Fawkes held—"with gun and blade, if matters should come to such. I heard in town the gent that owns this place had hired seamen, so here we be."

"Here we be." Half-Jim continued smiling but did not lower the gun. "Where in town?"

"An apothecary, his name is Kegley. We did some trade in his shop, spoke of the sea life, and he mentioned some seafaring men come to him from time to time, buying materials for the owner of this place."

Fawkes grinned. "Did you come here looking to find me, Spider?"

"No," Spider answered with a shrug.

"Because there are some who might want to track me down, might hire a gentleman such as yourself to hunt me and gut me."

"We sailed with Bent Thomas, you and me, long enough for you to know I am not one to go hiring on as an assassin."

Fawkes nodded. "So you've said. But I've seen you fight damned hard. And I have left more than a few angry men in my wake. Some of them might have hired someone to track me down."

"You can check my purse." Spider said. "Empty as ever."

Fawkes grinned.

"I've fought when I had to," Spider said. "And I'll take work where I find it. But I am not here for blood. I was told of a wounded sailing man working here, but whether it was you or no, I had no thought.

Half the men I've ever known on the sea are injured. Tough work. I never felt no love for you, Jim, it's true, but I never had reason to hate you, neither. You did your work, fought as hard as anyone, and never cheated me as far as I know."

"Fair enough," Half-Jim said. "Whatever become of Bent Thomas?"

"*Lamia* went down in a storm, and I presume the cap'n with it," Spider said. "A devil-spawned storm, it was. Me and a friend was lucky to get to land, near Boston. My friend died after. Ain't seen anyone else from *Lamia* since then, neither, so I figure they all died, by the sea's doing or by the noose."

"Dangerous work, sailing." Half-Jim sighed. "Stingo, fetch your horse up to the barn and sit a spell, grog if you like. Reward for paying attention to these gobermouchs. Then get your ugly hide back to the road."

"Appreciated, Jim." Stingo lowered his musket and headed back toward the gate.

"Do not imbibe too much," Fawkes growled. "You are known to do that."

"Aye."

"As for you, Spider John, we'll drink a tot to the memory of Bent Thomas and his lads, later tonight by a nice fire. Unless the master wants me to shoot you. Then I'll drink alone." His grin returned.

13

Three more men emerged from the woods, each from a different direction and each with a flintlock at the ready. One was black, with a face heavily tattooed with dots that resembled nail holes. His bright eyes darted back and forth, and gave the impression they never missed a thing.

Of the other two, Spider decided one was Spanish and one was French after listening to them exchange brief greetings with Fawkes. The Spaniard focused more on Fawkes than on the captives and carried a sabre sheathed on a weapon belt. The Frenchman, blond, aimed his gun back and forth between Spider and Odin, and smiled at the prospect of shooting one of them. He had no sword, but the fingers of his free hand hovered close to an oversized dagger tucked into his belt.

Their gaits spoke of the sea, and old scars marked their weathered faces. They wielded weapons like experts, and stayed alert for possible trouble from other directions.

The makeup of this small band confirmed for Spider that Fawkes had gathered his fellows from the ranks of pirates. That was the way of life on the account; men came to the sweet trade from many places and for many reasons and found unity while trying to elude the law and stay alive.

All the drawn weapons made Spider nervous. He silently prayed Odin would not do anything rash, and apparently his prayer was answered. The old man spat, rather casually, but did nothing to provoke violence.

Fawkes had kept his own gun trained on Spider until his cohort arrived, but now it was tucked away. He switched the crutch quickly to his good arm and growled. "Let us all go see the master," he said.

"These fellows are not Mister Wilson, Jim, and they don't look like village rabble," said the Spaniard.

"I know that, Raldo," Jim snapped. "But we need to take them to the master just the same. Once we get these gents to the house, the rest of you can return to searching the grounds. And I advise you to do exactly that, Raldo. Exactly that."

Raldo spat. "Of course, *mi capitán*."

They all began trudging up the road, Half-Jim leading the way and setting a quicker pace than might be expected, given his crutch. The man's agility did not surprise Spider, though; he'd seen Fawkes hobble across a heaving deck in a strong gale and wield the crutch as a weapon in battle. Half-Jim Fawkes was not the sort to worry about obstacles.

Half-Jim's team brought up the rear, guns at the ready. They followed closely enough to improve their odds of putting a ball in their prey, but not so close as to give Spider or Odin a chance to pounce and turn the tables—yet another sign that these were experienced fighting men.

"So, your master," Spider said, "hires seafaring men? What's the job?"

Fawkes paused and turned, grinning. "If the master wants to tell you that, he will, but I'll say this much. It's not your skills with a hammer, nor your friend's with a knot, that the master prizes." He turned to continue, humming to himself. That, Spider decided, was to let them know he had no fear of showing his back to them.

Their path was leveling off, and a large house of three stories loomed in the distance. Bars of iron on the upper-floor windows gave the entire place the aspect of a prison, and a turret on the northeast corner lifted a dark spire like a raised sword. Shingles were cracked in many places and missing in others. Spider could not tell from this distance whether an ink-black streak on the spire was a hole or merely rotted wood exposed by a heavy wind.

"Ghosts here," Odin whispered.

"I don't believe in ghosts," Spider said quietly, but not sounding as confident as he'd hoped. The place did have a haunted look.

More goes on here, perhaps, than might be usual for an English country manor, Spider thought. He decided to press Fawkes a bit for information. "Who is your Wilson?"

The wounded buccaneer laughed. "Wilson? A fool villager. He thinks we are killers and thieves. Well, we are, but he has it wrong, nonetheless. We're not killing and thieving against the likes of him. Are we, lads?"

"Aye," they answered in chorus.

"But the master will tell you more of that when the time comes, if he chooses." Fawkes moved onward.

"Looks like you buried something," Odin said, pointing toward some mounds in a clearing. "A few somethings."

Three graves, Spider noted, shuddering. An image of Hob flashed in his mind.

Fawkes stopped, whirled on his wooden leg as though it were a maypole, and planted the crutch into the road with such force that it almost snapped. He put his hand on the flintlock holstered on his crutch. "Sometimes, men die," he said. "When they do, we bury them. You two should ponder that hard truth before you ask any more questions."

Spider and Odin exchanged a glance. Odin's expression said he was tired of these bastards and wanted to start some gunplay. Spider's raised eyebrows reminded Odin they were outnumbered and were not facing off against a bunch of virgins. Spider hoped Odin understood that. The old man probably did understand, he figured, but possibly did not care.

But Odin made no unwise move.

"Aye, sorry," Spider said, turning to look back at Half-Jim Fawkes. "You've got your duties, sir, and those don't include answering to strangers. We'll save our talk for your master, and see if he wants to answer. Is he a reasonable man, this Oakes?"

Half-Jim nodded. "Wise, Spider John. Wise. And the master is a reasonable man, with limits, and perhaps so learned that he thinks he reasons more than a man can." Fawkes grinned and exchanged glances with the Frenchman, who tapped a cross of gold hanging from his neck.

"But your friend, he seems less than patient. I've allowed you to keep your fighting tools to this point, just to see what you'd do. But maybe you two had best drop your weapons here on the road after all."

Fuck and bugger, Spider thought. He complied, slowly, dropping his coat first, but he did not release his grip on a single weapon until he'd confirmed Odin was relinquishing his. And he let Hob's knife drop last.

Fawkes smiled darkly. "Raldo, gather these toys, would you? Now let's all see what the master wants done with you two."

Raldo did as ordered. Spider watched the man examine Hob's knife before tucking it into a leather sack he wore on a shoulder strap.

They marched onward, following Fawkes, and Spider was glad the leader's necessarily slow pace gave Odin some respite for his leg. Fawkes began humming a chantey, but not one Spider recognized. Odin knew it, though, and took up the song himself, humming along and muttering a line of the lyric now and then.

"... *And they sailed beyond the horizon,*
Beyond the lowering sun,
They sailed beyond the lives they knew
And then their days were done."

The other men ignored the music and whispered among themselves, but the occasional backward glance told Spider their discussion was not distracting them from their guard duties. They were fully prepared to fill bodies with pistol balls, and they had sharp blades to finish the job if necessary.

The home, all good old stone and much neglected wood, topped the hill like a battered crown, its gleam dulled by time. Spider could make out more details now. They approached from an angle, and Spider could spy the west and north walls; there was a cellar entrance along the north face.

The place was large, and they had no idea how many men Fawkes had under his command. A quick, violent raid to free Hob—if he still lived—would be impossible, Spider realized. He and Odin would need time for scouting and laying a real plan.

The land around the house was clear for a good distance, rendering a stealthy approach difficult by day or on a moonlit night. Spider imagined himself dashing across that clearing, musket balls flying around him. It was a hell of a distance to cross, and men with muskets would have plenty of time to bring him down. Salvoes from the high ground of the upper floors, or from the turret, would be devastating.

Spider tried to peer between the bars and into the windows, hoping to see a familiar face. *Was Hob working here, pressed into service under Half-Jim's command? Or was Hob a prisoner, kept inside by steel bars and brigands' guns?*

Or, Spider wondered again with a look over his shoulder, *was Hob under one of those new-dug mounds?*

He shivered. *Don't think that way. Believe he's alive. Believe you can get him away from here. Then do it.*

A voice, totally incongruent with Spider's dark musings, arrested his attention. It was a female voice, child-like and tinkly as a harpsichord.

"Mister Fawkes, have you brought me new friends?"

14

Spider stopped studying the house and turned toward the musical voice. He'd expected to see a girl of eight or nine. Instead, the question came from a young woman, perhaps of twenty years. She was slender and blonde and wearing a white nightdress. She held a wriggly white kitten in her arms, deftly maneuvering to prevent its escape. Her green eyes were wide with fascination as the men approached.

Half-Jim Fawkes halted, leaned on his crutch, and held his hand palm up toward the woman. "Miss Daphne, you know you are not supposed to wander outdoors on your own. Nor are you to play with the kitten unless someone is there to keep watch on you." Fawkes turned to Spider and whispered. "She strangled one, a week ago."

Daphne smiled. "But he's so pretty. And I did not choke a cat, Mister Fawkes."

"Your sweet little hands were locked around its little throat, missy."

"I was coddling him. I love kitties."

"Well, I'm told that one was struggling, and you dropped him when Peter saw what you were doing, and it ran like bloody hell once it hit the floor," Fawkes said. "And I have not seen that little black shit around here lately. Have you, Raldo?"

The swarthy man spat. "Hell, no. I think she cooked him and ate him. She is crazy, this girl." Raldo, leering at the girl, looked crazy, too, Spider thought.

"I did not!" She cuddled the cat in her arms closer and nipped its ear with her teeth.

Fawkes shook his head. "You know what the master has said. He has been kind to you, given you some freedoms and all, but you are not to take advantage. Do you wish us to wrap you in sheets again?"

The blonde scowled and dropped the cat. It hurried away and vanished around the home's southwest corner. "Mister Fawkes, you are vile and mean."

"I am only doing as the master tells me to do, Miss Daphne." He doffed his tricorn and tilted his head forward in a courtly gesture. Then he popped the hat back onto his head. "For my own part, I do not care if you strangle every damned cat on the property, just so long as you do not try to strangle *me*. That would end very badly for *you*."

He smiled as he said it, and Spider clenched his teeth. Spider had seen many women treated ill on the Spanish Main, and he had an idea just how badly things could go for Daphne.

The girl, however, seemed to take no note of what Fawkes said. She bit her lip and tilted her head, and Spider wondered if she was, indeed, pondering the demise of many cats.

"If you kill all the kitties, you'll have to do their mousing, I suppose. Ha!"

The woman looked up at Odin and her eyes widened. She rushed forward and ran a hand across the scarred tissue of his face. "Oh, my, sir. Was this painful? The loss of your eye?"

Odin stepped back. "To be honest I didn't feel a goddamned thing when it happened. I was dead to the world."

"Dead to the world," she repeated, softly. "Dead to the world. Oh, my. How was *that*? Was it terribly cold, terribly dark?"

"My face hurt like a kick to the balls when I woke up," Odin said. "Still hurts now and then, when the weather is cold or the wind has a lot of salt on it. But when it happened—a cannon blast, and me knocked right in front of the goddamned thing—I did not feel a thing. Just a bright flash, and then I woke up hurting. In between, nothing."

Spider looked on, dumbstruck. "That is the most you have ever said about your face, and the most honest I have ever heard you sound, and I've known you a long time. You just met this pretty snip, and you are telling her everything."

Odin grinned. "I like her."

Half-Jim Fawkes maneuvered his crutch between Odin and the girl, then wedged himself between them. "Let this man be, Miss Daphne. He and his friend are going to see the master. If we don't kill them, perhaps you can play with them later. So long as that play doesn't get too amorous." He cast a glance over his shoulder at Odin. "That might be dangerous for you, both from her, and from the master. He decrees hands off of her, and he means it."

"Aye," Odin acknowledged.

The girl tiptoed on her bare feet to peer over Fawkes' shoulder. "When we can, we shall play cards. And you must tell me all about the loss of your face. And your pain. You must promise!"

Odin nodded. "Do you play chess?"

"No! But is that not the game in which one kills the king?"

"Aye."

She clapped her hands. "Will you teach me?"

"Aye."

Fawkes snarled and leaned close to the girl's face. "Where is Missus Fitch, Miss Daphne?"

"Daphne!"

The cry came from beyond the southwest corner of the house. "Daphne!"

"We have her in hand, Missus Fitch," Fawkes yelled. "And no critters dead, that we've found, anyway."

A tall woman, moving quickly although she was possibly as old as Odin, rounded the corner and hurried toward them. "Girl, you will be the death of me yet."

Daphne laughed. "Death of her!"

Mrs. Fitch halted by the girl and caught her breath. "Oh, my, I should not have used that turn of phrase with you, girl."

"Why?"

"Never mind why. You promised me you would remain by my side and help with the meat pies, Daphne."

"Meat pies are my favorite," the girl said, smiling. "Meat used to be alive."

"Good Lord," Mrs. Fitch muttered. Then she noticed Spider and Odin and caught a gasp in her throat at the sight of the latter's disfigured face. "Oh, my, have you come to see if the master can help you with that? He may be able to ease pain or something."

"No," Odin said. "I came looking for work."

"More new hires, Mister Fawkes?" She looked at him sternly.

"That's for the master to say," Fawkes answered. "We might be feeding them, or we might be feeding them to the fish in the pond." He chuckled at his own joke and cast a sidewise glance at Spider. "Big fish."

Mrs. Fitch took Daphne by the arm and began leading the girl away. "Come, girl, we've more work to do. We'll have to make the food we have stretch, is all. I haven't the time to watch this one all day and cook a larger meal, especially without proper notice."

"We might just kill them now, then, to save you trouble, Missus Fitch." Fawkes laughed, and his men joined in. The woman muttered under her breath, but Spider could not make out what she said. He could discern her displeasure, though, in her rapid pace and the shaking of her head. Daphne, meanwhile, simply looked back at Odin in awe.

Daphne practically had to be dragged, but the women eventually vanished around the corner.

"Well then, Spider John," Fawkes said, grinning. "You begin to see what sort of ship we run here, aye? Not precisely shipshape, is it? Let us proceed inward and meet the master, Mister Oakes, shall we? Hugh, run on ahead and tell the master what we are bringing him."

The Frenchman ran ahead, and Spider caught a whiff of whisky in the air as the man passed him. "God, for a drink," he said.

"If the master decides to keep you around, I will pour you a libation myself, Spider John, and we shall drink to old memories and dead friends. If not, I shall pour dirt upon your face."

Fawkes led the way, and the gunmen remained behind them. Odin leaned toward Spider and whispered. "What the bloody hell goes on in this place?"

"I don't know, Odin. But I might leave you here." Spider winked.

The attempt at humor had been intended to calm Spider's own nerves. It didn't work. He glanced up at the windows as they entered the building, hoping to see Hob's face peering back.

He didn't.

15

They climbed a short set of steps, entered the home through a door with badly rusted hinges, and were directed by Fawkes to a drawing room on the right. The chairs, tables, and divans all had been elegant once, but now showed signs of much wear—minor stains, loose threads, small gashes in the wood. A massive blunderbuss mounted above the fireplace had gashes in the stock, but otherwise looked lethal.

"I want it," Odin whispered.

"Shhhhhh," Spider admonished.

Raldo placed the sea coats and weapons confiscated from Spider and Odin on a large oval table near the massive fireplace. He noted Spider's gaze and slowly withdrew Hob's throwing knife from the pouch. He placed it on top of the rest, then walked away. He took up a station near the door and crossed his arms.

"If the master hires you, then you'll get those toys back," Fawkes said. "You'll need them to do the work." He winked. "If he decides not to employ you, well, those are some nice-looking pistols and I shall put them to good use. I think Raldo wants that pretty knife, but I am not of a mind to let him have it."

Fawkes and Raldo stared at one another for moment, both grinning, but there was menace in their eyes.

Raldo turned away first, and Fawkes chuckled.

Hugh entered the room. "Master is coming, *mon capitaine*."

The leader nodded. "Seat yourselves, gentlemen."

Fawkes waved toward a divan, and Spider sat. After an awkward moment of glaring at Fawkes, Odin mimicked Spider's actions. Spider realized he'd been holding his breath, wondering if Odin might pick a fight. He exhaled slowly.

"So then," Spider ventured, "what sort of work is it being done around here?"

Fawkes turned toward the fireplace. "Light your pipe, Spider, and clench your teeth on it to keep yourself quiet. The master will ask the questions."

"Well, then," Spider said, taking up his pipe. "Might I borrow some tobacco?"

"Raldo," Fawkes said. The man tossed a pouch at Spider, who caught it deftly. The man then fetched a brand from the fireplace. Soon, Spider had a good smoke going and his nerves began to calm a bit.

They sat in silence for several minutes, during which time at least one man had a gun trained on them every moment. Spider noted, too, that they spread about the room, preventing any sudden attack from disabling more than one of them at once. Fawkes apparently had trained his men well.

When the door opened, Spider noticed that all the men—except Half-Jim—snapped to attention.

"Well, Mister Fawkes, we have been busy, have we not? Did you slip away and hire more men of arms while I was unaware?"

The man who had entered the room and asked the question was bloated, whale-like, with a stomach that shoved his white shirt forward beyond the high-collared black coat. He was almost as short as Spider, which emphasized his excessive weight. He was hairless, too; Spider had difficulty even making out the faint white eyebrows.

"Ha!"

Spider shot Odin an angry look, then returned his attention to the man who had entered the room. The black man brought the newcomer a glass. "Brandy, sir."

The man took it without a word of thanks, and without offering anyone else a glass. Spider caught scent of the brandy, though, and inhaled deeply. He determined to return to this room when he could and smoke out the bottle. A dram of liquor would do him good about now.

"We have been busy, indeed, sir," Fawkes said, deferentially. "I did not go looking. These gentlemen arrived today, and say they seek employment."

"Do they?" The man looked about, then began pacing like an admiral on a quarterdeck. Fawkes' men steadfastly avoided looking the man in the eyes. "How many men are still patrolling the grounds?"

"Three, just now, on the grounds, and Stingo will be on the road again soon. He trailed these new fellows back here after he saw them on the road and got suspicious," Fawkes answered. "We're light on hands, just now. Some are away, you'll recall."

"We'd best bolster the patrol, then. You men," the fat man said, pointing at the others. "Go back to work and join your fellows. Keep an eye out for trouble."

"Aye, sir," they said, leaving quickly.

The fat man stepped forward, swirling his drink. "Gentlemen, allow me to introduce myself. I am Ambrose Oakes, healer and philosopher, delver into unknown knowledge . . ." He looked at them, furled his brow, and shook his head. "You would not likely understand any of that."

Arrogant prig, Spider thought.

"This place is my home and my dream." He spun slowly, arms wide. "Here at Pryor Pond I provide sanctuary for troubled souls, the deluded, the crazed, the sick of mind." He took a sip of his brandy, closing his eyes and licking his lips afterward.

"Like that girl, Daphne?" Spider took a puff from his pipe.

The man tilted his head. "Do you know her?"

"We met her outside. She seems . . ."

Fawkes intervened. "The girl went wandering again. She is back in Missus Fitch's care. No dead cats."

Oakes nodded. "I do not think she killed the kitten, Mister Fawkes. Your men wag tongues. They are paid to guard my property, not to trouble my patients with accusations and rumors."

"Aye, master."

"She seems troubled, the girl," Spider said.

"Troubled," Oakes said. "Indeed, our Miss Daphne suffers from much morbid rumination, a fascination with pain and death that is most at odds with her youth and beauty, and likewise at odds with the wishes of her parents. They have entrusted her to my care, and we have made progress, mark my words. We may be able to help her yet. There is a bright flower inside her. We shall entice it to bloom."

He sized up Spider and Odin, staring coldly. Spider felt the pressure of that gaze and wondered if the man was looking for signs of mental instability. He also wondered if he was finding any.

Oakes stepped toward Odin, with the same scowl Spider had seen on the face of many a captain or shipwright staring at a bit of hull rot. "Old. Disfigured."

"Lame, too," Fawkes said. "Limping a bit."

Odin grinned. "Aye, I am old, because nobody's been able to kill me yet. My leg will heal, just took a bit of a blow. It sounds as though you have rough work for us. If you like, let one of your fellows take me on." Odin's grin widened. "I can't promise I won't ruin him for you, though. I take no half measures in a fight."

Oakes looked up at the high ceiling, as though pondering Odin's suggestion. Then he looked at Fawkes.

Half-Jim shrugged. "I do not know him, but I have sailed with the other gentleman. Spider John, he is, and a right quick hand in a fight."

"Is he, now?" Oakes turned his hard gaze toward Spider. He nodded approvingly. "Not yet thirty, I'd wager. Experienced hand, are you?"

"I know my way with guns and swords and knives," Spider said, "if that be what you need. And I am a carpenter as well. You could use one about this place, I reckon."

Oakes paced. "Pryor Pond was uninhabited for a long time," he said. "I came into it to find it in a state of neglect. And I admit my work takes priority over attention to the household. Perhaps you will be of use in that regard."

"My friend here, Odin, is mean and tough as a shark," Spider went on. "Sailed with Blackbeard. Ed Teach is dead now. Odin is not. I've seen him fight many times, and I rely on him. I think Odin is more than the match for any of the men I've seen here."

Oakes grinned, and paced some more. He finished his brandy and placed his glass on a table. Finally, he spoke. "Well, we shall not waste any good blood in foolish demonstrations. What made you think I might hire you?"

Spider cleared his throat. "Well, sir, we heard in the town . . ."

"Which town?"

"Lymington, sir."

"Continue."

"We heard that you had hired some sailing men . . ."

"From whom?"

"Who did you hire them from?" Spider pulled the pipe from his jaws and pointed it at the man. Oakes was trying to control the conversation, firing questions at him like a broadside. Spider was determined to slow things down. "Oh, I see. That's not really your question, is it? You want to know who told us you was hiring, I suppose. Well, we stopped at an apothecary to get something to stop Odin's horrible itching . . ."

Odin pointed at his scarred face.

"The man's sack, it itches from whores, it does, and his pickle itches, too . . ."

Oakes closed his eyes, and his jaw quivered. "Who told you . . ."

"That you was hiring seamen? Well, the apothecary, a Mister Kegley. He told us a wounded sailor came in regular, to pick up supplies, and that the men accompanying him had the manner of sailors about them, they did. So, we being sailors who would prefer not to be on the sea for a while, me and Odin, but needing coin and quarters, as it were, we thought we'd see if you had work for us."

"Is that so?" The man opened his eyes. "Did Mister Kegley tell you anything else?"

"No," Spider said. "Just that he valued your trade."

"Very well." Oakes turned to Fawkes. "And you know this man?"

Fawkes pointed at Spider. "I sailed with him and fought beside him. He's fast, and a right devil with a knife, and he don't want to die so he fights hard."

Oakes nodded. "What do you think of the other fellow?"

"One eye, old as Moses, and he limps," Fawkes said. "I see no use for him."

"Fawkes, I have seen you prove many times that a wounded man can be very dangerous."

Fawkes nodded, and grinned. "Aye, Spider John. I suppose you have."

"Odin is tough as the devil," Spider said. "We're not fools, Mister Oakes. You had men about on your property, standing guard. You've got enemies, it seems. Well. Odin and me, we've been in the thick of it, smoke and oakum, blood and fire, more times than you can imagine. If you don't think Odin can protect your grounds or wrestle a crazed patient to the ground, well, give him a knife and someone to fight. I know who I would bet on, if I had money."

Oakes and Spider stared at one another for a long while, with Oakes casting the occasional glance at Odin.

Fawkes shrugged. "I can vouch for Spider John, sir. As for the other, if he can't fight we'll likely know soon enough and we can always have Michael and the boys dig another hole. I suppose John is worth a gamble on the old man."

"Very well." Oaked grasped his hands behind his back and continued pacing. "I have need of men who can handle themselves. Some of our patients will flail and bite and scratch, and their madness lends them a strength and determination that will often catch an inexperienced man off guard. Mister Fawkes has helped me procure men who are accustomed to violence, and who will not flinch."

Fawkes nodded in agreement.

"In addition, there are those beyond my acres who, being ignorant fools, view our operation here with suspicion. Every time a crime is committed, every time some drunken fool wanders off, they blame our patients, as though we allow them to simply wander about freely doing harm as they will. They do not understand us, so they fear us."

Oakes paused. "Most, being afraid, keep their distance and spur their horses when they pass our grounds. But not all. Suffice it to say that there are spies and prowlers who creep across my property, blaming me for this odd death or that odd vanishment, and intending to do me mischief. I will not have it. Part of your duty will be to see that no one interrupts my work or interferes in any way. Do you understand?"

"Aye," Spider said, Odin nodding beside him.

Oakes inhaled deeply and turned to Fawkes. "We've seen no further sign of this fool Wilson?"

"Not since we chased him off," Fawkes said. "But he may well return, and you've many acres to guard."

The fat man paced, quietly, and stared into the fire for a while. Finally, he turned to Spider.

"There is a man named Wilson who blames me for the death of his son. Twice he has come on these grounds, intending to do me harm. I have work for a carpenter, as you noticed, and one who can fight serves me doubly well. I will give you and Odin an opportunity."

"Aye," Spider said, with Odin nodding. "Thank you, sir."

"Mister Fawkes will tell you your pay, and we can provide you some additional clothing. You both look like tavern dregs who have traveled long and hard. I'll give you your weapons back, and you can patrol the grounds. Learn the faces of my men here, and if you should see anyone you do not recognize prowling about, I want them captured or killed. Can you do that?"

"I am not accustomed to take men alive," Odin said, "but I suppose I can try my hand at that. Ha!"

"You will be posted outside, and you will answer to Mister Fawkes. He will tell you what is needed, what is to be done. Spider John, you shall be posted in similar fashion for now. We shall see about repairs to the home later. Mister Fawkes . . ."

"Aye, sir."

"Give these men their weapons, and their orders."

"Sir," Spider said, "we've walked a long way, on little food."

"The men will eat soon," Oakes said. "and so shall you."

Oakes strode toward the door but paused there before exiting. "Fawkes, if these men make you nervous in any way, or show the slightest sign of working on behalf of Wilson or anyone else . . ."

"I'll present to you a gift of their balls, in a pretty crystal goblet, sir." Fawkes grinned.

"I do not require their testicles, Mister Fawkes," the fat man snarled. "And I may have a use for them alive, well, the young one, anyway, even if they prove to be spies."

"Aye, sir."

16

Mrs. Fitch's meat pies, porridge, and bread proved filling, and Spider puffed away at a refreshed pipe. Fawkes and his men, about a half-dozen of them, had hovered close by throughout the meal, crowding the kitchen and leaving no opportunity for Spider and Odin to talk privately. Stingo, who apparently had not returned to patrol and who seemed a bit drunk now, cast suspicious glances at Spider.

Odin glared at the man. "Are you not supposed to be back on the road?"

"Are you in charge?"

Fawkes rapped the table with a calloused knuckle. "Get back on the road, Stingo."

"Aye." The man's eyes never left Odin's face as he crossed the kitchen to leave.

Spider's mind was itching with questions.

Was Hob one of the hired men here? The boy was young and strong and dearly loved a good fight, and so might fit in well with this rough crew. The job rather lacked the appeal of the high seas, though, and Hob's head was stuffed with longing for pirate gold and glory. Spider doubted the fool would willingly trade a life on the Spanish Main beside the beautiful Anne Bonny for a billet here with Ambrose Oakes.

But willingness might not enter into it, he thought. From what Spider had learned so far, Hob and the other smugglers had been taken captive, not hired. Did Oakes need men so badly that he gathered them via press gangs, much as the Admiralty swept the taverns of Plymouth to round up sailing men for Naval duty, their wishes be damned?

If that were true, then Hob might well be somewhere on the grounds, doing his duty or seeking escape. Or he might already have fled; the lad had a daring nature, and if he was determined to escape he would not dawdle.

Hob also was reckless, though. Had he already attempted escape, and failed? Was he lying now within one of those fresh graves?

Mrs. Fitch passed out cups, and the men passed a bottle around. Spider filled his and was glad to discover it was strong whisky.

"No water today, lads," Fawkes said. "A bit of a nice welcome for our new mates. Ahoy!"

They all drank together, and Spider's eyes followed the bottle to the cabinet where Mrs. Fitch tucked it away. Spider was trying to drink less—alcohol had bedeviled him in the past, and he wanted to keep his wits about him—but the whisky had helped to settle his mind and he thought a bit more settling might not be a bad thing.

Outside, a ship's bell clanged.

"Well, then," Fawkes said. "Let us relieve our mates on the watch. Odin, your station is the main gate. Stay near it, but out of sight. If anyone should come through, confront them. If they make you suspicious, detain them and raise an alarm. Men will come to your aid. Should you meet any of our own coming off watch, the byword is 'lamb.' They will know it if they are ours. The proper reply is 'wolf.' Do you have it?"

"Aye." Odin checked his weapons and headed out the door. Spider moved to follow, but Fawkes clapped him on the shoulder.

"You, Spider John, shall have the south wall. Patrol it, east and west, and take note of passersby and lingerers. If anyone climbs over, hold them. Shoot them, if need be. Raise an alarm if you are outnumbered or otherwise need aid. You heard the bywords."

"Aye," Spider answered, trying to hide his disappointment. He had much to discuss with Odin.

"But I promised you a libation, did I not? And you shall have it."

He opened the cabinet, took out the bottle and filled Spider's cup, then his own. "To Bent Thomas and poor *Lamia*."

"Aye."

"You still crying every night over a woman in Nantucket, John?"

"I still aim to get back there, aye," he answered. "And to my son. Wondering if he may be taller than me by now."

"Most men are," Fawkes quipped.

"Little Johnny is not yet a man. He was still in Em's arms when last I saw him. He would not know me if he saw me." Spider was feeling the whisky now.

Fawkes poured him some more and watched him drink it. "So you did not come here looking for me."

"No," Spider said. "No reason to do that."

"No one hired you?"

"Just you and Oakes."

"Hmmm." Fawkes drank deeply. "It has been a long time."

"That peg on your leg, that is not the one I made for you."

"I fell off a ratline and broke that one," Fawkes laughed.

"That one you have now is in poor shape. Big cracks. I can make you another."

"Duty first. Go patrol your wall."

"Aye." He rose and felt the whisky a bit more.

Spider did not like his posting. He desperately wanted to discuss things with Odin, but he understood why Fawkes would separate them. If he could not stand watch with his shipmate, he would have preferred a station in or near the house so he might look for Hob. Patrolling a damned wall would make that impossible.

He would have to bide his time. Spider stepped out of the kitchen and hurried off at a quick pace, but Odin's hiss soon arrested him. The old man was hiding behind a stout tree.

"Here, Spider," Odin said, tossing a leather flask. "A fellow named Ira might be wondering where that went."

"Obliged," Spider said, tucking the flask under his belt. "Why aren't you at your post?"

"I am making sure Half-Jim doesn't kill you."

"He didn't. He's suspicious, though, I think."

"Don't drink it all too fast," Odin said, turning to go. Spider headed off to his own station.

Soon, he realized Stingo was following. Spider turned to face him.

"Your friend gave you a flask. Will you share?"

"I can spare you a swig, I reckon." He tossed the flask to Stingo, who took a healthy drink and handed it back.

"Thanks, mate."

"You are supposed to be on the road."

Stingo grinned. "Half-Jim does not know everything that goes on here." The man stumbled forward. "And he doesn't need to, does he?"

"I reckon not," Spider said.

"Good. Some advice to heed," Stingo said, slurring. "Don't go upstairs."

"Why?"

"Just don't," Stingo said. Then he laughed. "I am sick of digging."

The man spun, nearly falling, and staggered away, laughing.

Spider stared at the upper floors. "Don't fret, Hob. If that is where you are, I'm coming." He resumed his course.

The lowering sun threw long oak shadows across the grass. Spider paused beside a thick tree and looked back at the house. Other men moved about, as did several dogs. Spider hoped to spot Hob's long-legged gait among the men but was disappointed.

A familiar pressure at the back of his skull made Spider freeze. He knew how a gun against his head felt.

He raised his hands slowly. "Lamb," he said, quietly.

"And I am the wolf," came the answer, in a feminine voice that caught him further off guard. "You'll need to be more attentive."

"Aye," Spider said, turning slowly. The woman before him wore a slouch hat, a man's blouse with billowing sleeves, and a leather vest that likely would turn away a knife thrust. Spider assumed she wore breeches and boots but did not let his gaze wander. Instead, he focused on the icy blue eyes and the gun still aimed at his head.

"Spider John," he said. "New hire."

The woman, perhaps close to his own age, blew aside a stray dark strand of hair. "Ruth."

"Pleased to meet," Spider said. "I am for the south wall."

She lowered the gun. "I'm back from the south wall. Quiet day. Why do you dawdle here?"

"Just eyeing the place, to get my bearings. I was hired on only today."

"Well then, best get to work." Ruth headed toward the house. "And I'd best get to my meal. Pay more attention to your surroundings, Spider John. I'd hate to be shot in the head while I slept because someone slipped past you."

"Aye," Spider said, noting she had three knives on her belt. He watched her walk away, and rather enjoyed it. If Hob was here, he no doubt had noticed Ruth as well, randy pup that he was. This woman would bear questioning when Spider got the chance.

When such an opportunity might come, Spider had no idea. Half-Jim Fawkes had always been a cautious fellow, and his separation of Spider and Odin—along with this business of bywords—showed that he remained careful today. Half-Jim would be watching closely.

Once he reached the wall, at the corner overlooking the road to Lymington and close enough to the pond that he could smell the fishy odor, Spider sat on the flagstone wall and took a sip from the flask. Stingo had lightened it considerably. Rum, it was, but watered down. That disappointed him but did not keep him from taking another swig.

He looked back but could not see the house from here. The road bore no traffic, and soon it would be dark enough for travelers to require a lantern. He listened a while, heard no horses or whip cracks or creaking wheels in the distance, and so he headed east along the wall. He rather hoped to find Hob sneaking over it on his way to freedom.

An hour or so of boring duty, however, brought no such luck, and no surprises. Spider sat on the wall, listened to the night birds, and slowly emptied the flask. He held a pistol at the ready, lest one of the owl hoots became a shrill cry of attack.

He reckoned the bell signaling relief would come by dawn. It would make for a long night, but he'd stood long watches before. And it was not as though he planned to sleep anyway. He planned to seek Hob, and get the hell away from Half-Jim, his rough crew, and that blubber man, Ambrose Oakes.

Sleep could wait.

17

The clanging of the bell woke Spider from a deep slumber, and the first thing he noted was morning rain dripping from his hat.

He had not meant to sleep, but the combination of boring duty, thick darkness, and weary bones had done him in to the point that he'd slumbered through a light rainfall. The booze played a role, too, no doubt, and he cursed himself. He'd promised Odin he'd quaff less.

Spider shook the water from his hat and noted the rain had stopped. He got to his feet quickly and peered through the dawn light to see if anyone had noticed his dereliction of duty. He did not actually care whether anyone stole from Ambrose Oakes, or even if someone murdered the fat bastard, but he did not want to be tossed aside from this job before he found Hob.

No one was nearby, so he wandered toward the pond and emptied his bladder, scattering a trio of catfish. He shivered in his wet clothes and hoped the sun would lift above the trees soon and warm him. He glanced around before trekking uphill toward the house, but no one else was about. He headed toward the kitchen door and spotted Half-Jim kissing Ruth deeply before slapping her arse and sending her on her way to her duty.

The woman passed Spider but paid him no attention.

Fawkes grinned, watching Ruth walk away. "I have no idea whether she can really fight like she says," he told Spider. "But she is quick, and sneaky, and has other skills besides."

"She is a right handsome lass. Where did you find her?" Spider stepped away from the door to let men coming and going pass. Fawkes followed him. Spider looked among the passersby for Hob but did not see the lad.

"I was harbored in the Turks," Fawkes said. "I was hiring crew for my cap'n, Ruggard Blake, and she begged to come aboard, said she wanted the hell out of there. Showed me she could use a gun, and a knife, and shall we say she convinced me to sign her on." Fawkes winked. "We had no real trouble on that voyage, though, so I have not yet seen her in action, and all the nooses make me nervous about resuming life on the account, so unless we see action here I may never see what she'll do when blood flows." Fawkes sighed. "Pirate days are done, Spider. They've hung or killed all the famous ones. Blackbeard. Calico Jack. Roberts. And you tell me a storm probably claimed Bent Thomas. Seas are dangerous, I think. I'm for being a landsman."

"Aye."

"So now here I am, working for my old shipmate Oakes, and I have that pretty thing Ruth to keep me from getting sad about the old days."

"All these hands former shipmates of yours?"

"Most. Hired others in Lymington. Surly gents, like most pirates. You can't really trust them unless you are carrying a gun and a sharp blade."

"I won't offer trouble, Jim."

"See that you do not, Spider John." Fawkes looked off into the distance, where Ruth had vanished. "A right fine lass, you said? She is that. Kept me warm in the night when you lads were getting rained on. I have to keep my hired lads from sniffing around her. I don't want her warming anyone else up. You look cold."

Spider nodded. "Cold and dead tired. I don't think I could hoist the flag now if I tried." He yawned.

Fawkes leaned toward Spider. "Don't you go sniffing after her, be warned. What's mine is mine."

"I've been wet before, and I'll keep myself to myself where Ruth is concerned."

"See to that," Fawkes said. "Tired, Spider John? I know it was a long day and night."

"Weary to my soul," Spider answered.

Fawkes sighed. "Your soul." The man gazed off into the distance. "Are you certain you have one?"

"Well, I've been told so by men that studied the Bible more than I ever did. Sailed with a couple of preachers, last voyage. They did not agree on much, though, and I'll be damned if I know the truth of such things." Spider shook his head. "Can't say for sure about my soul, I reckon. It might belong to the devil more than it does to me."

Fawkes laughed. "Maybe we will know before long. Maybe!"

With that ominous note, the man spun on his crutch and wandered off, still laughing. Spider followed the scent of fresh bread into the kitchen.

18

"So, have you found the little whoreson?"

"If you mean Hob, no," Spider whispered. "Sit and keep your tongue still." Although the other men had gone off to their bunks or to their stations, leaving Spider and Odin a chance to converse, Mrs. Fitch still hovered about washing plates and putting things away. The kitchen was quite large, feeling especially so to men accustomed to cramped galleys on ships where every cubic inch of space was used to best advantage, and every move meant a risk of banging one's head on a hanging kettle. But the kitchen here was spacious, and now and then the woman would move away to place something in an oven or take something from a pantry. They used those moments to talk. Still, even then she was close enough to overhear them if they weren't cautious.

Odin placed a plate on the table and sat. Spider had already finished his meal of boiled eggs and crusty bread, so he snatched an egg from Odin's plate.

"For a small man, you eat a lot of my food," Odin said. "Did you learn anything?"

"No," Spider said. "Well, I learned that Jim really would prefer it if we kept our peckers away from his woman, and that patrolling a wall is a boring duty, and that I can fall asleep even without the sea's gentle rolling."

"Ha! Napped, too, I did." He cast a quick glance over his shoulder, then whispered. "Is she eavesdropping?"

"Probably," Spider said, tapping his egg on the table to crack the shell. "Keep it low. Laugh now and then, so it seems we're just telling stories."

"Ha!" Then Odin muttered. "Like that?"

"Not so much like an old witch, or you'll frighten her, but you get the notion."

The old man sighed. "I'll wager a bottle of rum Hob's already gone from this place," Odin said. "These sots are all action and attention when Half-Jim is near, but they're a lazy rum lot otherwise. Hob would be a handful for them."

"You can't afford a bottle of rum," Spider replied.

"Well, you owe me a bottle, damn you, and do not forget."

Spider glanced at Odin. The ancient mariner had been crotchety the day Spider met him and he'd never stopped, but the old salt had never fixated on something the way he obsessed over that chess game and the rum bet. That limp was bothersome, too.

Spider had no idea how old Odin really was, and now he wondered if all the years finally were catching up to his friend.

No. Odin's tough as good oak. He'll be fine.

Spider tried to get back to the matter at hand.

"You may be speaking truth, though, Odin, and I hope you do. Hob's a daring lad, and smart, and I have not seen a one here I thought could best him in a fight. Even if he is gone, though, I want to stay about and see if we can learn where he might have headed."

"You think he would have told anyone here?"

"You haven't seen Miss Ruth, have you?" Spider shook his head. "Part of Fawkes' crew. She's a sight, and a match for Miss Anne Bonny, I dare say. Good looking, probably dangerous, just the lass to turn that idiot Hob's head."

Odin grinned. "He does like the ladies. And I have heard tell of her, among the men a bit. Raldo says she is a right naughty baggage, but he sounded pissed. Maybe she won't be naughty with him."

"Aye." Spider bit off half the egg he'd filched from Odin. "And if Fawkes catches him with her, Raldo will be dead, I reckon. I plan to talk to the lass, see if she's seen Hob, see if the arse tried to arrange a rendezvous in London with her or some fool thing. Or a rendezvous on some pirate vessel, more likely."

"You think Jim's crewing a ship, maybe some voyage Oakes is planning?"

Spider chuckled to keep up the pretense. Mrs. Fitch turned her back to them and thrust a knife into a fat cabbage. "That's not a bad notion. Jim says most of this lot is old mates of his, and they all have sailor manners. I have not heard anyone say anything about a voyage, though, but Jim's not the kind to spill secrets before he must. So if there is something in the wind, only Jim and Oakes know it, most likely."

"Fawkes could be up to something on his own," Odin said. "Maybe Oakes has money here, and Fawkes plans a mutiny."

"Perhaps. We'll just have to poke around here, quiet like a pair of ghosts, and learn what we can."

"Well, then," Odin said. "I shall eat, and sleep, and wake up and sit by the goddamned gate again, no doubt. Against all odds, we have a plan. Ha!"

"How is the leg, Odin?"

"I will be fine," the old man said. "Don't go planning to saw it off just yet."

"I don't saw them off," Spider said. "I just make the pegs." He glanced heavenward in thanks. That unpleasant duty of amputation often fell to carpenters on ships lacking surgeons, but Spider had been fortunate enough to avoid having to use his saw for that purpose.

"I don't need a peg," Odin said. "I need the fucking bottle of rum you owe me."

"Why do I owe you a bottle?"

"The chess game! I was winning before you ran off to see who killed Missus Bonnymeade's husband and then led us to this goddamned hellhole. Do not suppose I will let you forget I won! Ha!"

Justice for Mrs. Bonnymeade, Spider thought. *That was a rash promise now, wasn't it? I'm here to find Hob, and I don't really give a seal's slick shit about Tom Bonnymeade.*

He did not mention any of those thoughts to Odin. "I do not recall the chess bet, Odin. And we never finished the game."

"You always recall the bets you win. I hope birds eat your eyes while you sleep."

"Do you know where we sleep, by chance?"

"Cellar," Odin said, pointing toward a hall. "First door on the left, or you can go in from the doors on the north wall outside. They've turned it into quarters for the men. You get a hammock or a bunk, and a chest. You'll find dry clothes, too. Mine fit fine, yours might not. Cramped quarters, it is, and smells like belowdecks without the salt and fish smells. Still got the piss and shit smells, though."

"It will feel like home, then," Spider said. "I'm off to sleep a while, then I'll explore a bit, see if I can find Hob." He popped the rest of the egg into his mouth.

"Aye. Did you finish the flask I stole for you?"

"Want to wager a bottle of rum on the answer to that?"

"You are a fuck, Spider John."

19

It was a short sleep, and troubled by dreams of Em and Little Johnny and Hob, all on a shore he could not reach because wind and tide kept drawing him away. But his involuntary slumber on duty the night before meant Spider had gotten more than enough rest. He rolled out of his hammock, noted Odin was snoring peacefully not far away, and grabbed his guns and knives from the chest that had been allocated to him. He spotted a pouch in another man's chest, held it to his nose and smiled. Virginia tobacco, if he was any judge. He tucked that into his belt, grabbed his hat and pipe from his own chest, and wandered toward the kitchen in search of a coal or a brand to light his smoke.

Soon he had a good fire going in his pipe and stepped out the back door. A horse whinnied from within the bowels of a large barn nearby, and chickens scratched at the ground.

Spider lifted his head, blew a cloud at the sky, and noted the black pirate who'd escorted him to the house the day before. The man was near the kitchen door, staring at him.

'I'm Spider John. Would you like some of this?" Spider lifted his pipe.

"No," the man said, before spitting violently. "No, I would not."

The man's gaze was ice, and Spider involuntarily reached toward Hob's knife. But the man turned away and strode boldly down the road.

Perhaps, Spider thought, it was the tobacco that had given offense. Blacks from the west coast of Africa had been captured by the thousands and shipped to the American colonies, many to work in the tobacco fields surrounding Chesapeake Bay. It was a harsh and violent life, and some of those who managed to escape found their way into piracy. This fellow may have walked a similar path, and Spider decided he would not smoke around him again.

After taking a couple of deep breaths and wishing he could smell the sea, Spider went back inside. He wandered about until he reached the central foyer and the wide staircase leading upward. No one seemed to be about, so up he went, Stingo's warning be damned. He halted briefly when he heard a pitiful sob from above. A man's voice, but too old and frail to be Hob's. Spider continued when he heard nothing further.

As soon as he gained the top, he paused to get his bearings. The stairwell opened onto a long hall with a series of doors on each side. Light poured in from a window at the end of the corridor. A stain of some sort—perhaps from water, perhaps from blood—on the wall to his left brought to his mind a shadowy face peering at him, and a low wail from somewhere toward the end of the hall almost sent him back downstairs. He'd told Odin he didn't believe in ghosts, but he'd known when he said it that he'd been trying to convince himself of that. He gulped and continued forward.

Daphne emerged from a doorway on his left.

"Mister Spider!"

"Miss Daphne," Spider said, stepping toward her quickly in hopes it would prevent her from speaking so loudly again and drawing unwanted attention. "You look to be in good spirits."

Indeed, she did. She wore a nightgown, fresh and clean, and she looked all scrubbed and shiny compared to the dregs of humanity Fawkes had hired, and to the ever rushed and sweaty Mrs. Fitch.

"I am feeling well today, thank you, sir. I was not wrapped in wet sheets last night! Nor did I have to drink from that foul bottle."

Spider tilted his head. "They wrap you up?"

"To keep me doing harm," she said, "although I have done no harm to anyone. I have not harmed any cats, either! Still, they give me awful medication, it tastes abominable, it does, and tortures. They mix it with brandy, which I detest, but the medicine is even worse. Worst of all is the sheets. I hate the wet sheets! So . . . cold. I can't move in them. Terrifying. I imagine it must be how death feels."

Daphne's smile was at odds with her words, though, and Spider felt a chill himself. He tried to step away.

The girl crowded against him. "Are you a pirate?"

"No."

"Oh, come now. Are you a pirate? Have you gutted men with your sword?"

Spider tried to push her away, but she backed him up against the wall.

She persisted. "What is it like? Tell me, please, I beg you."

"What do you mean?"

"To gut a man with a blade, or to run it across his throat, to shower in his blood. What is it like? It must be a singular experience!"

Good Lord.

Spider grabbed her elbows and put some distance between himself and Daphne, but she seemed familiar with the maneuver and twisted out of it. "Now, look, miss . . ."

Spider John had, in fact, run sharp steel through a man's neck and stood blood-drenched more than once, but he was trying to leave such experiences behind him and he sure as hell was not going to discuss them with this strange girl.

"Have you?"

"No, miss," he said, "I never done that. Not once. An honest sailor, that is me, hammers and saws instead of flintlocks and cutlasses."

"Half-Jim hires pirates, not honest sailors," Daphne said in a conspiratorial whisper.

"Do not call him Half-Jim, I beg you," Spider said. "He hates that."

"So you know him! You sailed with him! Pirate!" She jumped up and down as she said it.

"God damn, girl, would you . . ."

"Pirate, pirate, pirate!" She ran down the hall, yelling the word in a singsong fashion. A lean, bald man in a robe rounded a corner and stepped into her path, almost causing a collision, but she danced around him and vanished. The bald man paid no attention at all to Daphne, or to Spider. Instead, he peered through the window bars at the end of the hall and sobbed. It was the same mournful sound Spider had heard earlier.

Spider looked back at the face peering from the stained wall. It seemed to be laughing now.

Jesus.

Spider listened to the girls' echoes reverberating through the house and thanked God that Half-Jim and Ambrose Oakes already knew he had been a pirate, and that neither seemed to care.

The sobbing man vanished into a door on the right. Spider stood in the now empty corridor, stunned, and said a quick prayer for the man.

He uttered one for Daphne, too. *That girl has such an obsession with death*, he thought. *Could she be the one filling those graves?*

She was too small and frail to put up much of a fight against the rough company Fawkes had hired, but that did not rule out stealth. A fetching lass with a devious intent could prove to be a deadly siren for the men here. *And for Hob. Especially for Hob.*

Spider moved to follow Daphne down the corridor, but two men emerged from a near doorway. They saw him, scowled, and moved quickly to block his path. Shoulder to shoulder, they glared at him.

"Don't try her," said one of the men, who wore a large leather apron and held up his hands in a sign of warning. His hair was cut short, and he bore no weapons Spider could discern. He was powerfully built, though, with muscular arms.

"What?" Spider raised his own hands to indicate he wanted no altercation.

"Don't try her," the other man said. Like the first fellow, his height topped six feet and his hair was cropped short, but he wore no leather apron. He, too, was unarmed. He was thinner than the other man, and lacked the impressive muscles. One or both of these men smelled like Kegley's apothecary shop.

"She's pretty, and no doubt juicy, but don't try her," the second man added.

The first man stepped forward. "Billy tried her, and she nearly clawed out his eye. Master says hands off her since then."

"Aye," Spider said. "Hands off." As he spoke, he smiled, all the while deciding that he could get a foot between the strong fellow's legs, trip the bastard toward the thin gent, topple them both and get a knife in play in a couple of heartbeats—if it came to that.

"I'm Simon," the first man said. "He's Gold Peter."

"I am Spider John."

"Why are you up here? And with weapons? No weapons upstairs unless master orders it," Simon admonished. "And he never orders it, because it is a fool idea. The crazy people tend to snatch at guns and knives, some of them, and they don't care who they kill or why. Hell, they don't even know they are doing it."

"You certainly do not wish that girl to grab anything sharp, or anything filled with powder and lead," the other man said. "You do not want that."

Spider stepped back. "Have patients here killed their caretakers?"

"Not yet. We see that they don't," Gold Peter said.

Simon leaned forward. "That girl hurt Billy, though. Scratched him deep."

"I shall be careful, then. I'm new," Spider said. "I'm a carpenter, as well as a hired guard. Thought I'd come up here and look at the place, see what needs fixed. This place has not seen a lot of care. It would be really nice with a lot of hard work."

"We'll give you a list of things to fix," Gold Peter said. "A long list. But you don't come up here without orders. If you were on day watch, I'd know it. You are not on day watch."

"Aye, it's night watch for me," Spider said. "But it is easier to spot wood rot by daylight, and I can't inspect the house if I am out marching up and down along a wall, can I?"

Gold Peter stepped forward. "Go downstairs. Now. If the master wants you up here, he will tell us."

Spider stared at him. Peter had no long hair or earring Spider could snatch at. Still, the man's stance left his belly and balls wide open to a swift kick or a quick knife, and Spider reckoned he'd be able to end any fight the moment it started. But there were two adversaries here, not one, and they'd repositioned themselves just enough to render his first plan of attack useless. Besides, beating this snotgoblin into the floor would not find Hob, so Spider stepped back.

"Noted, gents. Just learning my way here. Let's not fight, aye?"

"Downstairs. Now," Gold Peter ordered again.

"Aye." Spider turned slowly. He passed the face stain; now, it looked amused.

Spider descended the steps. Once he reached the bottom, he glanced back upward.

Gold Peter and Simon still watched him. Somewhere behind them, a man moaned like a wolf. But the men ignored that, and remained focused on Spider.

Spider left, but the wolf howl followed him.

20

Spider found a hot coal and a supply of tobacco in the kitchen, so had his pouch refilled and his pipe going by the time he'd stepped out the door and wandered toward the wooden frame that held the ancient ship's bell used to call men to duty, or back from their posts. Odin was there, leaning against the frame and scratching his head.

"Did you sleep well?"

"Aye," Odin said. "Ungodly dull duty, though, sitting near a gate on a dark night waiting for some fool to sneak through. And nothing to do off-duty save snoop. I wish I were on a ship, Spider, up in the trees where I can feel the wind and see the horizon all around me and listen to the snap of sails and the hum of the stays."

"Aye," Spider confessed quietly, puffing on his pipe. "A ship bound for Nantucket, with Hob on board with us, would suit me."

"We could find a ship easier than finding Hob," Odin growled. "I don't know that he is here."

"And I don't know that he is not," Spider snapped. "I have had plenty of time to think, but it did no good. I can't fathom what goes on here." He looked around. Mrs. Fitch was watering plants toward the front of the house, and a tall fellow who looked like a scarecrow with a blunderbuss patrolled the road leading to the gate. Upstairs, a bald man peered between iron bars, his hand caressing the window glass as though it were a lover.

"This place makes me wonder if you are correct about ghosts,

Odin. Let us take a walk about the grounds," Spider said, trudging off. "We need a chance to talk."

Odin followed him.

Spider headed toward the north wall, opposite of his station from the night before. He was happy to notice Odin walked with less trouble than he had the previous day. Once Spider deemed they'd put the house and any prying eyes and ears far enough behind them, he spoke.

"This place is thick with something."

"Ghosts, as you said," Odin replied, his eye widening. "I heard them, in the night. Coming from the house, pitiful wails that traveled all the way down the hill to the gate. Sorrowful, mournful like a low, slow fiddle tune."

Spider exhaled pipe smoke into the sunshine. "Not ghosts. Probably." He wished he felt more confident saying that. "Most likely, you heard patients. They get treated upstairs, apparently, and it's a sad place. I saw one empty-minded sort, and of course there is Daphne. Some rough gents are standing guard up there, too, and they don't much like strangers wandering about, so if you do go up there hide your knife and such. I did not see any weapons, but they both look like they can fight. The girl, Daphne, tells me they wrap her up in soaked sheets, so she won't harm no one."

"You visited the girl, did you?" Odin leered.

"I went up there and she found me," Spider said. "I did not go see her for anything, you old leech. She found me. And don't you go visit her, either, though she thinks you fascinating, or some damned thing. She is not well in her mind, Odin. It would be wrong to take advantage."

"Aye, then," Odin answered, although he looked disappointed.

"Daphne," Spider muttered. "Haunting, she is. Or haunted, I should say. Blabbering on about death. I tell you, she bears watching."

"I won't mind that. Ha! Even if I can't touch her."

"I did not get to talk to her long before she ran off, bellowing about pirates. Then the guards showed up and chased me off, so I could not follow her. I'm wondering if she's seen Hob. That whore sniffer might have sought her out, I'm thinking, her being as pretty as she is. Hell, he might have gone after pretty Ruth, too."

"I've seen her now, that Ruth. If Hob's here, he's probably had both of them girls," Odin said. "He's still young enough to do that, hee!"

"Maybe." Spider inhaled from the pipe, realized it was spent, and knocked the dottle out onto the grass. "It is worth asking both of them about Hob. If he is here, though, I wonder why we've not seen him ourselves. Unless there are more bunks somewhere, Half-Jim has maybe a dozen hands, all told, as nearly as I can tell by counting hammocks and bunks and running two watches."

"A few are on liberty, a fellow told me when I woke up and asked a few questions," Odin said. "Off to Battramsley, he thought, to drink and fuck. So maybe fifteen hands or so, all counted."

"Aye, then," Spider said.

"Think we can take them?" Odin meant it as a joke but shook his head when it appeared that Spider was taking the question seriously.

"I do not want a skirmish," Spider said after some thought. "They know the grounds and the house better than we do, and we're only guessing at their numbers. We'd waste a great deal of time shooting and stabbing and we'd likely be dead before we ever found Hob. Too many rooms to search, and a whole third story above we have not even sniffed at. So, no. We've got to carry on and explore and play along like good hired ruffians."

Odin nodded. "Aye, then. Do you really still think the lad is here?"

"I hope he is here, and I hope he is alive," Spider answered. "Little Bob had Hob's knife, and he told me Hob and other smugglers had been rounded up, and our trail has led us here. So, then, this is the only place I know to search. I still don't know why Oakes or Fawkes would capture smugglers, though, but I am not sure I care so much about that if I can just find the young fool."

"Pressed men?"

"It could be," Spider said. "With this Wilson fellow that Oakes frets about raising trouble, maybe Oakes needed fighting men in a hurry. Or maybe he plans a voyage, like you reckoned. I have not heard any of these gents grumbling about being pressed, though, have you?"

"No," Odin said, "and I have never met a man who was pressed stop complaining about it. Never! Damned slavery, it is! Goddamned slavery!"

Spider raised his eyebrows. "I am going to guess you were pressed into the Royal Navy at some point in your long life." The more he journeyed with Odin, the more Spider wondered about him. He knew the man claimed to have sailed with Blackbeard and to have seen the famed pirate die, but he had no idea how Odin himself had escaped the noose if that tale was true. He knew the man claimed to be a Scotsman, but he'd heard him claim at least once to be Irish. And he had no idea what Odin's real name was. The man steadfastly refused to share it.

"Aye. Caught me in Plymouth, they did, me just a lad and having a bit of liberty after a voyage to the Mediterranean. I was on a merchantman crew, I was, and us docked for repairs, and I was in Plymouth getting my throat wet with booze and my whore pipe wet, too, ha! And the damned Navy came along and decided I was going to rig sails for His Majesty, whether I liked it or not. Bugger that bastard, I say!"

Spider wondered how much of that was true, but he decided not to push. "And here you are, still grumbling about it."

"Ha!" Odin nodded. "These lads here, Fawkes' boys, are lazy as any pirate when there is nothing to steal and no one to fight, but they do not grumble. They like the food and the easy duty."

"Aye," Spider said. "Men here get a place to sleep, decent food to eat, and, so far, the Admiralty is not sniffing about here for pirates. A lot of men would accept that, wouldn't need to press them, just tell them about the job. Maybe they were pressed, but don't mind because the food isn't full of maggots."

"Aye," Odin answered. "Do you think Hob would accept such duty?"

"Not much glory or adventure in it," Spider said, "and so he might have run off. The duty here is nothing to one such as Hob. But that Ruth, he might stick around for her, or for Daphne. He follows his pecker wherever it points, he does."

"Aye."

"Maybe we can ask a few gents if they got pressed without raising too much suspicion," Spider mused. "Maybe some of them sailed with Bonny. We know there was some of her men about. Fawkes has to be finding his men somewhere, I reckon. You could count on a bunch of gentlemen who sailed with Bonny to be the kind Fawkes would hire, men who are able to handle trouble."

"Not Little Bob. He can scarce handle his prick without falling off his bunk. Ha!"

Spider laughed. "That reminds me, Little Bob killed Tom Bonnymeade because he thought Bonnymeade betrayed the smugglers to their captors, we think. If Little Bob has any mates about smart enough to trace their way here like we did, they might plan a sneak assault or something. Pirates are not known for forgiveness. Lead and blood might fly, my friend. Lead and blood might fly."

"It would feel more like familiar territory if so, Spider John. Ha!"

Spider realized he was still holding his empty pipe and poked it into the band of his hat. "So where is Hob?"

"Could be he is one of the hands away on liberty," Odin said. "I believe they are expected back tonight."

Spider raised his eyebrows. "That's a thought. I forgot about that. Wouldn't that be a fair wind? Do you think we'll receive the same posts tonight? If you are posted at the gate, maybe you can plug the young bastard over the head when he comes back and carry him away from here. Hell, I will join you at your post. It ought to be just a few fellows coming back, aye? Maybe even drunk? We can handle those odds, for certain. And if we find Hob we'll snatch him and all run like the devil is at our heels!"

"Suppose we don't get the same orders tonight?"

"Fuck and bugger that! I say we disobey our orders and choose our own posts, for our own purposes," Spider said. "I do not rightly care if someone sneaks into the house and disturbs Ambrose Oakes. I don't care if someone shoots him in the head. Do you?"

"Ha! No."

"I care about Hob, and that is it. You were right, Odin. No need to poke our noses into the affairs of other folks, especially one such as Oakes. We'll take care of our own, we will, and the devil take the rest!"

"This is the most sense you've made since I met you," Odin said.

"Very well. We have a plan. While we wait, let's both explore, quietly, and see what we may see. If either of us learns anything of use, head to the ship's bell. It can be our rendezvous."

"Fine," Odin said. "I am going for the barn and stables back east of the house, see if maybe there are more bunks or signs of a larger force here. I'd like to know how many men I have to kill if it comes to that."

"If you ask any questions, be subtle," Spider said. "Don't go waving a pistol or poking your knife into anyone's eye."

"Do you think me crazy, Spider John?"

"Aye, I have no fucking doubt of it, really. I'm thinking of wrapping you in a wet sheet to keep you from trouble."

"Aye, then. I will go about pretending I'm not a real man who can fend for himself, then, and just meekly ask my questions, like a goddamned psalmist or something."

"While you do that, I will seek out Ruth. It seems Half-Jim and she are bunkmates, by the way."

"So he's not cut in half down there, then."

Spider ignored that remark. "If Half-Jim and Ruth are together and Hob got in the middle of that, the lad might well be under one of those mounds."

"Spider John, I have seen Hob fight, and so have you. I know you think him a little puppy, but he knows gun and blade as well as anyone, and what's more he actually loves to fight. Ha! I do not see a one-armed, one-legged man besting Hob. I truly don't."

"I have seen Half-Jim fight, too." Spider shook his head slowly. "He's mean, and tough, and he has no fear."

"I'll bet you a bottle of rum Hob wins," Odin said.

"We can't pay for a bottle of rum between us."

"You still owe me a bottle, from the chess."

"Just trust what I say about Half-Jim, and do not ever call him Half-Jim."

21

After they parted ways, Spider took a roundabout path back to the house. At this distance from the house, he spotted no sheds or outbuildings that might serve as a brig for a young trouble-maker like Hob, or as a hiding place if the lad was on the run. He was about to give up when he saw a tall young man leap over the north wall.

The man ran swiftly for the cover of a wide oak, and Spider took up a similar station. His first thought was that this was an assault, perhaps Mister Wilson or even one of Anne Bonny's crewmen on a raid. But the sun was bright, and Spider could not make out a single weapon. If this was a raid, it was poorly planned.

The mysterious man loped to another tree, and then another, and it seemed his aim was to avoid being seen from the house. Spider drew a knife and followed at a distance, taking care to avoid being seen.

The man he chased was big, and wide-shouldered, and his bare forearms showed the kind of muscles that came only with much hard work. Long blond hair hung in a ponytail across his broad back. He took a zigzagging path toward a point behind the barn, and Spider wondered immediately if Odin was still poking about in there. Spider scouted a path that might get him unseen to the barn—and past the goddamned chickens—before the interloper could catch Odin in there, but the odds were not good.

Once the man was behind the barn, though, and in a place where he could not be seen from any of the barred windows in the house, he walked into the open and strode confidently toward the barn. The man rounded the corner just as another man—not Odin—emerged from the building, and they exchanged friendly waves.

Was this one of Fawkes' men, then, come sneaking back after taking an ungranted liberty? Spider rushed to another tree, to be close enough to aid Odin if the old pirate was caught hiding in the barn. He could now see inside, where the giant man was brushing the mane of a brown mare. He saw no sign of Odin.

Spider watched the man work until he figured there was no way Odin would have patiently remained in hiding for so long, then snuck off himself to ponder this new mystery.

22

*H*ead down and meandering like a pup sniffing out a place to pee, Spider wandered near the pond and the south wall. He was hoping to find Ruth on watch. Instead, she found him.

"What are you doing?" She approached without a weapon in hand.

"I was posted to patrol here last night, and I lost a good knife," Spider lied.

She brushed hair away from her face and smiled. "Is that so?"

"Aye," Spider said. "It is so."

"Not looking for something else, then?" Her attitude seemed flirtatious to Spider, but he realized that might just be a wishful thought on his part. Spider also noted her hand stayed close to the pistol tucked into her belt. He remembered she also carried knives at the small of her back.

"Just the knife," Spider said. He winked. "I am sure you have plenty of attention from the gentlemen, but I saw you with Fawkes earlier and I have no wish to cross him. No wish to cross you, either, I dare say."

"See that you don't," Ruth said, without a trace of coquetry.

Spider had hoped speaking about attention from the crew would lead her to mention any previous attempts at dalliance, perhaps even some attention from Hob, but she said nothing. Instead, she spun about slowly, peering at the ground in search of Spider's fabricated knife.

"How many hands in Jim's crew?" Spider continued his ruse of seeking the blade. "And are they all shipmates of his?"

"Some are old mates, but I do not know how he met them all. Shy of twenty of us. Fawkes goes to Lymington on errands from time to time and does some recruiting while there, and now and then a fellow drifts away, as they will, so he hires a replacement. Most of them seem the rough sort."

"Aye," Spider said. "Seafaring men, all of them, I dare say. Better food here, though, than on any leaky bucket I served aboard. I like the fresh eggs. I had a cap'n once who thrashed a man for making chicken stew because stewed chickens can't lay eggs. I didn't care for that cap'n much, but I wholly agree with him on the quality of fresh eggs."

Ruth laughed, and Spider thought it somewhat magical. *Sorry, Em*.

"Did your cap'n really thrash a man over eggs?"

"Aye, indeed," Spider said, "although, to be entirely honest, he was the sort of bastard who looked for reasons to thrash his men."

Ruth laughed again. "I have known the sort."

"Oakes and Fawkes seem to treat the men fairly."

Ruth's mood darkened. "The *men* are treated well," she said. She started to say something else, seemed to reconsider, then continued. "They know enough to not spur a mutiny, Fawkes and Oakes do, although Jim can be rough if he's not obeyed."

"Aye," Spider said, noting the sudden change of wind but having no idea how to navigate it. "Good food, easy service. No need to press men into service here."

Ruth went back to looking for the fictional knife. "Jim always says give a man leeway but keep a watch. Treat him honest and see if he treats you honest in return. Most of them, he says, won't."

"Aye," Spider said.

"So Jim says be ready to shoot or thrust if they turn on you, but be fair before then. A man treated well might steal from you or betray you, Jim says, but a whipped man will certainly bite you, make no mistake."

"These gents all have a pirate look about them." Spider continued. "I have not seen any of my own mates here. I sailed with a young man who supposedly has family near Lymington. His name is Hobart, but we called him Hob. Young, fair-haired, good-looking fellow, strong and quick. Have you seen anyone like that about?"

Ruth stopped looking for the knife and looked up at Spider. "Is that why you came here? Seeking an old shipmate?"

"Well, no," Spider said, though her sharp gaze made him think he was foundering on hidden rocks. "I found myself in Lymington because the sea became a bit of a hazardous place for me and my friend to be. Plymouth seemed a bit hot, with lots of the king's lads rushing about, you know, and so many hangings in recent years. The sweet trade ain't so sweet now. Odin and I did not want to be next."

Ruth fixed him with a piercing stare. "A lot of men have been dangled, it is certain. A lot still ought to be."

He blinked. "Well, I hope the Admiralty never catches up to me, whatever I may deserve."

"If I should happen across an officer, I'll keep your secret, so long as you deal with me honest."

"Good, and should it ever chance to pass I will not tell them about you. Though I do not even know your full name."

"Ruth Copper."

"Is that your real name?'"

"What do you think?"

"I think it is a wise pirate who does not give her real name to any buccaneer who smiles at her."

"Are you flirting with me, Spider John Rush? If that is your true name?"

"I am not," he said, realizing it was a lie. "I know Jim Fawkes well enough to know that he would not respond well to that, and I suspect you might not like that much, either."

"Well, then," she said, "you were telling me how you did not come here with some secret purpose, even though you pay attention to everything and always seem to be wondering."

"Do I?"

"Aye," she said. "You seem a right sneaky fellow to me, always peering at the windows and listening to conversations."

"Ruth, I came here to this place because I heard there was work, no other reason. I do seem to recall my friend Hob mentioning a home near Lymington, though. Thought maybe he'd found work here, too. That is all."

Ruth did not respond to Spider's claim. "I have dallied here too long, I think. I am going to continue my patrol," she said. "I hope you find your knife."

"Very well, then," Spider said. "Thank you."

Spider pretended to search until Ruth was out of sight, then he turned back toward the house. There was no sign of Odin near the ship's bell behind the kitchen, so he veered toward the graves not far from the front of the house.

The clearing contained three mounds, and it seemed to Spider they all had been dug recently, but not at the same time. One had the beginnings of grass growing atop it and had begun to settle. The newest one was piled highest and still dark brown. None of them were marked in any way, but each was a bit wider and longer than a coffin.

The idea of being buried in the ground unsettled him. He'd always imagined his own death would be a violent one at sea, and that his body would be cast overboard to sink into the briny depths, perhaps with a Bible reading but most likely not. Most of the deaths he'd seen had ended that way, with no marker and no place where mourners could come to pray. Those deaths ended in a splash, in a place no one would ever find again.

These unmarked graves were not so different, he realized. They only did their work more slowly. Soon the mounds would settle and the grass would obscure them. No one passing would know the dead rested below.

Spider knelt by the graves and prayed. *Don't be down there, Hob. Don't be down there.*

23

The ship's bell rang, calling the day watch in from duty and the night watch to assemble. Spider, who had learned little else of note that day, headed to the kitchen for a quick meal before heading out to his post. No matter where he was told to patrol, he would find his way to Odin's side near the gate in hopes that Hob would return with the away party. If so, they would all flee from this madhouse together, and they would cut, stab or shoot anyone who got in their way. The idea that Hob might be among the men returning from liberty buoyed his spirits, and he almost looked forward to a little action to ease the tension.

Just let them try to stop us!

Platters of hot bread and cold chicken awaited him and the other hands on the large oak table, along with some onion slices. To drink, there was watered-down rum.

"That's the last of the liquor until the lads return," Mrs. Fitch said. "Still some tobacco left on the shelf there. Do not fight over it."

Spider stuffed his tobacco pouch, elbowing a couple of fellows away in the process, then tucked some fowl and onion into a hunk of bread. Odin selected a chicken leg and pointed to a hunk of cheese Spider had somehow missed seeing. Food in hand, they headed outside.

Fawkes was standing with Ruth near the ship's bell. "How is the leg, Odin?"

"Better," the old man said.

"Good. Gate duty again for you. We are expecting three men back from town with some casks of ale and rum and whisky, along with some other stuff the crew don't care so much about. They should have been back before this, and they had better arrive tonight. If they do, be sure they know the byword. And make sure no one is hiding in the wagon. Those lads are not the brightest."

"Aye." Odin headed toward his station, and almost trotted. Spider figured the old man was simply trying to demonstrate the fitness of his leg after Fawkes' question. He also noted that Odin seemed to limp a bit after a few steps.

Fawkes turned to Spider.

"Spider John, I had thought to assign you to the north wall so you could get to know another part of the grounds, but I hear you have been a-wander today." He grinned, as did Ruth.

"I like to know the territory I might have to fight on, Jim." Spider took a bite of cheese.

"Aye, I suppose that is wise. South wall again for you, though. Perhaps you will find your knife."

Ruth kissed Fawkes on the ear, setting the gold skull earring there to swaying, then sauntered into the house.

"Aye, sir. South wall." Spider headed in that direction without looking back, but he felt Half-Jim's gaze boring into his back. He tore into the bread and chicken, imagining it to be the bastard's neck.

Clouds soon cloaked the moon. Spider stayed at his station until it was good and dark, then headed north toward the gate. He moved slowly and quietly from oak to oak, careful not to trip on a root in the darkness. After an hour or so of slow progress, he found Odin behind a tree himself, just a few steps from the gate.

"Odin, it's me," Spider whispered.

"Did you bring me the rum you owe me?"

"I owe you no rum, we never finished the game."

"You were beaten, you lobcock."

"I will steal you a bottle when I can."

"That reminds me, I stole you a flask yesterday. You owe me two bottles of rum."

"You berated me for drinking too much after we all ended up marooned. Now you steal me bottles."

"It's just a habit," Odin said. "And you are too dour when sober."

Spider eyed the road beyond the low wall. "Have our wayward hands returned?"

"No," Odin said. "I am so bored I might just hike back to the house and kill Half-Jim."

"Well, if Hob is among our returning mates, as we hope, we might well be fighting our way out of here tonight. I doubt that will be dull duty."

"Aye. Ha! Did you talk to your girl Ruth?"

"I tried, but if she has seen Hob she is not prepared to discuss it. She keeps her secrets locked away like a cap'n's liquor. Did you find anything in the barn?"

"A pair of wagons, a couple of smelly horses, two ugly cows, and a bunch of hay. I think I'd rather smell a man three days dead in the bilge of a foul ship than ever smell horse shit again, Spider John."

"Just keep an eye for Hob," Spider said. "And be careful we do not shoot Hob, if he is with them. He does not know we are here and might take aim at us if it comes to a fight."

"Aye."

They sat in silence another fifteen minutes or so, until Spider heard a noise on the road leading down from the house and to the main gate. Spider placed a cautionary hand on Odin's shoulder, and they both listened. They both pulled guns from their belts, too.

The sounds grew louder, and Spider soon discerned a certain cadence. A sound like a shovel plunging into dirt, then a barely audible grunt, followed by the heavy fall of a booted foot.

"It's Half-Jim," Odin whispered.

"Aye. Do not call him that. Go talk to him."

"Why?"

"Because he is expecting you to be nearby, but he is not expecting me. At least, I hope he isn't. Anyway, it would look perilous strange if he was able to hobble right up to the bloody goddamned gate without a peep from the man he left guarding it, aye?"

"Aye," Odin grumbled. "You make a mean cap'n, Spider John."

The old man stepped out of cover and walked toward the road while Spider made sure he himself was hidden.

"Halt!" Odin brandished his pistol.

"Wolves, lambs, all of God's creatures," Fawkes said, slurring a bit.

Odin lowered his pistol. "Ahoy, master."

"No sign of our wayward gents? They ought to have come home by now." Spider had heard Fawkes slur this way before and knew the man to be more vicious when drunk. Spider prepared Hob's knife in his right hand, and a flintlock in his left.

Odin spat. "I've not seen a bloody thing until you came along, cap'n."

Fawkes proceeded on toward the gate. "Might as well come along with me," he growled. "I aim to raise a bit of hell, and I might need you to help me raise it. If those bastards are not back soon, I may form a party to go find them and string them up. Would you want to come along and carry the rope?"

"I would not mind a bit of a journey and action, sir," Odin said.

"Indeed," Fawkes answered. "Is that leg up to it? You still limp."

"My leg is fine, goddamn it."

"We can always cut it off and give you a chunk of wood like mine if it is not." Fawkes laughed. "Your friend Spider John made me a leg once. Didn't crack and weather like this one."

Odin growled. "No one cuts off my leg."

Spider watched the two men proceed to the gate. The idea of Odin left unsupervised with Half-Jim Fawkes made Spider nervous, and he started trying to devise a pretense for joining them. Nothing plausible came to mind, however, because Spider was supposed to be elsewhere on the grounds. So he waited, and listened, and hoped Odin did not start a fight. He crept closer, as quietly as he could and staying in the shadows.

He estimated half an hour had passed, during which Odin and Half-Jim did not come to blows, when he heard a chantey from the north. The sound, consisting mostly of bad harmony, seemed to emanate from the road to Battramsley.

Spider watched as Half-Jim opened the gate and stepped into the road, followed by Odin. The light from a lantern glowed in the distance, and soon Spider heard horses and the creaking of wheels. Drunken, singing voices rose above it all:

> *"Then he took her to the parson,*
> *And, of course, home again.*
> *There they met her father*
> *And seven armed men.*
> *Let us fly, said the lady,*
> *I fear we shall be slain!*
> *Take my hand, said the soldier,*
> *And never fear again.*
> *Fa, la la la, fa, la la la*
> *Fa, la la la, fa, la la la!"*

Fawkes bellowed. "Belay that noise!" The approaching wagon halted, and three men stepped down from it. Spider exhaled sharply. Hob did not seem to be among them. These fellows were all too skinny. But it was difficult to be sure in the darkness, and he had not seen Hob in a long while.

The men stood before Fawkes, between the lantern light from their wagon and Spider's hidden perch.

"You were away longer than expected." Fawkes barked it at them, and leaned on his crutch, wedging the handle in the pit of his mangled arm. That freed his hand to snatch up a pistol, Spider noted.

"Our business took longer than expected," one of the men answered.

Spider crouched low to the ground and crept toward them, trying to remain as concealed as possible along the way. He did not wish to reveal himself, but he would not leave Odin to fight alone if things went badly.

"You are to take as long as I say you can take," Fawkes said.

The three men approached Fawkes, and Spider was now certain none of them was Hob. One of them, the spokesman, drew within just a few feet of Fawkes. Odin remained three steps behind Fawkes and a bit to his left, leaving himself a clear shot if he had to take one. His hand rested on the butt of a pistol in his bandolier.

"Well, Fawkes, we are here with the supplies, as ordered, and no harm done," the spokesman said.

"Plenty harm done, Oliver." Fawkes raised his chin. "Discipline is harmed. My word is harmed, for I told the master you'd be back before this. My patience is sore harmed, that is for certain."

"Well, we don't see as we had any unreasonable delays, Half-Jim." Spider winced.

Fawkes lunged forward on his one good leg and the cracked peg, heedless of balance, and wielded the crutch like a sword. He wedged the end of it between the legs of the fool who'd used the hated nickname. A twist of the crutch sent both Fawkes and his adversary tumbling to the ground.

Odin drew his pistol and moved to the left, away from Fawkes.

Spider dashed to the wall, making far more noise than he wished.

Fawkes abandoned the crutch and snatched the dirk from his hatband. He jammed that into his adversary's neck and rolled away from the resulting red fountain. Then, lying on his back, he drew a flintlock pistol.

The two remaining men from the wagon raised their hands.

"Jim, Oliver held us up! Delayed us, he did! We've got no quarrel with you!"

Fawkes shot one of them anyway, putting a dark hole in his forehead. The other man turned to run. The horses reared in loud protest, and the wagon rolled backward.

Fawkes dropped his spent pistol, turned his face toward Odin and roared. "Kill him!"

Odin aimed his flintlock and fired just as the man tried to duck behind the wagon. The man screamed and tumbled in a heap on the dirt road. He clutched his leg.

"Calm those horses, Odin." Fawkes crawled to his crutch, rose in a swift maneuver he obviously had practiced many times, and spat on the dying man he'd stabbed. "I'll require my knife back when you are done bleeding," he said, as the man on the ground coughed and spasmed.

The other man rolled wildly, tried to rise, and fell. The wagon nearly rolled over him as Odin tried to calm the frightened horses.

The animals paid little attention to him. Odin cooed at them softly and snatched at the harnesses. The horses stomped and bit at the air, but they did not bolt.

Fawkes, meanwhile, hobbled on his crutch toward the man Odin had shot. That man implored for mercy. "I beg you, Jim, don't kill me. I begged Oliver to come back, I tried. And I was not going to fight you. I swear."

Fawkes came to a halt a few feet away from the man and tucked the handle of his crutch into the pit of his partially severed left arm. Then he drew the pistol from the holster attached to the crutch. "This man that shot you, he's new. His name is Odin. Came with another fellow, gentleman named Spider John. Good seafaring men, they are, and I now know Odin won't flinch and is a fair hand with a pistol. So, I do not believe I will be needing you in my crew now, Jack."

"No, Jim, wait . . ."

Fawkes did not wait.

"I am not going to waste a shot on you, though." He holstered the gun, then braced himself on the crutch. He leapt on the good leg, and planted the wooden peg of his maimed leg squarely on Jack's face. Jack began twitching.

Fawkes repeated the maneuver twice, balancing on the crutch, even though the first sickening crunch had likely been fatal.

Spider sheathed his weapons and hoped he'd forget the hammer-blow thunks he'd just heard. He clutched at his shirt and felt Em's pendant beneath the fabric. *Lord, I am trying to leave all this in my wake!*

The horses still protested, and it took both Odin and Fawkes to calm them.

"I am taking the wagon up to the house, Odin. Gather up my pistols, will you? I'll send some fellows down to take these poor dead bastards up to the house. We'll dig some more holes." He clambered up onto the wagon and took up the reins. Then he grinned and laughed harshly.

"I suppose these men are too dead to be of any use to the master."

Spider blinked. *What the bloody hell does that mean?*

Fawkes guided the wagon slowly up the hill, with the light from the lantern swinging near his face lending him a demonic aspect. He took up the song the three dead men would never finish:

"Then he took out sword and pistol
And caused them to rattle.
The lady held the horse
While the soldier fought in battle.
Hold your hand, said the old man,
Do not be so bold!
You shall have my daughter
And a thousand pounds of gold!
Fa, la la la, fa, la la la,
Fa, la la la, fa, la la la!"

Fawkes was still laughing wildly when the wagon disappeared in the darkness on its way to the house.

Spider met Odin at the wall. "I owe you a bottle of rum, Spider."

"Why?"

"I am not certain Hob could take that crippled bastard. He is mighty quick. Like a goddamned snake."

"Aye."

"You owe me a bottle, and I owe you a bottle, or maybe two bottles, so I guess we'll have to steal three bottles somewhere. Or four."

Spider appreciated Odin's levity, but there were three dead men in the road. "Did you have to shoot that fellow? We are trying to become honest men, you'll remember."

"I reckoned I'd miss, to be truthful, in the dark and far away and him on the run," Odin snarled. "Also, since I am, as you say, an honest man, I didn't know the son of a whore nor care much whether I hit him or not. What I cared about was Half-Jim not shooting me."

"Aye," Spider said. "Understood. And you have it right, I reckon. Half-Jim would have shot you if you'd not followed his command. And if you'd shot Half-Jim, well, that would leave us with many things to explain and little chance of staying on here and finding Hob."

Odin spat. "Do you think Hob fought that bastard?"

"Lord, I hope not." His gaze aimed involuntarily up the hill, toward the graves beyond the oaks and the shadows.

24

Spider had not remained behind to watch Fawkes' man gather the slain. Instead, he'd gone to the pond, trying to make sense of what was happening here.

He returned to the house when the morning bell rang. The crewmen who had collected the corpses from the road were now piling earth back into a fresh grave—one pit for all three of them, which forced Spider to consider the number of previously buried bodies might be higher than he'd reckoned. Bitter and tired, he went to the kitchen.

Mrs. Fitch stayed as far from the table as she could and moved platters and kettles about for no reason Spider could divine. "Too much," she muttered. "It's all too much."

Odin had arrived in the kitchen before Spider and was buttering a hunk of bread. He put down the knife, tore some fowl away from the platter with his fingers, and stuffed the poultry into his mouth. He started to approach Spider, but the latter waved him off. He wanted a chance to talk with Mrs. Fitch, and thought he might have more success without Odin's presence. She was already rattled, and Odin was never soothing by nature.

Odin gave Spider a quick nod and left the kitchen.

The men broke their fast with chicken, cheese, and bread, with some boiled eggs as well. Spider noted that Mrs. Fitch was boiling more eggs even as the last crewmen were finishing their meal. *She might well know a great deal about what goes on in this house*, he thought, so he dawdled over his meal. Once he and Mrs. Fitch were alone, he struck up a conversation.

"We appreciate the meals, Missus Fitch, we truly do."

"Thank you, John." She had paused awkwardly in the middle of her sentence, as if pondering whether to add the word "Spider." She went back to her work, as though to end the talk.

"You have many mouths to feed, do you not? Crew, plus patients upstairs. How many up there?"

"What?" She looked over her shoulder as she hovered near the boiling kettle. Rising steam moistened a loose strand of hair, and it was losing its curl. "I'm sorry. This business in the night, men dying. It's horrible. Five, at present. Patients, I mean. Five patients. Not so many as a month or two ago."

"Oh? Did some find cures, and leave?"

"No," she said quietly. "Some found death and were buried, God rest their souls."

"I see," Spider said. "The graves."

"Aye, the graves, for the bodies. But their souls are in a better place now, in the Lord's mercy." She lowered her head and closed her eyes a moment. Her lips moved but Spider could hear no words emanating from them. Then she glanced at him. "And three more dead today, I am told, although these by violence and not sickness."

"I've heard how the men died last night," Spider said. "Bloody awful business, that. But the patients, did they die of violence, too?"

"No," she said. "They died on their own, though the master tried to save them."

"Some sort of accident?"

"Why, no," she said, looking away. "They departed this world one at a time, they did. Poor wretched souls."

"How many?"

She looked at him suspiciously. "You ask questions, don't you?"

Spider nodded. "I am curious. Odin says I should stop."

"Odin looks like the very devil."

"He takes some pride in that. So how many patients died?"

"Four," she said. "All young men, bless them. Better men than these who lost their lives last night, I am certain, whatever their ailments might be that put them here."

Spider said nothing.

She shook her head. "I told the master of the house these were wicked men, I did. I told him. I doubt very, very much their souls are in a better place today, John. No good could come from such rough . . ."

She stopped suddenly and looked away from Spider.

"Fear not, Missus Fitch," he said. "I am a rough sort, I know. Like most seafaring men. Scarred, missing a finger, missing some teeth. But looking rough don't make me rough, if you understand me. I avoid violence when I can, although I've often thought of my own soul and where it might be headed . . ."

He touched Em's pendant beneath his shirt. "I am wondering if I shouldn't go from this place. Might be too rough for me."

"I have had the same thought," she whispered. "I have worked for Mister Oakes a long time, at the old place for three years before we came here, and I do not mind cooking and cleaning for the poor souls upstairs, especially Miss Daphne, bless her. But that Mister Fawkes, and the men he brought along . . . it cannot lead to anything worthy, I say. I should just go."

"How did the master meet up with one such as Fawkes?"

"I do not know for certain, although the master was a sailing man long ago. I suppose they met at sea."

"Aye, that could be. Once shipmates, always shipmates, or so I've heard. Some fellows I would as soon never see again, though, for my part." He winked and hoped the gesture might be reassuring, or even charming. It seemed lost on Mrs. Fitch, though.

Spider tried a new course. "Where would you go?"

"What?"

"If you left here. Where would you go?"

"That is a good question," she muttered.

She wrapped her hands in cloth and lifted the kettle from the stove, setting it onto a large cutting board. Next, she ladled steaming eggs into a bowl. Spider counted ten eggs. "Can I help you crack them open?"

"No, thank you. I can manage."

She let them cool, glancing at Spider now and then suspiciously. "Have you no place to be, John?"

"I am not weary," he said, preparing a pipe. "And I love the aroma of a good kitchen. Not something I get to enjoy much at sea."

She nodded. "Very well. Forgive me if I work rather than chat."

"Forgiven."

She shelled the eggs, then mashed them in a bowl while Spider lit his pipe. "Easier for the patients to eat," she said, when Spider asked about the mashing of the eggs.

"Are they restrained? Daphne told me of being wrapped in sheets."

Mrs. Fitch shrugged. "They are, most of the time, locked in their rooms, although some are allowed out for exercise. Perambulations, the master calls it, says it does them good. If they get out of hand, Simon or any other fellow up there will wrap them up or tie them down, as need be. But sometimes they chomp on their food so, and eat so violently and thrash about, that we fear they may choke. So they eat mashed eggs, and mashed potatoes, and soups and such fare as that."

"And is there an illness among them?"

"What, sir?"

"An illness among the patients, to account for the deaths? Some fever or such? Or do they take their own lives?"

She wiped her hands on a towel and seemed to be gathering her thoughts. "Illness, yes. Mister Oakes says they died of illness, not by their own hands. It comes on slowly, and they waste away. He tells me I need not worry about me own self, that there is no contagion. It is a consequence of their mental afflictions, he says, some of them being so mad as to not cling much to life. You may hear some howling, John, some sobbing at night, from those wretched souls. Tucked away here, they are, out of sight from their respectable families, and Mister Oakes doing what he can to help them and yet . . . and yet they moan so, and they howl. Lost, they are, and perhaps better off with the Lord than ignored here on Earth by them that are supposed to love them."

Spider nodded. "It is good to know there is no illness that might spread," he said. "All those graves, I had to wonder."

"Contagion or none, still, I avoid going up there. You should, too."

"I see." Inwardly, Spider shuddered. The road to Hob was a nightmare path, first murder, followed by pirates and smugglers, then a madhouse, and now a series of deaths. *And Hob might not even be here,* he thought. *This whole quest might just be a fool's errand, needlessly keeping me from Em and my boy. It might be for the best if I just burned this hellish place to the ground.*

"He, Mister Oakes, shows no fear of being around the sick patients himself," Mrs. Fitch added. "And he works like the devil to save them once they catch ill. Sometimes he goes without sleep for days, stays right by them."

"You must have seen many deaths, though, over the years," Spider said.

She frowned. "What?"

"You said you've been with Mister Oakes a long time. I reckon that means you've seen patients die often. Much sadness for you to endure."

Mrs. Fitch seemed puzzled. "Well, come to think of it, there was not much death at Gayle Fields, that's the old place. Just that Mister Lamb, and he was nearly ancient and not long for the world even had his mind been whole."

Spider pondered that. "So, these poor souls dying, that'd be a new thing then?"

She nodded. "But we had fewer patients then, it was a much smaller house. That is why the master moved us here, you know, so he would have more room for more patients, do more good in the world."

"I wonder that patients here die, but not the ones you had at the old place." Spider scratched his beard. "What would the difference be?"

Mrs. Fitch shook her head. "I don't know, really. I just never thought much about it. I . . . well!"

"Yes?"

"The poor ones that took ill mostly came from those Mister Fawkes fetched. A couple before that, they came in separate from each other and died, but then Mister Fawkes came back from somewhere with half a dozen all at once. And a couple of those have died from that batch. Maybe they all had a disease in common?"

"Maybe," Spider said. "That ever happen before, a whole batch of patients at once?"

"Heavens, no."

"Where do the patients come from?"

"Families bring them, usually," she said. "Sometimes Mister Fawkes goes and fetches them." Then she sighed heavily. "I honestly think, in some cases, certainly in poor Daphne's case, the families just want the poor souls out of the way. They pay Mister Oakes and then have done with them, other than sending funds for their boarding and food. No one even comes to mourn them when they die, or to take them home to be buried."

Spider spotted a tear on her cheek.

A rap on the door drew her attention, and she opened it quickly, seeming glad to have the interruption. A giant of a man, wild blond hair dangling across his face, strode into the kitchen carrying a heavy bucket. Spider recognized the man instantly as the fellow who had leapt over the north wall and snuck to the barn.

"Fresh milk," the man said. His voice was barely audible, and it seemed to Spider the man struggled over the words. He did not struggle with the bucket, though. He hefted it onto the table as though it was filled with air, and did not slosh any milk over the top.

"Thank you, Michael. You are a dear." She tore a hunk of bread from a partial loaf and handed it to him. "I'll help with the chickens, in just a while. Wait for me."

Michael, who seemed to be perhaps twenty years old, at most, nodded and gave Spider an awkward glance. Then he scurried back out into the yard.

"Don't mind him," Mrs. Fitch said. "He is shy, because he is none too bright and he has difficulty with words. But he sees to the cows and the chickens and does many chores for us. A good lad, Michael is."

"I think I saw him earlier, sneaking over the wall."

Mrs. Fitch blushed. "I think he must have a lass nearby. That's what Raldo says, anyway. Raldo thinks everyone is . . . well, let us call it courting. He thinks of little but women and supposes all other men to be the same. But I have teased Michael a bit, you know, he's such a dear, and I think in this instance Raldo has the truth of it. Michael has a sweetheart, and he sometimes is not around when he ought to be."

Spider mused upon that point. "Indeed."

Mrs. Fitch whirled. "You will not say anything to the master, or to that dreadful Mister Fawkes, will you? I would hate to see anything happen to Michael."

"I shall keep my mouth closed, Missus Fitch, you may rely upon it. I have no reason to wish your friend ill."

"Thank you." She returned to her work, using a ladle to fill a pitcher with milk. Then she took a key from a peg near the door and unlocked a cupboard. She pulled out a bottle, then the cork, filling the room with an enticing scent of rum that drew Spider's attention. She poured a bit into a wooden cup, then added some water from another pitcher. Next, she returned the bottle to its place.

"Might you and I share a drink?" Spider pointed toward the bottle.

"I do not drink," she said. "I think rum is the devil's tool. I would not give this to the poor souls upstairs, I would not, but Mister Oakes says it is medicinal. Nor would I serve drink to the men, but . . ."

"But we would mutiny if you did not," said Gold Peter, walking into the kitchen. Daphne followed in his wake.

"Aye," Mrs. Fitch said harshly, locking the cupboard.

She pointed to the bowl of mashed eggs and the pitcher of milk. Peter placed these on a large platter, scowling at Spider.

"And this," Mrs. Fitch said, holding forth the cup of watered rum, "is for the sick Irish lad. The master says it will lift his spirits."

Daphne took the cup and did a curtsy. "I will see to it, ma'am.

Bram will have his special cup." The girl saw that Spider was watching and covered the top of the cup with her hand, as if to block anyone from even taking a whiff. "This is not for you. Not for you."

"See that she does as she is supposed to do," Mrs. Fitch said quietly to Peter.

"Aye," Gold Peter growled. He carried the food and drink out of the kitchen. Daphne started to follow but glanced at Mrs. Fitch and saw the woman's attention was elsewhere. She strode toward Spider, lifting the cup as though it were a magical elixir. "Quickly," she whispered, "and mind you, just a sip."

Spider winked, lifted the proffered cup, and took a small swallow. Then he gave it back to the girl, who dashed out quickly.

Mrs. Fitch hummed quietly across the room.

Spider shook his head. "Is that a good idea, Missus Fitch, trusting the girl with liquor? Won't she drink that herself, or use it to bribe Gold Peter or Simon for some favor?"

"The master says it is an important part of her treatment, to show some trust. So we allow her some chores. Peter will see to it she does as she is told."

"I am not so sure any seafaring man can be trusted when it comes to rum."

"Well, the master is likely awaiting the cup by the patient's side, so all will be well, I am sure."

Spider doubted that. *All will be well? How much freedom does death-obsessed Daphne have? Does she come and go as she pleases?*

"I am off to help Michael feed the chickens and choose a few for the pot," Mrs. Fitch said, exiting through the back door. She paused. "Thank you for the company, John. It is a rare thing here. Rather gentlemanly."

"Thank you for the company and the food, Missus Fitch."

She left. Spider puffed away at his pipe, took up the key from the peg, and opened the cupboard. It held only three bottles, and he had no doubt Mrs. Fitch would notice if one vanished. So instead of taking one, he merely helped himself to a swig or two, then locked up and replaced the key on its peg.

"Never a good idea to trust a seafaring man around liquor, I warned her. To bed, then," he told himself, "and let there be no nightmares."

25

*B*efore he reached the cellar, a voice halted him.

"Spider John."

Spider turned to see Ambrose Oakes at the end of the hall, one hand holding a bottle and the other opening a door. "Sir?"

"Fawkes tells me your old friend gave a good accounting of himself last night," Oakes said. "Shot a man on the run, in the dark. That is no easy task."

"Odin is a tough bastard and a fair hand in a fight, sir," Spider said. "I told you that." He also wondered why Oakes was not upstairs with the patient, as Mrs. Fitch had supposed.

"Come, John." Oakes stepped into the room. Spider followed and discovered it was a library, complete with a wide desk and a wooden mechanism that resembled two wagon wheels on an axle. Slats mounted between the wheels held open books, six of them, and Spider soon surmised the wheels could be turned to bring whichever of the books was desired to the top. All the shelves were on axles, too, and were rigged so that they always remained perpendicular to the floor.

"This is beautifully done, sir," Spider said, running a finger over the smooth maple.

"Oh, yes, you are a carpenter. Yes, I have had that a long time. I had it made when my library was much smaller and space was difficult to come by." Oakes moved a candle on the desk, placed his bottle next to it, and removed two glasses from a drawer.

"I might try to build something like this for ship use," Spider said. "I've made travelling desks, but nothing like this. Charts would be most at home on one of these, I dare say."

Oakes poured two glasses of dark wine and handed one to Spider. "This is Spanish, and quite excellent. To our newly dead."

Spider drank.

Oakes did, too, then sighed. "So quick, that transition between life and death. One moment a breathing man with dreams and fears, and the next . . . cold, lifeless. And especially so when dying by violence, would you agree?"

"Aye," Spider said. "I've seen too damned much of that in my life."

Oakes sipped again. "I do not much care for the ruffians surrounding me, Spider John. I mean no offense, of course."

"Of course."

"I must have protection, though, if I am to do my work—my vital work—and so I do as I must. Mister Fawkes, himself a rough fellow but one I know, hired them on my behalf."

"You have known Jim a long time?"

Oakes nodded. "If one man can really know another, yes. We were adrift once, he and I, almost thirty days in a launch, with a few others." His almost hairless brow furrowed. "We watched men die slowly, then. Hunger. Tremendous thirst. Fawkes and I, we were young then, and survived the deprivation, but the others . . . you could watch them dying, and almost predict the moment their souls would escape."

The man's head tilted, as though he was watching a ghost ascend.

"So, I do know Fawkes, to an extent, and he knows me, if men reveal their true natures under duress. We see what men do, hear what they say, but their minds remain unfathomable, castles that can never be breeched and their souls likewise a mystery. Or so they say. I dare to believe otherwise. I assail impregnable castles, Spider John."

The fat man drained his glass and poured another.

"Those deaths," he pointed toward the west, where Fawkes had left three dead in the road, "are regrettable. Men of the caliber and, shall we say, attitude I require are not easy to find, and I would prefer not to squander them through senseless violence. But those men were malcontents."

He inhaled deeply. "We'd hoped sending them to town for supplies, and giving them a brief taste of freedom, might appease them somewhat. Well, so I believed. Mister Fawkes was of another mind. I hope this mess does not lead to mutinous thoughts?"

So, Oakes takes a sounding, does he?

"I have heard no grumbling," Spider said. "Men who have lived on the account know violent death very well, and they know a fellow who disobeys is likely to bring it upon himself. If you started treating them all badly, or did not pay what is owed or something like that, they'd rise up. If they think a mate has been dealt unfair, they might rise up. But if they wager these men bought their own deaths by crossing Fawkes, well . . . they likely do not care."

Oakes considered that. "That is somewhat reassuring, John. I'll rest my mind where mutiny is concerned. We still have lost hands. But . . . your friend apparently is capable, and Fawkes speaks well of you. Perhaps the two of you are more than equal to the three we lost last night."

"We will serve well, sir."

"You look weary, Spider John. Go to your rest. As for me, I have a patient upstairs awaiting my attention." The heavy man opened another drawer, frowned, then opened another.

"Aye, sir." Indeed, it had been a long night, and Spider's head seemed to be spinning a bit from the rum and the wine. He left the room. Behind him, Oakes bellowed.

"Missus Fitch! Where is the sedative?"

"I believe the woman is out to the barn, doing something about chickens," Spider answered when Mrs. Fitch did not.

"Confound it," Oakes muttered. "Thank you, John."

Spider headed toward the cellar, chose a hammock next to the snoring Odin, and soon plummeted into a deep sleep.

* * *

"Spider."

The hammock rocked like a boat on a turbulent sea.

"Spider!"

He forced his eyes open—his eyelids seemed anchored, somehow—and peered into Odin's face. It seemed the old man was spinning, lending his ghoulish face a more sinister aspect than usual. Then everything blurred, and Spider saw worms crawling from Odin's wounds.

"Lord!" His stomach heaved, and hot fluid rose in his throat, but he coughed hard and choked it down.

"It will not be long until duty, Spider John. You've slept an unusual long time, you bastard. Are you ill?"

Spider blinked and shook his head. "I do not feel right." He looked at Odin, and saw only the familiar hideous face of his friend.

"I slept ill, and had strange dreams, Odin." Indeed, night memories swam in his head, visions of Em, holding the hand of a boy who looked like Hob, both of them shouting words he could hear but not understand as Half-Jim Fawkes thumped his peg leg and crutch into the sand while pacing behind them, laughing maniacally.

Spider attempted to roll out of the hammock and onto his feet, but somehow ended up on his knees. His stomach seemed filled with bilge, and he began to cough. Small splotches of gray fluid hit the floor beneath him and glinted in the lantern light.

"Jesus," he said. "Oh, Lord."

"Spider, do you need help standing?" Odin lifted him. Spider coughed a bit more, and Odin blinked against the spray.

"There is illness here, Odin." Spider walked uneasily toward the chest where his weapons were kept. "Scurvy, or some plague, I know not. I should not have gone upstairs. Stingo warned me."

"Lord," Odin said.

"Missus Fitch says that's what filled those graves out there, a sickness," Spider replied. "She says Oakes told her it was no worry, just something related to the patients and their afflictions, but . . ."

"I don't trust him any more than I trust a ship's purser, or a fucking shark."

"Nor do I," Spider said. "The man hires killers and thieves and pirates."

"Like us."

"We are former pirates, Odin." Spider closed his eyes. His head was slowly halting its mad spin.

"Not former killers, though, if that is what it takes to get out of here. Let us go, Spider. We have not seen Hob, have we?"

Spider shook his head. "If I have to dig up those graves to make certain Hob is not in the cold, cold ground, that is what I'll do ere I leave this house. I do not hold you to any promise, though, Odin. You've been a true friend to me, but I can't ask you to stay here and catch ill."

Odin spat. "I'll stay. You have been a true friend to me, too, and I am not accustomed to that, by thunder. Most men keep their distance."

"You are a frightening son of a whore, Odin."

"Ha! But if I get a pox and die, Spider John, I am going to haunt you until the end of your days, and maybe beyond."

Spider laughed weakly. "I suspect you are going to haunt me no matter how you die. Besides, my mind stops spinning now. I can stand." He did so. "Oakes is up there with patients a lot, and Gold Peter and Simon, too. They all seem healthy. Perhaps I simply ate too much of that cold chicken."

"Perhaps."

"Or," Spider muttered, grasping Odin by the shoulder, "Shit! I'm a lubber, Odin. Maybe I didn't eat too much. Maybe I drank too much."

"You always drink too much."

"Aye, and I always hold it better than this, don't I? So what might be different this time? I think . . ."

The doors leading out to the grounds opened, flooding the room with sunlight. Hugh, the Frenchman, leapt into the cellar and landed with a flourish. "I thirst, my friends!"

He dashed between hammocks and hurdled a sea chest, then stopped at another and lifted the lid. He took out a small pewter flask.

"It is wine from home, and I have only a few precious drops left," he said as Spider and Odin watched him pop the cork. He looked at them suspiciously, and held the bottle out of reach. "Pardon me, but I have not enough for sharing."

"I've had enough to drink, I believe," Spider said.

Hugh drank deeply enough to indicate he had a bit more wine than he had claimed. He wiped his lips and winked. "Enough, you say? No, no, no. There is never enough of this. Say, you will not tell *notre capitaine*, will you? He will take it amiss if he knows."

"I saw nothing," Spider said.

"I am half blind. Ha!"

Hugh smiled. "You please me, my new friends. A fair man, Fawkes is, until he has caught you breaking his rules. Then, you would not want to be the man who broke the rules. Those three last night, they broke the rules."

"Aye."

"I break rules, too, though I do it wisely, and quietly!" He emptied the flask. "I had some wine coming to me, and I hope it was in the wagon. Our shipmates, they went for supplies, and I asked for supplies, too. But they cannot tell me, alas, if they found my wine. If they brought me my wine, not so good as this from my home, but wine is wine, and if they brought me my wine I shall offer a sip to the both of you."

Spider and Odin nodded.

"You did not help to unload the wagon? Were there some bottles?"

"No, we did not unload."

Hugh sighed.

"Well," Spider said. "Maybe you will find it. And we will share any good fortune that comes our way, as well. But fortune don't favor us, usually."

Hugh smiled. "Fortune. She is a fickle bitch!"

"Did you sail with Fawkes?"

"I met him a year ago, serving with Ruggard Blake. Fawkes was first mate. Hard men both, Blake and Fawkes. But the law was catching up to us, and we dispersed. I stayed with Fawkes, because Blake was coughing blood by then. He is dead now, most probably."

Spider nodded. "I sailed with Fawkes, too, a while back. Bent Thomas was our cap'n, back then."

Hugh smiled. "Then you know Fawkes, and you know to never"—he looked around quickly, then continued—"never call him Half-Jim."

"Aye. He does not like that."

"Very well, my friends! I am now fortified to return to duty." Hugh placed the flask back in his trunk and left the way he came.

Odin tapped Spider on the shoulder. "I woke you because if you wish to seek Hob or ask questions before we get sent out to our posts, you are losing time."

"Thank you," Spider said, heading up the cellar stairs. "How is the injured leg?"

"Better than your stomach. Ha!"

"That reminds me, don't drink a dram of liquor, nor water unless you bring it up from the well yourself."

Odin scratched his nose. "Why?"

"Poison, I think."

Spider rushed up the steps.

26

Between his attempts to sneak upstairs in search of Hob, Spider did a lot of thinking.

He did not for a moment believe those graves outside held men who had died of illness. It was too much of a coincidence, and the illness did not behave like any he'd heard of in his sailing life. He'd heard tell of sickness ravaging entire crews and accounts of Naval vessels that had been turned away from ports because of some horrid disease. But he'd never heard of any illness that claimed one life at a time, as Mrs. Fitch had described. If some malady upstairs was killing men, it seemed likely Oakes would be taking more precautions.

Those thoughts were still tossing in his mind when Odin beckoned from the front door. Spider hurried out.

"Is something amiss?"

Odin shook his head. "No, I just wondered whether you'd made it up to find Hob."

"No. Those ruffians upstairs seem ever alert."

"Damn," Odin said. "I am tired of this place. I have been thinking about poison. Why'd you get sick from it, and I did not?"

"Because I drank from a bottle Missus Fitch keeps tucked away, supposedly as medicine for patients that have taken ill." He quickly told Odin about all he'd learned in the kitchen.

"So, poison in that bottle, then?"

"Perhaps, Odin, but maybe not." Spider inhaled deeply and gathered his thoughts, then looked around to make sure no one was close enough to overhear as they strolled.

It was true enough that Spider knew nothing about mental afflictions, but he'd sailed with many a buccaneer who was clearly not right in the head—and none of them had died wasting in their beds. He'd seen a man walk right off the bowsprit and sink into the arms of death below, and he'd seen a man put a flintlock to his temple and pull the trigger. But he'd never seen a crazy man simply waste away and die in bed. Poison seemed more likely, and this sudden stomach trouble of Spider's reinforced that notion.

"Rum never made me churn like that, Odin."

"This is true, by thunder."

"It could have just been medicine, though, something in the bottle to treat the patient that hit me amiss. Remember old Doctor Boddings, in his cups and lecturing. A medicine given proper would save a man, but a wrong dose or bad circumstances and it would kill him." He pictured Boddings, pontificating while in his cups aboard *Plymouth Dream*, and wondered if the old man lived. He had been quite ill himself. He was still of sound mind when last seen, though, and was a surgeon of long experience who seemed to know his business.

Odin grinned. "I thought Doctor Boddings just told us all that because he had booze in those bottles and wanted to keep us out of them."

Spider nodded. "Aye, he liked his drink and hoarded it away. But he seemed a right good doctor, though, and probably spoke true about his profession, I think."

"Did Missus Fitch give you the drink? Was she trying to kill you?"

"No," Spider said. "I snuck it, when I had a chance. But there is more. Daphne gave me a sip from a cup she was supposed to take up to a sick lad."

"Was she trying to kill you?"

"Jesus might know. I do not." Spider rubbed his hands together. "And for that matter, Oakes gave me a bit of wine, too."

Odin scoffed. "Everyone just pouring you drinks all day, then?"

"Makes for murky waters, it does. Let us head back to the house, I want to make another try to find Hob."

They walked in a broad circle that reversed their course. "Spider, maybe ask why someone might be killing people here, instead of worrying whether it is poison or medicine or what."

"Aye, Odin, good thought."

"So why would Missus Fitch poison people?"

Spider considered. "She feels sorrow for those poor souls, Odin, the mad ones upstairs. She thinks death might be a release for them, send their souls to a better place." Spider snapped his fingers. "And I heard Oakes yell for her, wondering where some medication had got to."

Odin scoffed. "She does not seem a killer to me, and there is that little Daphne. She seems a right better suspect."

"Aye. She might poison anyone, for any reason. And she is let to walk about, it seems. Some notion of showing trust, Missus Fitch says, part of her treatment."

"Trust is a foolish notion," Odin said. "Piracy drove that nonsense out of my head. Ha!"

"You trust me, don't you?"

"Not with my flask, I don't, nor do I trust your notions about helping people and figuring out who killed who and all that. I am just here because you and Hob both owe me, remember?"

"Aye."

"Would Oakes have a reason to kill people?"

Spider considered that. "He is here to help people, he says, and he makes his coin by caring for them. If he kills them off, I suppose that families would stop paying him, wouldn't they?"

"Aye, probably."

"And what reason might he have? He seemed a bit upset about the violence of last night. He's got an ego, for certain, but I don't know why he'd snuff people like candles." The man, indeed, had seemed remorseful when discussing the deaths in the night, but Spider knew that could have been an act. He'd seen many a smiling man sneak a knife into a belly.

"Fawkes?"

Spider shook his head. "Knife or gun, for him. Not poison."

"One of these other brigands?"

"Maybe. There is a farm hand that sneaks about, as well, large fellow."

Spider sighed heavily. He was glad Odin was here to discuss things with. The old man's prying questions and eager ears had, in the past, helped Spider settle things in his mind when pondering one puzzle or another. But they could not keep tossing ideas back and forth like clouds in contrary winds. He longed to find Hob, and it would be folly for both Spider and Odin to try to get upstairs.

"I am going in again. Wish me good fortune."

"I don't think I've ever had a prayer heeded, Spider, but hell. I'll try." The old man scooted off, barely limping now.

Moments later, Spider was making his fourth attempt at a foray upstairs when he felt a tug at his sleeve before he'd ascended a single step.

He turned to find Ruth smiling at him. "Come with me, will you?"

Spider blinked. "Does Fawkes summon me?"

"No," she said. "I do."

She turned and strolled toward the sitting room where Spider had first encountered Ambrose Oakes. She had no weapons Spider could see. He followed her, a bit too quickly. His head throbbed a bit still, and something in his stomach swirled.

"Aren't you still on watch, Ruth?"

She smiled again. "Jim gave me leave to come off watch early. And I have questions for you."

"Questions?"

"Aye." She smiled. "You are not like these other pirates here. I can tell. You are looking for something, Spider John. Or maybe you are hiding something. I cannot decide which."

"No," Spider said. "I have dark deeds in my past I am trying to outrun, like most of these gents, I suppose, and I came here seeking honest work. The work I found don't seem quite so honest, I reckon, but I have meals and a roof and there has not been a goddamned Navy frigate come sailing by, so it suits for now."

She shook her head and stood a bit closer. She smelled clean, and he noticed her dark hair was a bit damp.

"No, Spider. You have some purpose. I see it in the way you glance about, the way you listen to everything being said."

"I just pay attention because noticing things has kept me alive, so far."

"So far. I noticed that you noticed me."

She stepped forward and kissed him. He had his arms around her before stopping to consider whether that was a good idea. His hands searched for the three knives he recalled seeing previously at the back of her belt, but they were not there.

"I am supposed to be on watch soon," Spider said, "and Fawkes has not given me no leave."

"He certainly won't give you leave to do this." She kissed him again, more urgently.

Spider noticed his body responding quickly. It had been a long, long time. Ruth's mouth opened to his, and he pulled her tight against him.

I'm sorry, Em.

Ruth's right hand raked his back, slowly, starting from the base of his neck and moving downward. The stroke made it almost halfway to his belt before Spider remembered he had knives tucked away there.

He stepped back quickly, only to realize Ruth's other hand had grasped his belt buckle. He backed against a bookshelf, and she pressed him against it.

"Did you think I was going for your knife? You are not supposed to carry one of those upstairs, you know." She winked at him. "It is against the rules. It is a very good thing I caught you before you climbed the steps."

"I know. And yes, I thought you might be trying to take me unawares, as they say."

"If I meant to fight you, I'd have brought a knife of my own. But I am not carrying any right now. I don't need a knife right now. Do I?"

Spider blinked. "I reckon you do not need a knife."

She smiled and opened his weapon belt buckle.

"So why resist?" She kissed him again.

When he managed to pull his lips from hers, he said, "because Fawkes likely would kill me." *Also, there's a woman I love and have not seen in years,* he thought, *although that hasn't stopped me before, so . . .*

"Oh, yes, he certainly would kill you," she said. "Have no doubt. He probably would kill me, too. But he is away from the house, I know that for certain. And the master is upstairs, working with a sick patient. We won't be disturbed."

Her hand reached into his breeches, and she clutched him.

"Ruth," Spider said, "I do not think we should . . ."

"You are stronger than me," she cooed, her right hand moving down his arm. Her left hand moved, too. "If you truly wanted to pass up this opportunity, I think you would have cast me aside and escaped by now. But you haven't. Have you?"

Spider's head spun. He pulled her grasping hand away, and the friction resulting from that nearly toppled him overboard. "Ruth . . ."

She backed toward the divan. "Come here."

He buckled his belt, with some difficulty. "Is this what you do, play the whore and entice men when Fawkes isn't looking?"

He'd meant the remark to sting, to change the game a bit. But she simply smiled. "Why should I not have a bit of fun when I can?"

That convinced him she was up to something. This change in her attitude toward him was too sudden. Spider decided to play a game, too.

He stepped toward her. "No wonder Jim's men do not complain," he said.

She lifted her blouse over her head and tossed it on the floor. "I am no harlot, Spider John. I choose my mates as I will. And I am choosing you."

She cupped her breasts and smiled. "Will you choose me?"

Spider joined her on the divan and placed a hand on her breast. He kissed her, hard. She leaned into him and he was almost convinced her enthusiasm was genuine.

"Some of these gents were even captives, right? Taken in some sort of raid?"

She startled. "What? No, I mean . . ."

He had a knife at her neck in a heartbeat.

"I do not want to fight, but I think you are trying to start some trouble for me," Spider said. "Are you? Quietly now."

She blew aside a strand of hair. "I think you came here to Pryor Pond for some reason, and I am trying to find out what that is."

"Do you now?"

"Yes," she said. "My blouse, if you please."

Spider raked the garment closer with his boot, never taking his eyes from her face while she reached for it. Once she had it, he stood while she donned it.

Spider held the knife ready; it occurred to him she might have hidden a dirk between the divan cushions in advance of her little operation. "Does Fawkes know you are doing this?"

"Perhaps he does, perhaps he does not. I do, however, have my own mind. Jim is no fool, though."

Spider winced. "Well, then, I'd best avoid him."

Her eyes became icy. "What are you looking for? Are you a scout?"

"A scout?"

"For Wilson, or for Bonny's men?"

Spider stepped forward quickly, knife ready. "Bonny's men? So you know about that?"

She blinked. "That is it, then. You are here seeking revenge."

"No, no, no," Spider said. He lowered the knife. These were difficult waters to navigate, and he was still dizzy from illness and from Ruth's attempt at seduction. He took a moment to gather his thoughts.

"I did not come seeking revenge," he said after he and Ruth stared at each other for half a minute. "although if I find anything I need to avenge, well, by bloody goddamned hell I will avenge it."

"Why did you come here?"

"Bonny's men, the smugglers. I was not a part of her crew, but a friend of mine did sail with her. A foolish young rake, he is, his head easily turned by a good-looking woman."

"That just makes him a man," Ruth said.

"Aye," Spider answered. "I came here seeking him. His name is Hob, he is young and strong and better looking than me by a few leagues. Blond hair, horny as a cat in the summer. I'm sure he would have noticed you. Have you noticed him?"

She shook her head. "I have not seen anyone like that here."

"Fuck and bugger!" Spider spun around, madly. He'd thought himself close to the answer to all these mysteries.

Ruth stood, reminding Spider that she was a dangerous adversary. He focused his attention on her once again, and was happy to see her hands were not reaching behind her.

"Are any of these men working for Fawkes from Bonny's crew? Did he press them into service?"

"No," she said. "These men are, mostly, his old shipmates. One or two he met in Lymington or Bristol."

"Then why the bloody hell did Fawkes ambush a bunch of smugglers in the middle of the night? And my friend among them?"

"I do not know that," Ruth said. "I truly do not. I did not accompany Jim when he went to do that, nor when he arranged the whole thing. It was just a bunch of new patients, he said. Men who'd gone mad at sea after serving a mad captain. He said they'd been starved and lashed and driven mad."

"What I heard was Jim had made a deal of some sort with a taverner in Lymington, a gent named Bonnymeade."

"I've heard the name, but I do not know him, nor do I know anything about all this for certain." Ruth took a step toward him. "I do know that men who pry into Jim Fawkes' affairs do not live very long at all. He is a rougher man than you may know."

"You and he have an understanding, do you not?"

She crossed her arms. "Of sorts. It is not your concern."

"Aye."

"Spider, I give you credit. You turned tables on me. But I think if this conversation goes further, you and I might both find ourselves in dire straits with Jim Fawkes."

"I am beyond caring about that," Spider growled. "Where is my friend?"

"I told you, I do not know," she said through clenched teeth. "Oakes only speaks to Jim, and Jim tells people only what he wants them to know."

Spider's next question died in his mind when Ruth leapt to her right and placed a hand behind her back. Spider stepped to his own right and crouched, ready to fend off whatever weapon she had back there and wondering how the hell it had escaped his attentions when they were locked in an embrace.

But Ruth had no weapon. It was a feint, and now she could escape with ease. She smiled and bolted out the door.

Spider gave chase, and saw Ruth head out the front entrance. He froze though, when he heard Odin's voice behind him. The one-eyed sailor was emerging from the down the hall.

"Spider! I have news!"

"So do I, Odin."

27

Once Odin caught up to Spider, they rushed outside. Ruth had vanished.

"If you see Half-Jim, let me know."

Odin spat. "Why?"

"Because I almost diddled his woman and now she knows we came here looking for Hob."

"When did diddling and tattling become part of our plan, Spider John?"

"It was not a thing I . . ."

"So if one of us has to diddle a wench, can it be me?"

"Odin . . ."

"It should be me. I think I can manage to get my pecker wet without telling the lass our whole fucking . . ."

"Listen to me, you ugly, shit-stinking, cock-sucking son of an old whore's mule!"

Odin stopped complaining to Spider and stared at him. "You accuse me of cock-sucking, Spider?"

Spider sighed heavily. "Well, sorry. As for my actions, whatever damage I may have done it seems pretty Ruth is gone from us for now. Let's find a copse to hide in. Tell me your news."

"Aye," Odin answered. They walked, seeking cover. "I am supposing drink addled your brain, as usual."

"I do regret drinking this time, Odin, for certain."

"While you were drunk and horny and talking too goddamned much, I was rolling bones in the barn with some gents."

"Oh?"

Odin nodded. "Aye. One of those boys I was dicing with, Edward, says the folk in the town up north are convinced that Daphne wench, or some other crazed person, escapes from these grounds and kills young men."

"Is that so?"

"Aye. Three deaths. Well, one death and two disappearances. But everyone thinks the vanished lads are dead."

"Is that what this Wilson fellow is about, the man Oakes mentioned sneaking about his grounds?"

"His boy Joe was the one they found dead, yes."

Spider pondered. "Good cover here." They stepped into a space surrounded by five oaks with great, broad trunks, one of which sported a broken limb that dangled low and obscured the view from the house. "I have a story forming in my head, Odin. Trying to fit parts together, make a good dovetail joint between what you are telling me and what I've learned myself. Go on. How long ago was the most recent disappearance from the village?"

"Maybe eight months, maybe more. Lads were drinking, and arguing a bit."

"Hmmmm." Spider scratched his beard. "And they found no bodies?"

"Just Joe's. He'd been in a brawl and lost, they said." Odin lowered his breeches to take a piss.

"Was his death the last of the three instances?"

"Aye."

"What makes the villagers think Oakes is involved? Or Daphne, I should say?"

Odin finished and tucked up his breeches. "The very first lad disappeared not long after Oakes started boarding madmen, Spider. Not quite a year ago. Daphne was his first patient, they say. Rumor is they've seen a woman in white in the village, too."

"She escapes now and then, does she?"

"Aye, she gets out of the house sometimes, although the dicing boys tell me she ain't never got that far away. She's made it to the road a time or two, pestering passersby and asking for rides. But they say they always find her quick."

"I know someone else who gets off the grounds now and again." He was thinking of Michael, the huge farmhand. "Continue."

"The second disappearance was a few weeks after that first one. Both lads, first and second, just gone, one went to milk cows and never came back. The other had been courting a girl but went gone on his way home. And then the Wilson boy, killed in the middle of the night, a fortnight or two after that. They'd started a patrol at night, in the village, because lads kept disappearing, and he had the watch the night he got killed."

"And those deaths drew some attention, aye? Riled everyone up?" Spider crossed his arms and looked at Odin.

"Well, aye," Odin said. "Wilson and others have been peeping around here, sometimes sneaking, sometimes hollering for blood."

"You said the Wilson boy lost a brawl."

"Aye, they found him dead. Looked like he'd taken on Blackbeard or fucking Ned Low or some other scallywag. Broken arm, bloody face, deep gashes, lots of blood."

"That little girl Daphne did not do all that," Spider said. *But Michael could have done it.*

Odin shrugged. "Probably not. Ruth?"

"She probably could do it," Spider said, "but why would she?"

"Who knows why a woman does anything?"

"Not me," Spider said. "I reckon women know why they do things, though."

"Do they?"

The watch bell rang.

"Odin, we are in a deep smelly privy here. Ruth knows we are looking for Hob."

"Why did you tell her that?"

"I thought I might learn where he is."

"Did you?"

"No."

"Is that why you didn't fuck her?"

Spider grasped Odin's shoulders. "She knows why we are here. And Half-Jim is her man. She said he was away, busy or something. And I do not know if she spoke the truth. Maybe Jim told her to try to find out why I was here, maybe it was her that suggested it to him, or maybe she really just wanted to find out what we were about on her own. I don't know. As you said, who knows why a woman does anything? Anyway, Jim could be anywhere, he could have maybe even been in the next room listening to Ruth and me talking. Even if he wasn't, when she sees him she probably will tell him why we came here."

Odin considered that. "Will he care if we came here looking for a friend?"

"I have no idea," Spider said. "He might, he might not. The answer to that probably lies in why the smugglers were snatched in the first place. Jim won't like being lied to, though, I can vouch for that, but if it does not involve danger to Oakes—and it does not have to, if we can find Hob and get him away from here—then Half-Jim may not care much."

"So what do we do?"

Spider rubbed his hands together. "I do not know. I have an idea of what is happening here, I think, or at least a wee hint, and it is damned ugly, Odin. Damned ugly. That little girl might not have killed Wilson's boy—hell, I am certain she did not—but she might well be killing men around here. She might be the source of the illness that keeps killing patients."

"Aye," Odin said.

"Aye," Spider said. "She looks at death the way you look at a tart in Tortuga. She is fascinated by it. And she is allowed to take rum to the patients. Poisoned rum, it may be."

"Why would a girl do that?"

Spider shook his head. "Maybe she just wants to watch them be buried. Maybe she listens outside their doors while their breath rattles. I don't know. I just know she is a scary little wench."

"She is, indeed."

Odin shrugged. "Well, then. I am done with booze until we reach some civilized place, Spider John. What do we do?"

The watch bell rang.

"We'd best muster for our watches, I think, so we don't arouse notice. We will be late as it is, I fear. But let us go to our posts, and be ready for Half-Jim or Ruth or, fuck, everybody to come after us."

"Just like our old days on the account. Ha!"

28

Spider patrolled the south wall, after skipping the proffered bread and cheese. His stomach had settled, mostly, but well water had not been able to cleanse the burning feeling from his throat. He was no longer dizzy, though, and he was beginning to feel hungry, so he counted that a good omen.

Spider was still pondering some ruse that might get him upstairs to see if Hob was locked away in one of those rooms when a shadow dropped over the wall some two dozen yards away.

It was too small to be Michael again. A dog, perhaps.

Spider dodged behind a tree and watched the dark shape rush toward an oak and vanish there. It was no dog. It was a man, or perhaps a woman, intent on silence and on not being seen.

Spider freed a gun from his belt and crept toward the spot where the shadow had disappeared. He crouched, took three slow steps, and plucked free a dagger in his left hand. Just as he thought he was close enough to rush the interloper he saw a second shadow, and a third, drop over the wall.

Damn! This was an attack.

Spider little cared if Oakes or Fawkes or any of their hired fighters were ambushed. But Odin was out there in the darkness, and perhaps Hob as well, and there were Daphne and Mrs. Fitch to consider. Odin might curse that chivalrous thought, but by thunder, it was against the odds that both of them might be ruthless killers. Surely, one of them might be worth saving.

He thought about rushing the intruders himself but erased that thought almost as soon as it had formed. He'd seen three. He figured he could kill one quickly enough in an act of surprise, and perhaps finish the second in a head-on fight. The third, though, likely would kill him, and there might well be more coming over the wall soon. Or perhaps others had breached the wall further away, unseen. The attack could be coming from several directions, too.

Familiar feelings stirred within him. He had survived more than a few chaotic battles in his life as a pirate. Whatever happened next would leave him with regrets of violence, or it would leave him dead. The difference would be how quickly and efficiently he could stab or slash or shoot, without thought for the fellows on the other side of the fight. He'd learned that lesson well over the years.

Life or death also would hinge on whether these interlopers were expert skirmishers or angry villagers with no experience in a real fight. Whether these were Anne Bonny's men or a mob led by Wilson, Spider had no idea. Either way, the prudent course was to raise a warning.

So he crouched and ran as quietly as he could toward the house, using oaks and shadows as cover and praying he would not hear a shout of alarm or the crack of a pistol behind him.

He counted on his own familiarity with the terrain to help him move with haste in the darkness. The attackers, on strange territory, would have to move more cautiously to avoid tripping on a root or stepping into a rabbit hole.

A life of piracy prepares a man for action, so Spider was not quite winded by the time he saw the light in the window of the drawing room. He bounded up the steps to the front door, surprised his head was spinning a bit. *The goddamned booze.* He entered the house, rushed to the drawing room and found Oakes and Fawkes talking before the fireplace, brandy in hand.

So Fawkes is not away after all, he thought. *Fuck.*

"We are besieged, sir," Spider said. "Three men at least crept over the south wall. Likely there are more."

"Damn," Oakes said. "Wilson?"

"That man is not so bold," Fawkes said, grabbing the crutch that leaned against the hearth. He drained his brandy, set the snifter on the table beside him, and rose. "We'll fight them off, no matter who they be." If he had heard anything about Spider's intentions from Ruth, he showed no sign.

The more Spider thought about it, the more he suspected Little Bob and his friends had been able to trace the men who had ambushed Anne Bonny's smugglers to Pryor Pond. If they'd been angry enough to murder Thomas Bonnymeade, it would be no surprise to see them seek vengeance on the men who had snatched their shipmates. It would be far more surprising if they didn't.

Spider did not mention any of this to Oakes and Fawkes, though.

Oakes lifted his bulk from his chair. "I shall be in my laboratory, Mister Fawkes. I want this skirmish ended quickly!"

"Aye, master." Fawkes winced, as though he did not like his choices. "Spider John, go rouse the day watch, lead them out to meet the oncoming party," Fawkes said. "I'll sound the alarm and stir men to watch for flankers. Move!"

"Aye."

At the top of the cellar steps, Spider bellowed. "Attack coming, lads! Men with guns and swords! To battle, now! South wall!" Then he rushed to the kitchen and toward the back door, nearly knocking a large kettle out of Mrs. Fitch's hands.

"Oh, what happens, John?"

"We are under attack," he said. "Grab a big knife or a cleaver and hide yourself!"

"Oh! Oh!" She opened a drawer and pulled out a ladle. "Damn!" She threw that aside and withdrew a sharp knife. "Better!"

"Go hide!" Spider rushed out the door.

Fawkes was clanging the ship's bell in a cadence, three loud rings followed by a pause. He repeated this pattern as Spider and the day watch rushed past him, arms in hand. Stingo, Spider noted, wobbled considerably.

"Let none through, lads!" Fawkes' voice boomed like a cannon.

"Waste no powder, aim true and careful! I want to fill a few more holes tonight, I do!"

Spider ran toward the south wall. He felt the effort now, and pain clutched at his stomach. The remains of a fallen oak provided nice cover, and he dove for it. "Good place here, gents! They'll be up to us soon!"

A couple of men joined him, while others took up positions behind standing oaks. They all peered into the darkness, waiting for their adversaries.

Shouts rang through the night, first to the south where the attackers were approaching, then all around.

"They've heard the bell, boys, and they've given up on stealth!"

"They come in a rush! Meet them with lead and blades!"

"Blood and ruin, lads! Blood and ruin!"

Spider's two flintlock pistols were ready to go. In addition, he had Hob's throwing knife and two daggers, all sharp. He also counted on snatching weapons from anyone he killed.

He wondered how Odin fared. The old man could fight, but that injured leg worried Spider.

Spider lifted his head and peeked over the fallen trunk. Shadows rushed up the hill, gliding from tree to tree, boulder to bole. One of them seemed to be the size of a child.

"Is that you, Little Bob Higgins?" Spider muttered quietly. "I owe you a fucking knock or two."

So these are indeed Anne Bonny's men, come looking for bloody revenge. That would mean a real fight, not a bout with village amateurs.

Spider figured these buccaneers Fawkes had hired were up to the task. So was he.

He touched the pendant beneath his shirt and thought of Em. Then he closed his eyes in prayer. Even here, miles from the sea, he was about to be caught up in bloodshed, with no choice but to fight or die. *Will I never outrun my pirate past? Am I doomed to this, always, punishment for choosing to join the attacking pirates all those years ago instead of letting them heave me overboard to die in the deep?*

He opened his eyes. All he really knew was that he had to fight now if he ever wanted to see Em and his son. And so he would fight.

He placed one of the flintlocks on the fallen trunk, then took up the other. He wanted to shout to the other men and tell them to hold fire until the attackers were upon them, but he could hear the snaps of branches and the labored breathing of running men. He dared not reveal his own position. The attackers were too close now.

The interlopers rushed forward as best they could given the slope they climbed and the darkness. None of Fawkes' men pulled their triggers. Spider nodded, satisfied these men knew their bloody trade.

The fastest of the attackers was less than a yard away when Spider shot him in the chest. Guns erupted all around him as the dead man plunged forward, sprawling on the fallen tree with a gush of his last breath. Spider had to roll the bastard off his other gun to free it.

Once he had the second flintlock in hand, Spider leapt from concealment, sidestepped a cutlass thrust and jammed the gun into another man's belly. He pulled the trigger, winced at the thunder-crack, and felt the burn of powder on his arm, followed by the warm gush of blood. He used his shoulder to shove the dying man away as the rising smoke stung his eyes. Spider dropped the spent weapon as another attacker rushed him, only to find Spider's knife deep in his neck.

That man dropped a cutlass, and Spider snatched it up. He swung it hard twice, cursing as he detected a warp in the blade that spoiled its aim, but managed to slice a man's belly with it nonetheless.

Shouts from the north told Spider that reinforcements were coming, or that the attack was coming from multiple directions. Suddenly, it became impossible to tell which of the skirmishers around him belonged to Fawkes' crew and which belonged to the assailants. Spider found a place behind a wide oak and decided he would kill anyone who got too goddamned close, whatever side they might be on.

He looked for Little Bob but did not see him.

One shadowy figure zigged and zagged drunkenly, and fired a

blunderbuss without aiming. Stingo, it was, laughing with drunken madness. He flung his spent gun into the darkness. "I have a surprise! Oh, what a surprise!"

Stingo reached into a leather pouch strapped over his shoulder and lifted out what seemed to be a small stone. "Oh, what a surprise!"

The man spun and tossed the small object into the air, not seeming to care much which way it flew. Spider tried to follow the object's flight but lost it in the darkness. But a sudden flash of orange and green, accompanied by a rumble of thunder, erupted in the night, approximately where Spider judged the flung object should have landed.

"Holy Jesus," Spider muttered. He remembered Little Bob's description of the attack waged against the smugglers. Bob had mentioned explosions and flashes of light.

He turned back toward Stingo, who laughed madly.

"Boom!" He danced. "Boom!"

Then someone sliced the man's neck and Stingo fell, hard. He landed on the pouch, and Spider ducked in case the satchel contained more of those little bombs. It did not explode, however. Spider thought to grab the pouch, but the man who had cut Stingo came at him. Spider's cutlass made short work of that foe, but by the time that was done someone else had made off with Stingo's bombs.

Loud cries filled the night. Among the shouts, one voice stood out. It was a feminine voice. Ruth, it had to be, although Spider could not spot her amid the tumult.

Spider moved to the other side of the oak and nearly tripped over a bulk on the ground. He knelt and brushed aside a fallen branch. A dead man stared back at him.

It was one of Fawkes' men, Raldo, the Spaniard, dead and on his back. A small trace of blood had trickled from his mouth, but there was no sign of any wound that Spider could see.

Raldo's bad luck might well be my good fortune, Spider thought, looking about in hopes of seeing one of the man's weapons. He'd feel a damned sight more comfortable with a pistol in his hand. Nothing lethal presented itself, however, and he cursed the darkness and the ankle-high grass.

No one was rushing him, though, so he risked rolling the corpse over in hopes of finding an unfired flintlock. It took more effort than expected, because the body was oddly stiff, and cold.

He did not find a useful gun. He did find a lot of blood, though, and a knife, plunged into the man's skull, upward from the neck. Spider declined to take that.

Damn, Spider thought. *This death makes no sense. It does not fit the pattern.*

He had no time to ponder, however, because the battle continued in the night around him. As he rose, his hand brushed that of the dead man's, and against a scrap of cloth. The fabric, a ragged piece less than two inches square, clung to the man's fingernails. Spider snatched it, tucked it into his tobacco pouch, and cursed himself for letting this new mystery divert his attention from the fight.

A shadowy figure ran by, limping, and despite the confusion and turmoil Spider recognized him immediately.

Well, then. Opportunity after all!

Spider dove, caught the man by the ankle and sent him tumbling. Then Spider crawled atop his prey and put a knife to his throat.

"I have you, little bastard!"

"Damn and blast ye, Spider John!" Little Bob Higgins spat in his face and tried in vain to squirm his way free.

"I should have killed you last time we met, Bob. Put your hands where I can see them."

Spider felt a sharp scratch at his side and knew then that Bob had a knife in hand. Spider quickly ran his own dirk through Little Bob's neck and rolled away.

"You are welcome, Aggie."

He clutched his left side and felt warm blood, but only a little of it.

"Fuck and bugger!"

He crawled behind the oak, next to Raldo's corpse, and sat up. He could not see well in the darkness, but he removed his hand from his wound and licked it. It was not drenched in blood. He touched the wound, and winced, but was relieved to find it was not gushing. He decided he probably would live.

The gunshots had stopped, but the shouts of combat and the ringing of steel on steel echoed all around him. Spider stayed where he was but kept an eye out for Odin.

He saw the crusty old son of a bitch soon enough. Odin had gotten his hands on a bloody axe somehow and was spinning like a god-damned waterspout, hewing necks and arms and cackling like a witch. It was his way in any fight like this, to compensate for the missing eye.

"Like a top," he always said, "so I can see all around. And it keeps the blade moving, too!"

If the leg still bothered the old man at all, it didn't show. Spider watched Odin kill or maim four men—it was impossible to tell how badly he'd cut them in the darkness, but they all fell and remained still. Spider wondered if they worked for Fawkes or for the smugglers.

He decided it didn't much matter. They were all going to hell. All of them.

The sounds of battle continued around him. He rose, crouching to meet any assault, but kept spinning full circle while the battleground revolved, too, and everything became one blurred shadow.

Then Spider's battle was over.

29

Spider awoke on a hard bench surrounded by foul odors that immediately brought to his mind the apothecary shop back in Lymington. His belly felt hot and itchy on the left side, and his shoulder muscles ached from effort.

He opened his eyes, and once the bleariness faded the similarity of his situation to that of the druggist's shop increased. Morning sunlight illuminated shelves full of bottles and jars, and on a table nearby a candle's flame danced beneath a clay pot suspended above it on a metal frame. A skull beside it stared at him; after a moment or two, Spider decided it likely had once belonged to a cat.

He could not see it from this vantage, but he felt the warmth of a fireplace somewhere behind him and heard the occasional snap and crackle of burning logs.

He turned his head to the left and realized he was in the center of a large room. He saw a table covered with beakers, alembics and clay pots tucked between shelves containing books and more jars. Pegs above the table held sharp implements, curved and straight, some unusually short and others quite long. Leather hoses dangled between them. A stack of folded cloths filled the space between a tall vial of blue-green fluid and another that seemed to be filled with salt.

To his right, sunlight streamed between the iron bars securing a window, illuminating a shelves-and-wheels contraption much like the one Ambrose Oakes had shown him previously. It held open books, and a tall stand next to it held a jar of ink, a cup full of quills, and a jar of blotting sand.

Spider saw nothing at all of the grounds beyond the window, so he decided he must be on one of the upper floors. He had no memory at all of having left the battle, but he knew it must be over. He heard no gunshots, no shouting, no swordplay.

A quiet cackle in the opposite corner caught his attention. Spider looked and started violently when he saw a raven perched atop a coat tree. Instinct, fueled by his lifelong fear of all birds, told Spider to cover his face and get the hell out of this room, but he could not.

Fuck and bugger! I'm bound!

Indeed, ropes across his naked chest and across his thighs held him to the table. He tried to raise his arms, but found he was bound by the wrists as well.

The raven stared, mocking him.

"Jesus!" Spider's voice sounded weak, and very far away. He stared at the damned black bird, which lifted wings and teetered on its perch. The beak opened and closed, opened and closed, as though the bloody beast was trying to speak, or perhaps chewing on something. Spider raised his head as much as he could and glanced at his side. He saw grayish plaster, with a faint bit of crimson peeking through, which corresponded to the pain he felt. He did not see any sign that the bird had dug into his wound, nor did he see or feel any places on his body where the damned beast might have torn off a piece of his flesh.

Still, Spider wondered why the thing was not already eating his eyes.

He tried to shout for help, but his throat was raw and he could not draw a deep breath.

He closed his eyes tight and turned his face away from the raven. Tugging at his binds, contorting his body as hard as he could, he thought he might rock the table. *Topple it*, he thought. *Tumble to the floor, use the table as a shield!*

He kept it up for what seemed ages, wondering if his heart might give out with the effort and every moment imagining the beak and talons at his throat and eyes. The table legs drummed on the floor as he continued his frantic attempt to escape. But it was a heavy thing, and apparently well built, and he almost wept as he realized the attempt was foolish.

"Now then, Spider John, what is this?"

Spider halted his struggle, opened his eyes and saw the bulk of Ambrose Oakes standing in the doorway. "A raven! A goddamned filthy soulless raven!"

Oakes nodded. "You fear birds? Well, then."

"Fuck and bugger, man, I am bound for its fucking feast! Free me from this table before that black fiend tears at me!"

Oakes laughed. "Old Ben? Come now, Spider John." The master of the house walked toward the coat tree and coaxed the raven onto his arm. It perched there with dark wings spread.

"Ben here is quite old, Spider. Likely he will not be long among us, I'm afraid. He has lost an eye, like your friend, although Ben's was given up in a battle with a cat. The cat lost a good deal more." Oakes pointed across Spider toward the skull next to the heated beaker.

Spider's throat seized up. *This fucking bird killed a cat? God help me!*

"But you are not a cat and Ben has little life left in him, so you are quite safe." He chuckled and returned Ben to his perch. The bird danced there for a few heartbeats, apparently trying to decide whether to face the wall or face into the room. Then it dropped some wet, white dung onto a tray built onto the coat tree below it.

Oakes chuckled for a moment, then turned serious. "Have you always feared birds, Spider? I would like to discuss it with you, for such irrational fears fascinate me. Such fears are part of what induced me to establish this facility. I have treated a fellow who feared spiders—what would he have made of you, Spider John? I wonder. I wish he was still with us, to gauge his reaction upon hearing your name. He has passed on, I'm afraid."

"Get me off this table!"

Oakes scolded him. "That would be premature. This fear of yours, perhaps it is the lingering effect of some childhood trauma, a frightening incident or perhaps the swooping of a bird that seemed to presage some horrible event in your life. Do you fear all birds, John, or only ravens? Or perhaps only birds black in hue?"

Spider was in no mood to discuss the state of his mind. "Why am I bound?"

Oakes approached and glanced at Spider's side. "To keep you from fussing with the plaster I put on your wound. I know you itch, but I invested time and effort in stopping your bleeding and would hate to see you ruin my work." The man drew a finger lightly across Spider's injury. "Perhaps it still pains you mildly?"

"Aye," Spider said, while keeping a watchful eye on Ben. He did not trust anyone when it came to goddamned birds and doubted the creature cared what its master said about its behavior.

"I also wanted to question you, John. Did you suffer any blow to the head, or some other injury? Aside from that long knife scratch, which was not deep, I see naught but minor scrapes and contusions, nothing that might explain why you fell unconscious."

"I do not recall," Spider said. "I do not think anyone hit me."

"Hmmmm. You were lucky, Spider John," Oakes mused. "Your wound was slight. You lost some blood, but not a great deal. Had the blade bit you even a little deeper, it might have been different. As it is, I am surprised you succumbed to it, quite honestly. Judging from old scars, you've suffered wounds far more severe than this one."

Spider pondered that. At the time, he had considered the cut from Little Bob to be a mere scratch.

He was no stranger to injury, or to pain. Indeed, he'd learned quite early in his pirating days that it often was best to ignore the hurt and just keep fighting, and seek the surgeon later if you were still alive— if there was a surgeon, of course. That skill was rare on pirate vessels, and Doctor Boddings had been a rare luxury for wounded men aboard *Plymouth Dream*. On pirate vessels, often the best treatment to be had was from a former loblolly boy who did his best to recall what he'd seen while assisting a genuine surgeon on a Naval ship.

If Little Bob's blade had left merely a shallow wound, then why had Spider passed out? The battle against the intruders had been brief, a good deal shorter than many fights he'd seen in his day. And those melees had almost always been followed by hard work. Work such as carrying badly injured shipmates to the surgeon when there was one—or over the gunwale when there was not—or hauling booty from the prey vessel, repairing decks and bulkheads shattered by nine-pound balls, bailing from the bowels of a sinking vessel, stitching sails, hoisting up spars to replace those that had cracked or broken under enemy fire, rolling out a keg to celebrate victory and drink to the memory of the departed.

Blacking out after a fight was not a common experience for Spider John.

He gulped. "Might the blade that cut me have been poisoned?"

"Envenomed?" Oakes shook his head. "It is possible, I suppose, all things being possible in heaven and Earth, heh, but not at all likely." The fat man's large forehead creased deeply in thought. "I examined your wound quite closely. No discoloration or odor or anything else that cannot be explained by the presence of your own blood. I've had no chance to examine the knife, of course, and I'm told the men gathered a large number of weapons off the bloody grounds so there would be absolutely no chance of determining which one scratched you. But it's a fool who goes into a close fight with a sharp blade coated in something that can kill him, if I have learned anything at all in my association with the cunning Mister Fawkes. Would you carry such a weapon into a fracas in the dark, running across wooded fields?"

"No, I reckon I would not."

"No, Spider John. It would be a great risk. One might trip and cut oneself, and what then? No. In all probability, you were not poisoned."

Not by the knife, anyway, Spider thought.

"I believe you will recuperate well, John."

Spider sighed and prayed silently. He pictured Em, and his son—who looked remarkably like Hob in Spider's imagination. He would live. He would get back to them.

"My friend, Odin," Spider blinked. "Did he survive?"

"He did, indeed," Oakes said, nodding and laughing softly. "Your friend, I am told, is the very devil in a fight, despite his age. Accounted for himself with valor, according to those who saw him, an inspiration even to men Fawkes hired precisely because they had lived violent lives. I am told Odin wielded an axe that I assume he appropriated from my barn. I ought to scold him for that, but given the proficiency he demonstrated, perhaps I should simply reward him with the axe. He'd rather have some of the little bombs, though, or so Fawkes tells me."

"He is one who enjoys a skirmish, he is," Spider said, still casting glances at the raven. "Sees it as a matter of pride, I think, that he can still deal death, old though he be. And I saw those little bombs. What are they?"

"I make them," he said. "I learned some things from the Greeks, and from others. Quite handy, and Fawkes and his men love them."

"I am not surprised Odin wants some," Spider said. "I am glad he came through it unharmed. Shipmates, we are."

Oakes shrugged. "He fared well. Others fared worse. We killed nine attackers, unless there are bodies we have not found yet, and lost three of our own in the affair."

Spider, calmer now but still watching Ben, inhaled deeply. "Then manpower is a concern, I take it, and I am stretched out here. Might I return to duty now, sir?"

"Soon," Oakes said. "Be patient. I am troubled by your swoon. There may be an illness at play, something untoward that we should watch."

"I woke up feeling queasy, sir. I might have eaten too much. The food here is better than what we eat at sea."

Oakes nodded. "Indeed, I have had plenty a bad meal at sea, and a stomach tossed by wind and wave does not handle rough fare well." He paused and grinned as though recalling old times. "Perhaps you did merely eat too much. I suggest a day and night of rest, and just a little food, perhaps a bit of drink if you handle the food well enough. Let us give your wound a chance to heal before we send you out to duty again."

"Aye, sir, if you think it best, but I am accustomed to keeping busy.

Might I roam around and inspect the house? I've seen much that needs repair already, and I have not even seen most of the place."

Oakes considered. "That won't be necessary, I think. The primary concern, for now, is my security and protection, that my work is not interrupted. For that, I need you hearty, and I deem rest would be more beneficial than wandering about with tools and such. But thank you, John, for the suggestion. Perhaps when you feel better and people are not sneaking about on my property, we can see to repairs."

Damn it.

"Aye, sir. You know best, I reckon. Thank you for the patch. Are you a Naval surgeon, sir? Missus Fitch, she said you sailed."

Oakes grinned. "I never served as a surgeon. I was, however, a loblolly boy on a frigate, serving under a surgeon who knew his business well and who expounded upon it for all the time I was willing to listen. Those were wonderful days, John, wonderful days! The things I learned, the things I saw were worth every hunk of maggot-ridden bread, every storm-tossed night, every stern look from a surgeon who thought me a dullard!"

Oakes peered toward the ceiling, as though searching for memories. "A curious lad, I was, who paid close attention to the surgeon at his work. Doctor Myerscough, he was, a righteous and learned man, who brooked no laziness, no inattention. That was long ago, long ago."

Oakes smiled, then turned toward the bookstand and turned the wheels to bring a new book to the top. Then he snatched up a quill, dabbed it in the ink, and scratched some notes onto the paper. Spider watched and wished for perhaps the hundredth time he'd learned his letters. He'd met people over the years who had tried to help him, but it was difficult to find time to learn literacy while trying to keep a sloop afloat and dodge cutlass swipes and musket balls.

One day, he thought. *I will learn to read and write one day, and I shall write Em a love letter, or a poem.*

Oakes resumed speaking and brought Spider's attention back to reality. "My family did not want me running off to sea, John. My mother, indeed, wailed considerably. But I wanted to go, and so I ran off, changed my name, and set sail as a loblolly boy aboard *H.M.S. Spann*. It was such an education! A man can learn a great many things by paying attention, Spider John. A great many things. It is, indeed, the purpose God intends for me, I think. To learn things, to unravel puzzles and discover answers thus far denied to men. To ordinary men, I should say. To ordinary men, who dare too little and ask too few questions."

Oakes finished his writing and returned to the table, where he ran a hand along Spider's arm. "You are quite a strong man, are you not? Not large, but very well made."

"I suppose it is all the hard work, sir. Swinging hammers, toting lumber, climbing aloft." Spider wished he could move away from the man's touch. He wanted to get away from that goddamned raven, too.

"Indeed, hard work makes good muscles. And you learned more than carpentry at sea, no doubt. You fought well, I am told. You thought well, also. Raising the alarm as you did rather than engaging the attackers yourself was well done on your part. Some of these louts, I dare say, would have simply aimed a gun and pulled trigger and gotten themselves killed in a heartbeat, leaving the rest of us unaware. A cool head in a fight is a rare thing, Mister Fawkes tells me, and I've seen enough to believe it, although I am no man at arms, myself. You did well. I believe most of these fools, in your spot, would have fired a shot right at that moment."

"Thank you, sir. I've seen more than a few hot moments in my day, for certain. Why did they attack us, do you know?"

Oakes scrunched his forehead into tight lines and grimaced. "I do not . . ."

"Sir," said a voice at the door. It was Ruth, holding the door open for two men carrying a third between them. The carried man bled heavily from the leg. He was no one Spider had seen on the grounds before.

"This gent is one of the party who attacked us," Ruth said. "Took a ball in the leg and tried to crawl away. Left a bloody red trail across the grass plain as day once dawn came. I followed it and found him laying across the wall, trying to escape. Still got life in him, but barely. I thought to keep him that way, so you could question him."

"Well done, Ruth. Well done." Oakes snuffed out the candle, and moved it, the pot, and the cat skull to a shelf. "Men, place him here on the table and bind him."

"He ain't going to fight you, master," one of the men said.

"Bind him."

They obeyed, fetching rope from a trunk under the table.

Ruth appeared to have come through the fighting with no injury save a scratch on her cheek and a slightly bruised and cut lip. Her blouse was torn at the shoulder, and her breeches showed a splotch of blood—although that might have belonged to someone else. She shot Spider a quick glance, and he thought perhaps he was supposed to find a meaning in it. But whatever message she meant to impart was lost on Spider.

Oakes took a knife from the wall and walked toward the wounded man. He cut away the gore-soaked breeches to expose the wounded leg. "Oh, my. No saving this, I think."

Oakes walked around Spider and headed to the table beneath his hanging implements. He opened a drawer and lifted something out.

When Oakes turned, he was holding a saw.

"This will be unpleasant."

30

Spider had seen two amputations in his day—one a leg, and one an arm—and he had no desire to witness another. He turned his face away and closed his eyes.

Still, he could envision what was happening, and he could hear the operation as well.

"Open his jaws, there," Oakes said. That would be for the placement of a wood rod for the patient to bite down on.

"He's out like a dead pig," one of the men said.

"I have read Charrier, have you?" Oakes spat. "Do as I tell you, and do not attempt cogency. When I commence sawing, by God, he might well awaken, if he has any real life left in him. Do you want him to clamp his teeth down on a wooden dowel, or on your goddamned finger?"

"Aye, sir."

"Where is Peter, for the love of God? Where is Simon?" Oakes had to force the words out through jaws clenched in anger.

"Mister Fawkes ordered them downstairs, sir."

"Ruth, dear, we will need cloths. Prodigious amounts of cloths, more than we have here. This man has lost blood, but he still has more to lose. And a couple of buckets, please. And pass the word to Mister Fawkes, please. I will want him to help with the interrogation and to explain to me why my best assistants are elsewhere at a crucial time!"

"Aye, sir."

Spider watched her go, and in his helpless state he envied her. He envied the pair of knives on her belt, too. She was back almost instantly, though. "Mister Fawkes is here, sir." Then she ran off.

"Removing his leg, are you?" That voice, full of smirk, came from Fawkes.

Spider looked at Fawkes. The man had a nasty scrape on his cheek, fresh and red, but no other apparent injury from the fighting.

Oakes answered Fawkes. "Aye. He probably is going to die from the amputation, but he most certainly will die without it, and it will be a slow, agonizing, painful death. There is no good choice for him, I am convinced. And his odds are worse because, I understand, you sent Gold Peter and Simon off on some damned errand? They are the only men you've brought me with the intelligence to aid me competently!"

"I did send them downstairs," Fawkes said. "Someone trailed me to the house. I got no glimpse of him, and I tried to act unaware in hopes of luring him closer. Like the pirate hunters do, you see. Fill a merchant ship with fighting lads but keep them out of sight until the pirates pounce. My fellow did not pounce, however, so I came inside and sent Peter and Simon to spring a trap on him. They told me we had a captive up here, and I came to help ask him some questions."

Spider's mind raced. *Was it Odin who had trailed Half-Jim? Was that what Ruth had tried to say with her eyes? And why would she want to warn him of anything?*

"I need my assistants here, Mister Fawkes, not off guarding the property. You have ruffians enough for that duty."

"Our guards are in somewhat short supply of late," Fawkes said, seeming somewhat amused. "Why not simply wake this poor bastard so we can ask our questions? We do not plan to keep him alive after that, do we?"

"Do you question my judgment, Jim Fawkes?"

"I think you just want to cut this bastard's leg off and kill him now more than you want to know who attacked us, and why."

Silence, for twelve heartbeats. Then Oakes turned to his helpers.

"You, there is a wide blade on the hearth. Heat it, until it glows. And you, fetch me that." Spider watched the men move quickly to obey Oakes' orders. "Mister Fawkes, we know it was likely Bonny's men who attacked us, else a group gathered by Mister Wilson. It scarce matters who launched the attack, so long as you've fended it off. Have you? Entirely?"

"We have," Fawkes said. "And aye, Bonny's smugglers hit us, most likely, judging by the weapons they carried and the way they fought. We collected a few nice guns and shiny swords. But I'd like to know if they brought their full force, or if there be others out there somewhere who might come over our walls. This fool can tell us that, perhaps, if you don't kill him first."

"He won't awaken, I surmise, no matter what I do," Oakes said. "But he presents me an opportunity."

Fawkes laughed softly. "I suppose he does." He glanced toward the jars on the shelves, focusing on the row at the top.

Spider followed his gaze. The jars were all the same size, and each was corked with a small length of hose emerging from the top. Clamps held the hoses tightly shut. Some of the jars held dark fluid, in varying amounts, while others seemed to be empty. But all of the hoses were clamped.

One of the men walked around Spider's table and took a length of hose down from a peg. One end of it seemed to be attached to a mask of some kind. The man returned to Oakes. Spider, curious, turned his head to see what was being done.

"And that jar."

Another man fetched a jug, and Oakes fitted the end of the leather hose into a hole in the cork. "Some glue, please. Hurry."

One of the assistants fetched a small pot and a brush, and Oakes proceeded to place glue around the hose where it went through the cork. "Must seal it up proper," he muttered.

This was nothing like any amputation Spider had ever witnessed.

Once the jar was sealed up tight, Oakes handed it to one of the men. "Hold it steady. Do not drop it under any circumstances."

"Aye."

Next, Oakes fitted the mask over the wounded man's mouth and nose, working to make it fit over the short wooden rod in his mouth. Then he strapped it to the man's head and assured himself that the hose between the man's face and the jar was intact. "Good, good."

"What is this?"

"Not now, Spider John," Oakes said. "This is delicate work."

Spider looked over toward Fawkes, who only grinned.

"Here, sir." Ruth pushed her way past Fawkes and placed two buckets on the floor. One of them sloshed, the other was filled with fabric. "Hot water, and cloths aplenty."

"Excellent," Oakes said. "Will you stay and watch?"

"God, no," Ruth said. She glanced meaningfully at Spider again, then hurried out. *What is she trying to tell me?*

"Now, then," Oakes said, lifting the saw. "Let us get on with our gruesome work."

Spider winced. He had felt a sharp blade cutting him more than once, in battle. That always hurt like the devil's deep hell, but the initial sharp pain passed quickly. Spider tried hard not to imagine how it felt to have a sharp, serrated blade slice into you once, twice, thrice . . .

He hoped to hell the poor bastard on the other table was beyond feeling anything, or already dead.

"I must do this quickly," Oakes said. "Is the blade glowing?"

"Aye."

"Keep it in the fire and bring it quickly when I call for it."

"Aye."

"And you, wet cloths when I order it, direct on his wounds, do you hear?"

"Aye."

"Very well, then," Oakes said, checking the hose one more time. "Let's be done with it."

He lowered the saw to the wounded leg, and Spider turned away.

A ship's carpenter, Spider had heard the sound of a saw cutting wood many times. He had heard a saw cutting flesh and bone twice, and never wanted to hear it again.

But there it was, metal teeth through meat and bone. And the poor son of a bitch woke up, screaming through teeth clenched on a wooden rod. Spider could almost hear the teeth grinding into the wood.

"Fuck!" That was one of the assistants.

"Is he going to live through this?" That was the other.

"I endured it twice," Fawkes said.

"Silence," Oakes commanded tersely.

The sawing continued, the man screamed and Fawkes laughed. Soon, the wailing stopped, punctuated by a heavy thump on the floor. Spider knew that was the man's leg.

"The hot blade! Quickly!"

Spider expected more screaming once the searing hot metal was applied to the gaping wound, but there was none. He could hear sizzling blood, though, and smell burning flesh. It was a stench all too familiar to a pirate, one a man could never quite forget.

"Another jar, quickly, and a fresh blade. Hurry!"

Spider heard boots on the floor, glass tinkling against glass and soon a muffled scraping sound, like that of the last bit of honey being scooped from a pot.

"Put this aside. Cloth, please," Oaks said, less urgently.

Spider heard sloshing.

"Well," Fawkes said. "That man looks dead."

"Aye," Oakes said.

Spider turned around and opened his eyes. Oakes was peering into the jar and applying a clamp to the hose. Blood poured over the table's edges, some of it falling into a bucket but most spreading across the floor. One of the assistants tossed rags over the gore.

"We won't get to ask him anything, then," Fawkes said, laughing. "Will we see more attacks?"

"I wanted to ask this fellow that same question, master, remember? Now I can't."

Oakes said nothing, so Fawkes continued. "I am certain Bonny returned to sea after setting these men ashore to conduct business. She wasn't there when we ambushed them, and I don't see her hand in this attack. She'd have planned things better, no doubt. I don't know when she's coming back for her crewmen or where they plan to meet, but she can't have left too many men behind. They were supposed to conduct some business, not fight a war. We've likely killed or taken most of the bastards by now, I reckon. Still, it would have been a good thing to ask this dead gent about all that. I'd like to know if these gentlemen sent someone to rendezvous with Bonny, and if she might know about us and decide to lead a more competent raid on us."

Fawkes spat toward the bucket of gore. "I guess we'll find out when she slits our throats. What do you think, Spider John? Did you ever sail with Bonny?"

Spider peered into the man's eyes, wondering if he already knew the answer to that question. "I know her reputation well," he answered. "And met her briefly. Smart and ruthless, they say, and not likely one to forgive. Did you attack these smugglers of hers, steal their goods?"

Fawkes ignored that. "We aren't going to learn anything useful from this dead fellow, master."

"Well. I do not believe this man was destined to awaken enough to answer questions in any event, Mister Fawkes," Oakes answered. "And there is still the fellow you believe followed you, correct? Possibly more? So capture him, and maintain a strong guard, nonetheless. Look for anyone skulking about, and question them, I say."

"Aye, master." Fawkes pointed toward the jar. "Did you get it?"

Oakes peered through the glass. "I do not know. You," he said, pointing to one of the helpers, "hand me that knife."

The man complied, and Oakes deftly cut the hose just above the clamp. He peered into the jar again, then lifted the mask off the dead man. He carried both to the table between the shelves, under the watchful eye of Ben.

Oakes stripped off his bloody apron and added it to the pile of red cloths in the bucket. "Take this corpse and bury it. Have Michael help you," he commanded. "Free Spider John, but see he moves carefully. And tell Peter about this mess, have him clean it up." He left, and the henchmen carried the body—and the leg—out.

Fawkes remained. "I notice you did not watch, Spider John."

"I've seen it before."

"Aye."

"But I've not seen that bit with the jar and the mask. What the devil is that?"

"He didn't tell you?" Fawkes grinned. "He's trying to collect something. But he'll fail, though. Utterly."

Spider blinked. "I do not understand."

Fawkes laughed, heavily, and now Spider detected rum on his breath. "These men are like you and me, Spider John! Plied the sweet trade, they did. Pirates! Devil's already claimed their souls, and Oakes can't have them!"

Fawkes laughed so hard he coughed, throwing odors of booze and tobacco into the air. Once his fit subsided, he was leaning against a shelf near Ben's perch.

"You still deathly afraid of the birds, Spider John?"

Spider said nothing.

"Damnedest thing, a man as quick with a knife or a cutlass as you, ready for battle as any I've seen, and yet cowed by something almost light as air."

Fawkes placed his finger against Ben's talons, stroking them. He looked at Spider. "Even this one, old and mostly blind as he is, I can see he concerns you. Does he not?"

Ben lifted a foot and stepped onto Fawkes' finger. "Of course, your friend is old and half blind, and by God he killed a lot of men last night. So maybe old Ben has some death to deal yet. Aye, Ben? Aye?"

Spider inhaled deeply and strained against his bonds. "The master said to free me."

"Aye," Fawkes said. He leaned his crutch against the shelf, then hopped to Spider's bedside with Ben on his finger. He avoided putting weight on the peg leg, Spider noticed, but it thumped the floor twice nonetheless.

Fawkes leaned against the table.

"Jim, keep that . . ."

Fawkes placed the raven on Spider's chest. It flapped wings, and opened its beak. The bird's shiny black eye looked hard as marble.

"Jim . . ."

Ben turned, slowly, talons scratching at Spider's skin.

Fawkes laughed. "Ben won't hurt you." He freed a knife from his belt. "Ben won't."

Sweat filled Spider's eyes, and his throat burned with fear. Ben turned some more, and now the bird's empty eye socket loomed, like a small cave.

Fawkes brandished the knife. Spider struggled to fight free. Ben flapped wings.

The blade dropped suddenly, catching firelight as it did. Spider's left arm suddenly was free. Fawkes had cut the rope.

Spider swatted recklessly at the raven, which lifted into the air in a wild flurry of black feathers. Fawkes cackled dementedly.

Spider grabbed Fawkes by the wrist and twisted it, hard. The knife dropped from the man's hand, onto the table where Spider could not see it. He reached around blindly until he felt the hilt, then snatched it up and rammed it into the man's stomach.

He'd grabbed it backward, striking with the pommel.

Fawkes, off balance, fell to the floor as Spider cut free his right arm.

Ben cawed enough to account for an entire flock, crossing the room in random directions and toppling vials and candles.

Spider slashed at the remaining ropes and rose quickly, making himself dizzy. Standing, and clutching at the table lest he fall, he gazed right and left, his head lashing back and forth like a flag in a wild wind as he tried to keep both the crippled pirate and the damned bird in view. He backed toward the door, knife ready to strike at Ben or Fawkes if necessary. He nearly slipped in the dead man's blood.

Fawkes merely laughed. "Damnedest thing I ever saw! A fucking bird!"

Spider exited the room and tried to get his bearings. He heaved and thought he might vomit. Shaking, he headed toward the stairs leading below. He passed door after door and wondered whether Hob was behind one of them. He tried one, then another. They were locked.

Behind him, he could hear Fawkes crawling across the floor toward his crutch. Ahead, Gold Peter was ascending the stairs. Spider tucked away the knife.

"You lived, I see," Peter said, not sounding much like he cared.

"Aye," Spider said. "Lived to fight another day, as they say." If the man had recently crossed Odin, he showed no sign of it.

Spider pushed his way past Gold Peter and headed downstairs. He needed to find Odin and form a plan. If Hob was in this madhouse, they had to get him out.

And if the whole goddamned place burned to the ground behind them, the world would be better off.

31

He found a shirt that was not drenched in blood and was glad to find his hat and pipe on his hammock. Spider covered his naked torso and headed to the kitchen in search of tobacco and a light, and to ask about Odin.

"I have not seen him," Mrs. Fitch whispered, handing Spider a hunk of bread. "I hope your friend survived the fighting." She did not sound particularly sincere.

"I am told he did." Spider filled his pipe and lit it with a brand from the fire. Then he filled his pouch and found the ripped cloth he'd tucked there. Course thin fabric, possibly from a shirt.

"Who attacked us, John?"

He tucked the cloth into his hatband and filled his pouch with leaf. "I am not certain, Missus Fitch."

"It's enemies of these criminals," she said, shaking her head. "I am sure of it! Violence and crime swarm around these men like maggots crawling on a dung heap!"

She stared at Spider as though expecting to see maggots on him.

"I am glad no harm came to you, Missus Fitch."

He headed outside.

"Spider John, up and walking like a living, breathing man. Ha!"

Odin and three others knelt around an inverted bucket, using it as a table to toss crude dice. They used small wooden chunks, badly squared and badly painted. Spider doubted they rolled true and wondered if Odin realized that. Spider himself once had made a pair of cheat dice for his friend Ezra, with blunted corners that led to snake eyes more often than mere chance could account for. He and Ezra had won a lot of extra drinks and duff with those dice.

These fellows might be using cheat dice, too, but only a few coins dotted the bucket. The stakes appeared to be small, so Spider didn't make any accusations. Odin did not have much money to lose, by any account.

"I am feeling well, Odin, though a bit swirly in the head. Mister Oakes thought a slow walk about the grounds might do me well. Would you come along, should I need a bit of help?"

Odin picked up three coins. "Aye."

Once they were beyond earshot, Odin spat. "You fell like a god-damned slack sail last night. I thought you were dead!"

"I was not feeling well before the fight," Spider said. "Remember? I guess that's what toppled me. You fought like your old self, though. Where did you get that axe you were swinging?"

Odin laughed. "Stole it from the barn the first time I poked around, and hid it near my post in case I needed it. I certainly needed it last night, ha!"

"Aye. Did you try to sneak up on Half-Jim today? He said someone had followed him."

"I did. Followed him to the house, thought I might kill him and pretend I'd found him, killed by one of the attackers maybe."

"That would have been rash," Spider warned. "We don't want to show our hand too soon."

"You almost fucked his woman and told her what we were up to," Odin said. "Remember? So do not lecture me about patience you know I lack anyway. I didn't get the chance to stab him, though. I think he heard me or something, and he hurried and glanced about a lot. He reached the house, and I veered off. Didn't think I could get away with killing him in there. Rash, you'd have called that."

"Good thing you did not follow him inside. You were correct, he knew someone trailed him and laid a trap. Gold Peter and Simon were ready for you."

"I hope I'll have another chance at Half-Jim. Ha!"

"Those were Bonny's men, Odin, that attacked us."

"Aye. I saw Little Bob among the dead. I looked for Hob, too, but did not see him. If he was with that gang, he got away."

"Little Bob said Hob had been taken when the smugglers were attacked."

"Little Bob lied by nature. If he told me he was pissing, I wouldn't believe him even if my leg was getting wet."

"He had no reason to lie about this. If Hob was involved in the fight at all, it would have been on our side. But I think Hob's either run from here or locked away as a patient." *Or dead and buried.*

Spider tried not to think of that possibility. "Where are our weapons?"

"Gathered up after the fight, we're to get them when we go on post. But I got that knife of Hob's." He plucked it from his belt. "I know you have a silly sentiment toward that knife."

Spider took it. "I gave this to Hob."

"Aye."

"Anyway, Hob was attached to this knife, too. And if Hob and Little Bob was still part of the same group, Hob would've got this knife back."

"Perhaps," Odin said.

"I am certain of it. Do you see Hob letting Little Bob keep this blade?"

"No."

"No. So Hob was not among the attackers, then." Spider inhaled deeply and the pipe fired bright.

They came across a fallen oak and sat upon it. They were quiet for a while, both lost in thought, until Spider emptied his spent pipe. "We have a great deal to puzzle out, my friend. But I think I begin to see what we are against. Or, well, I thought I did. Then I found another dead man, Raldo."

"He was killed in the battle," Odin said.

"No. I found him dead, already stiff and cold, and the battle was just barely begun. He wasn't fresh dead. Someone killed him before the fight. Drove a knife into his brain, from behind. Up, like this." He made a stabbing motion with his empty hand at the base of Odin's skull to demonstrate.

Odin lifted a finger. "Well, suppose it was one of Bonny's lads scouting? Raldo catches him, and the fellow kills him."

"He was stabbed from behind, I said. If Raldo caught him, he'd have been facing him, aye?"

"Aye." Odin scratched his head. "So he snuck up on Raldo."

"Maybe," Spider said. "But maybe not. He could have been a scout, I suppose, and killed Raldo before reporting back to his mates. But a sneak attack from behind . . . well, why the base of the skull like that, then? It's an odd angle. I'd have gone lower."

"Aye, probably," Odin conceded.

"I'd have dragged him away, too, so as to not alert anyone an attack was coming," Spider mused. "Sunk him in that pond, not too far from where I found him."

"Aye," Odin said. "That would have been my way, I think."

"So this death, then, it wasn't in the battle and it won't fit nice into any part of the pattern," Spider continued.

"Pattern?"

"Aye. Missus Fitch, she spoke of patients getting sick and dying. Well, that is not the same as getting stabbed or shot, is it? So, I thought I had started getting the weather gauge on these murders, and now here is Raldo all dead by violence and shifting the winds."

"You're certain he didn't just die in the fight?"

"I've seen a lot of fresh new corpses, Odin. His wasn't. He was killed during the day, probably, not sooner, else he'd have been missed. And I don't see a scout like that operating by day, anyway, now that I think on it. Do you? Is that how you'd do it? Or would you sneak in by cover of darkness?"

"Aye, then. Dumb as Little Bob Higgins is, not even he would have planned it that way."

"Before I nearly tripped over Raldo's corpse, I thought I had part of this all reckoned out," Spider said after a while.

"So tell me."

"Young men are brought here, pirates and smugglers, but we don't find them. I think they are locked away as patients and end up in the ground."

"Someone pays Oakes to cure them of thievery?"

Spider shook his head. "No. It is something else entirely. Young men vanished first from nearby farms, raising a ruckus and drawing attention. Oakes did not like that, did he? What does a pirate do, when things get too hot where he's operating?"

"He sails to safer waters," Odin said.

"Aye. So then Ambrose Oakes sends his dog Half-Jim Fawkes to arrange an ambush on some smugglers and bring some of them back here captive. Hob among them."

"He was capturing young men here, then sent fucking Half-Jim to get him some men elsewhere once Mister Wilson started poking around?"

"Aye, Odin. Aye."

"Why does he capture men?"

"I think I know why," Spider answered. "But I shall be damned if I understand it. But ambushing a bunch of no-good, unloved smugglers gives him some fellows that no one is likely to come after. Aside from their shipmates, who is going to care if a few pirates disappear forever?"

Odin blinked his lone eye. "So, he's pressing them to serve him?"

"I do not reckon so. These men Fawkes hired did not come from Bonny's crew. No. They were hired to help protect the grounds, and to go get Oakes some captives he needs for a damned foul purpose. I began to suspect what that is, but I ain't reckoned it all out. But I think they were brought here and killed one at a time."

"Oakes murdered them, not some illness?"

"Perhaps. Perhaps, I say. But," Spider shook his head, "he did not kill me, and he easily could have. I was bound to his table, senseless, asleep, and yet he plastered my cut. He might have killed me then and there, but he did not. So maybe my wild notion of what goes on here is just that, a wild notion, and my mind is just not working right after being hurt."

"You fell hard, but that cut did not look so bad."

"Aye," Spider said. "I thought perhaps Little Bob had dipped his blade in venom or something, but Oakes says he did not."

"We both will go mad if we stay here. Ha!"

"Aye." Spider sighed. "You speak true. I am not sure I care who is killing who. Jesus, I just want to find Hob and leave this place behind us!"

"I never really did care who is killing who, or about finding that dumbass Hob, ha! He created his own problems, Spider John, when he followed pretty Miss Bonny across the ocean!"

Spider closed his eyes tightly. "I am of a mind to get our weapons and just confront these bastards right now, start slitting necks and bursting skulls until they give us Hob."

"I like a fight, you know that, but we are but two men. And these fellows are no newcomers to bloodshed, Spider."

"True, but there are not so many of them now as there were."

"Well, then, perhaps we remain under our false flag and reduce their numbers a bit more?"

"No. Our time is up already, I think. Maybe we can snatch up Oakes, or Fawkes, and put a gun to a head and make these bastards bring Hob to us. I don't know. Ruth knows we are looking for a ship-mate, and it is a . . . fuck and bugger!"

Spider pointed toward a fat oak. A man crouching behind it suddenly broke cover, running hard for the house.

"Do you think he heard us?"

"Yes."

Spider was already on the run, Hob's knife in hand. The fellow was swift, but so was Spider—and Spider did not need to cover the whole distance between them.

Once he was close enough, Spider halted, poised himself, and threw. It was a skill he'd developed during the long periods of boredom between action on the Spanish Main.

Hob's knife, designed for throwing, plunged between the man's shoulder blades and he fell instantly. He was still squirming and crying when Spider got to him.

"Spying on us, are you?"

"One of Oakes' boys," Odin said, catching up from behind. "I've seen him about. Don't recall his name, though."

Spider watched the man die, then hung his head. He wanted more than anything to leave all the killing behind, but the violent life seemed to cling to him. He told himself that this man would have raised the alarm, warned Oakes that Spider and Odin were up to something and ruined any chance they had of rescuing Hob, if the lad still lived. Knowing that did not keep the bile from rising in Spider's throat, though.

Of course, Ruth may have warned Fawkes anyway, because of my foolish maneuver.

"You had to kill him, and Half-Jim recruited all these men from the sweet trade," Odin said. "This fellow has probably known for years a blade or a ball or a hangman's noose would be his end. His soul is not worth your mourning."

"If that be true, then our souls are beyond mourning, too," Spider muttered. "Such things are likely to be our ends, too. But not before we get Hob."

"So we get our guns, and some extra guns, and then take the fight to them! Oh, and we get whatever Stingo lobbed at them! The explosions! Jesus, whatever that was, I want some!"

"Something Oakes cooked up in his laboratory. Little Bob mentioned something similar when he talked about the assault on the smugglers. But we can't just go in like madmen. Not yet," Spider said, looking at the dead man. He freed his knife from the body, and wiped it on the man's breeches. "I have a notion this man's death may help us even the odds a wee bit more."

32

"We found him, dying," Spider said. He and Odin held the dead man between them, his arms over their shoulders and his feet dragging. "He told us he saw two men before he died."

Fawkes, far more sober than the last time Spider had seen him, nodded. "Farewell, Timothy." Then his voice boomed like a cannon. "Men! Alarm! We've more of those bastards on the grounds! Weapons, lads! Guns and balls! Both watches to duty now!"

That prompted groans as tired men scurried for weapons.

Spider and Odin dropped their burden, then wiped at the man's blood that smeared their clothes. Men gathered about them, the ship's bell rang out, and guns and swords were passed about. Spider and Odin each found themselves with two guns, of Spanish make and already primed. Spider still had Hob's knife.

"Each to his usual post and scream bloody hell if you see any of these pricks!" Fawkes threw a weapon belt over his shoulder, then looked directly at Spider. "I am in a killing mood," he said. "You might pray I am able to indulge it before we meet again." He tapped his belly where Spider had hit him. Spider hoped that was the only reason Fawkes had to confront him, and it seemed likely. *If Ruth's already told him why I am here, he'd just shoot me.*

"Praying might be a good idea for us all, Jim." Spider ran out, followed by Odin.

"The ruse worked, Odin. Everyone is scattering. Head toward your post, but tack to the barn when you can," Spider whispered.

"Once they scatter, we go in and find Hob. If he's alive, he's in one of those rooms upstairs. If Gold Peter and Simon get in our way, well, so be it. All the rest of the men are scattered. So we find Hob. And then we are done with this goddamned place."

Odin's lone eye gleamed. "Almost as much fighting here as on the old ships," he said. "Ha!"

"Is your leg still troubling you?"

"No. The pain has passed, Spider John. I am fine."

They parted company, and Spider headed toward the south wall. He spotted an oak that looked easy enough to climb and decided to make all the years of climbing ratlines and maneuvering his way across yardarms pay off. Soon, he was high enough to see the house and had a commanding view of the surrounding grounds.

Half-Jim was out front, pacing as well as a one-legged man with a crutch could pace. He had two guns in the weapon belt across his shoulder, and the leather holster mounted on the crutch held a third gun. To complete his small arsenal, he had a goddamned farm sickle, a small one, tucked into his belt behind his back.

"I know a better place for that sickle, Half-Jim," Spider muttered.

He paid no attention to Fawkes' men rushing to their stations, not even sparing a longing glance at Ruth as she rushed toward the south wall, but he winced when he saw Michael run into the barn and shut the doors. He had forgotten all about the giant and the way he snuck away at times, and had said nothing much at all to Odin about him. If Michael was involved in the killings, and if Odin had already reached the barn . . .

He need not have worried. Odin waved from behind a large oak not far from the barn. Spider waved back and dropped from his perch. He took a roundabout path to meet his friend.

"That is one big bastard," Odin said, pointing toward the barn.

"Aye. Half-Jim is near the front entrance," Spider said. "I am guessing he's got no one in the house except Gold Peter and Simon, judging from all the lads I saw dashing about on the grounds. I say we go in through the kitchen, give Missus Fitch a nice story to keep her quiet, and we go find Hob. If we have to kill anyone on the way, try to do it quiet."

"Aye," Odin said, grinning. The old man dearly loved action.

"I mean it."

"Aye."

"Well, then," Spider said, glancing across the grounds. "Here we go."

He dashed across the open ground toward the kitchen, then put his back to the wall next to the door. Odin, limping less than previously, took up a similar position on the other side.

Spider listened intently, then signaled Odin to remain quiet. He could hear Mrs. Fitch working inside.

"I will talk our way past her," Spider whispered. "Follow me."

Spider lifted the latch and stepped inside. "Missus Fitch, did no one tell you there are prowlers on the grounds?"

"Aye, sir, there is a ruckus. Mister Fawkes, he has the men out searching." She piled diced potatoes into a massive kettle atop the stove, dropping them quickly and pulling her hands away from the steam. "It seems the normal state of things here, does it not? Always hiding from one raid or another, or the men fighting one another, or some other ruckus. I am sick of it, John! I shan't hide away anymore! I have my chores. I cannot abide a constant uproar of battle. I just . . . All this just . . ."

"Aye," Spider said. "We have our chores, too. Thought we'd head upstairs for a lookout, it'll be like perching in a crow's nest, won't it, Odin?"

"Aye," the one-eyed man answered. "Ought to see well from there, no doubt."

"Damn," said a man, and Spider at once recognized the refined voice of Ambrose Oakes. A glance behind him confirmed it; the bloated man entered the kitchen, mopping his florid face with a towel. "That boy has turned for the worse, Missus Fitch, so this is a horrible time for this new assault. I tire of it! It cannot be helped, I suppose. I must do my work as you must do yours, interlopers be damned."

"Yes, sir," Mrs. Fitch replied.

"It is good you are here, boys," the man said, nodding toward Spider and Odin. "Peter and Simon are preparing the laboratory now, and you two can help me get the patient there. It will save precious time. Hasten!" He grabbed a stack of towels and turned away, bellowing excitedly. "Missus Fitch, I will be in there with the lad for God knows how long. Pass the word to Mister Fawkes that we must not be disturbed!"

"Aye, sir," Mrs. Fitch replied.

Spider's heart did a beat to quarters in his chest. *Could the boy Oakes referred to be Hob? Was this rescue effort too late?*

He followed on the heels of Ambrose Oakes, with Odin in tow. Oakes tried to bolt up the stairs, though he was not built for such action.

"We must act before he expires," Oakes said. "Before the final moment."

"What boy is this, sir?" Spider stayed close behind Oakes.

"The Irish lad, Bram by name. He hasn't long to live, it seems."

And I doubt preventing his death is your goal, Spider thought. The name Bram gave Spider no real comfort; it would not surprise him at all if Hob had used a false name. The lad had seen Spider use an alias many, many times, as it was habitual for many pirates.

Spider gulped. "Blond fellow, strong?"

Oakes paused at the top of the steps and looked confused. "Dark, he is. And thin. Thinner now than when he came here."

"Ah," Spider said, trying to hide his relief. "Thought I saw a young blond lad about."

Oakes shook his head violently. "We dawdle, and we must not. A soul is at stake. Come!"

He led them past his laboratory, where Gold Peter could be seen arranging buckets and dangling a leather hose on the end of the table Spider had occupied previously. The other table had been wiped up, but still was stained red, as was the floor beneath it. Simon stoked the fireplace.

Spider and Odin followed Oakes to the end of the corridor, which intersected with another perpendicular hall. Turning left, Oakes removed a key from a vest pocket.

Odin peeked through a barred window that looked out onto the back of the grounds, and the barn. "None of the men seem to be close," he muttered in Spider's ear.

Spider was less worried about Fawkes and his crew than he was about listening for Hob's voice. He imagined he might hear it over the drumming of their footsteps in the hall.

"The boy is in here," Oakes said, halting by a door on his left. Like all the other doors, this one was of good solid oak and very damned sturdy.

Oakes turned the key in the lock. "Bring him to the laboratory, quickly! And fear not what you see, there is no contagion!" Oakes raced toward his laboratory. "Hasten!"

Spider went into the room. He'd seen forecastles more elegantly furnished. This room had a single cot along one wall and a small trunk along the opposite wall. A lone window, barred like all the others, looked out over a courtyard.

The cot's occupant was perhaps fifteen years of age, but too dark and skinny to be Hob. He curled up on the cot like a dog, precariously, and nearly fell to the floor when Spider crouched beside him. Heat rose from the lad's face and sweat dripped from his limp hair. He moaned softly.

"Bram," Spider said. He tried to lift the young man to his feet, but the fellow's legs were slack as rope.

"Poor man. Odin, grab his blanket. We shall roll him onto that and carry him."

"Aye," Odin said, stepping forward. As he did so, he kicked something on the floor that rolled away in a wide arc.

Spider picked it up. It was a wooden cup. A sniff told him it had recently held rum.

"Missus Fitch sent this up with Daphne, like I told you," Spider said. "A cup of rum. She said it was medicine for him."

"Medicine? Ha!"

"Aye," Spider said. "Poison, I am sure of it."

"Why give him poison? Isn't Oakes supposed to treat people?"

"I think the man has another purpose entirely. I think . . ."

"Spider John! Odin! May God damn you! Bring the lad here before he expires!"

Spider winced. "We'd better heed Oakes. Roll Bram onto the blanket!"

Once they had their ill cargo in hand and were headed toward the laboratory, Spider whispered. "If I am right, you may soon see what Oakes is up to, and why he had Fawkes fetch him some smugglers, and why they keep digging new graves here."

Oakes was waiting outside the laboratory door. "Does he live yet?"

"Aye," Spider said.

"Good! Get him on the table!"

They did as ordered, and Oakes nearly shoved them aside. Simon stacked towels on a side table and arranged the glue pot and other items. Gold Peter held small coils of rope.

Spider cast a glance at Ben, but the bird seemed to be sleeping.

"This boy was strong when he came here," the philosopher said, taking up the mask-and-hose gadget Spider had seen him use during the amputation. "I believe I will succeed this time. I do!"

Spider pointed to a small jar on the floor beside the table, and his finger traced the path of the hose that protruded from its cork and up through Oakes' hands and on to the mask he had just placed on Bram's face. Odin watched the maneuver but looked baffled.

Simon left the room, as Gold Peter secured the lad to the table. The man had obviously learned his ropes well at sea and made short work of it. "He's snug, sir. No need to worry about spasms or such."

"Thank you, Peter. Join Simon, watch from the windows and shout if any intruders come our way. Spider John, Odin, go find Mister Fawkes and get your orders. I can handle what needs to be done here."

"I wish to remain," Spider said. "This fascinates me."

Frightens me near to shitting, I should say.

Odin scowled at Spider.

Oakes turned briefly toward the two shipmates. "Truly?"

"Aye, sir. What I saw before makes me curious."

"Curiosity! So few men have it, I dare say. It is surprising and refreshing to find it in one of your sort. Very well, you may remain. Odin, go aid Mister Fawkes."

Odin shot Spider a quick glance. Spider tapped a pistol, nodded at Odin, and the one-eyed man exited the room.

"He breathes yet," Oakes said. "All is well." Then the man grinned. "Do you know what I do here, Spider John? The aim of this?"

"You want to catch his soul."

Oakes looked stunned, then laughed. "By God, you've a brain, indeed! Yes, man! Yes!"

Spider checked his weapons once Oakes turned his attention back to Bram. "What will you do with it?"

"Why, we advance knowledge, Spider John. What use is intellect if we do not use it to grow our garden of knowledge?"

Spider backed away and leaned against the table where the other man had died, the one who'd lost a leg. Spider felt the stickiness of the man's blood beneath his hands.

Oakes placed his hands on the mask, holding it firmly to Bram's face. "Can't let it escape, can I?"

Spider looked at the corked jars arrayed on the shelf. "Are those souls?"

"Possibly. Those are unconfirmed previous attempts," Oakes said. "It is gruesome work, I confess, but true advancement comes at the end of much toil. I do not know that I succeeded. But there may be souls in them. You see," he glanced over his shoulder, "souls seem to be invisible. A true hindrance to detection, let me admit. But I may defeat it yet, so long as I increase my supply. I must take advantage of every opportunity fate delivers into my hands."

Odin crept into the room while Oakes was diverted by his conversation with Spider. The old man's lips formed silent words: "Kill him now." Then he silently moved behind the other table and hid.

Bram's chest still rose and fell, but slowly.

"I started with collections of blood," Oakes said, softly. It was almost as if he was talking to himself. He turned back to the dying man. "At the moment of death, blood was collected into a jar. 'For the life of all flesh is the blood thereof.' Aye? Do you know that verse? And another: 'but by his own blood he entered in once into the holy place.' Blood, I thought. Blood. Might the blood be the very place where the soul resides? Was that the key? It seemed likely."

Oakes checked the fitting of the hose into the mask and stared hard at the lad's face. "So, some of those jars contain blood, and perhaps souls. I've attempted to verify the presence of the soul. I've boiled some of the blood, to see if a soul separated from it. I've swirled it. I've filtered it. But, thus far, to no avail. Thus far. But I shall persist."

Spider rested a hand on the butt of a gun.

"That jar," Oakes said, pointing toward his desk. "Contains marrow. Scooped from the amputated leg of that wretch. It was a sudden thought, and perhaps I had it too late, the man being too far along the road to hell, but the marrow might yet yield interesting results."

Spider remembered the scraping sound he'd heard during the amputation and winced.

Oakes continued, apparently unaware of how ghastly this all sounded. "And I can perfect my techniques for future attempts, of course. I am always learning, Spider John. Always."

Dear God, let me find Hob alive!

"I refuse to be defeated, and I realize I might go down many wrong paths before I reach my goal. After the blood attempts failed, I reasoned anew. If not the blood, then perhaps the breath! Perhaps that is where the soul abides! Does not the Bible speak of the breath of life, Spider John? And so now I collect their very last breaths, in hopes that their souls ride upon them. And I weigh the contents of these jars." He nodded toward a scale on the table between shelves. "I weigh them before and after, but perhaps souls have no weight. I mingle the contents with gasses, heavy and light. I heat the jars, and peer into them with lenses, shine light through them with prisms, but alas! The souls elude me. Thus far!"

He glanced over his shoulder. "But I shall not give up!"

Spider gulped. "I think harvesting souls is for the Lord, and the devil. Not for a man."

Oakes spat. "Why gift a man with intelligence if he is not to probe God's secrets?" He returned his attention to Bram.

"He will die soon," Oakes said. "But he is strong, and young, so he holds on. I select such as him with purpose, deeming their souls to be likewise young and strong, and more likely to survive my processes, and perhaps more vibrant as well, to aid detection. Your devilish friend Odin, though, he gives me pause! To have lived so long in a violent trade. Perhaps his soul is made of sterner stuff than those of these young ruffians!"

Good luck getting a soul out of Odin, you bloody goddamned devil.

Spider had heard enough. He drew a gun and placed the end of the barrel at the back of the man's head.

"Lift your hands in the air."

Oakes complied, slowly. "What is this?"

"I am looking for a friend. I believe him to be here. And he had better not be in one of those graves."

Oakes froze.

"I'll be damned," Odin said, rising and drawing two pistols. "The devil bought my soul a long time ago, you son of a whore. Ha!"

"This is important work, men," Oakes said. "Think of it. If we can capture the soul, we might yet store it away, repair the body from whence it came, restore it . . ."

"Madness," Spider said. "Dead men don't come back."

"Headless Blackbeard swam around his ship three times before he sank, he did!"

"Not now, Odin." Spider drew his second gun. "Oakes, this is madness."

"This is inspiration, Spider John! This is learning!"

Spider shook his head. "There is only one soul I wish to salvage. A young man named Hob, blond and strong, just the type you've been killing. You had best pray you have not already buried him, because the only thing that will keep me from killing you is knowing that Hob lives. Is he here?"

Oakes sneered over his shoulder. "So you came here under false pretenses?"

Spider pressed the gun hard against the fat man's skull. "Is he here?"

An odd cadence of thumps outside the room told Spider that Half-Jim Fawkes was approaching, as rapidly as possible for a one-legged man on a crutch.

"Fawkes!"

The rhythmic thumps quickened at Oakes' cry. Spider wrapped the man's neck in his left arm, squeezing tightly, then pressed the gun in his right hand hard against the mad philosopher's temple. Oakes struggled ineffectively.

Ben leapt from his corner perch, cawing madly. Odin shot at the damned bird, which vanished through the door in a black streak. Wind from the bird's wings stirred the smoke from Odin's gun.

Fawkes appeared a moment later, blinking in the smoke and ducking the bird. The crutch fell behind him, and he leaned against the doorframe, gun in hand.

"I'll kill him, Fawkes," Spider said. "Don't think I bluff."

"And I'll kill him," Fawkes said, aiming his flintlock at Odin.

Odin lifted his other gun and fired. Wood splintered near Fawkes' face. Fawkes fired in return, and the brimstone tang of burnt powder filled the air.

Spider turned so that the gun in his left hand aimed at the door, but kept his left arm locked around his captive's throat. Spider pulled the trigger, but the goddamned gun merely sputtered.

Fire erupted in Spider's leg. He glanced down to see a scalpel plunged into his thigh. Oakes had grabbed it from the table while Spider was distracted.

Next, Fawkes lunged into the room and Spider, Oakes, and the one-legged pirate all fell in a heap. Spider's head collided with something hard, and his right-hand gun fired impotently into the air. Oakes rolled away, and Fawkes reached toward the hearth.

The next thing Spider saw was Fawkes lifting a coal shovel above his head. The last thing he saw was the shovel's blade descending on his face.

33

*H*e was bouncing, and apparently upside down, and his head felt like it had been fired from a long nine.

Spider opened his eyes, and realized he was being carried over a man's shoulders. He looked down at the hardwood floor, and immediately recognized the boots of the man carrying him.

He also recognized the limp.

"Odin," he whispered. "Put me down."

Odin did so immediately, placing Spider on his arse with his back against a corridor wall. "If you were a bigger man, Spider John, I'd have left you back there."

Spider glanced around and realized he was still upstairs, not far from the laboratory. Gold Peter was bleeding all over the floor outside the laboratory door, surrounded by shards of Fawkes' shattered crutch. Behind him, in the intersection of hallways, Simon sat below the window with a red hole in his forehead. The window was stained red, and dripping.

"Is everyone dead?"

"I don't know," Odin answered. The man was breathing hard. "Blubber whale Oakes took a knock when he fell, like you did. I left him there. I stabbed Half-Jim in the back, then grabbed the gun from his crutch holster. Handy, that. Grabbed this damned thing, too."

Odin hoisted the small sickle Fawkes had carried behind him. "This might be better than the axe. So Peter and Simon came rushing," he continued. "I shot one and busted the crutch on the other, then I snatched you up and decided we did not need to remain here one god-damned minute longer. I am for leaving, Spider John."

"You are one tough bastard, Odin. How is your leg?"

"Better than your leg." Odin pointed at a bloody cloth wrapped around Spider's thigh. "Oakes poked you. You've had worse pains, though, so don't dawdle. Let us flee!"

"No. I do not yet know what became of Hob." Spider touched his nose. It was swollen, and his hand came away bloody, but the nose did not seem to be broken.

Odin spat. "I knew you would say that."

Spider rose, slowly, wiping his sleeve across his bloody face. "Is everyone else still out chasing ghosts? Or did the gunshots bring them all running?"

"I have been a might busy killing everyone while you took a nap, Spider John. I have no bloody idea where they all are."

"Aye. Well . . . Wait. Do you hear?"

Spider pointed toward the steps. Someone was rushing up them.

Odin and Spider prepared knives. Spider was poised to throw and Odin set to pounce when Ruth appeared at the top of the stairs.

"Spider! Odin!"

Neither man attacked, but both remained ready. The woman had a flintlock in her right hand, and two good dirks on her belt.

She lowered her gun. "I came to help you." She glanced over the dead men in the corridor, caught her breath, then looked at Spider.

"Help us?"

She nodded.

Spider tilted his head. "Last I talked to you, woman, I was a mouse in a cat's jaws. I thought you planned to betray us to Half-Jim?"

She bit her lip. "I . . . I thought then that you were with Bonny's men. Or maybe Wilson's hire. I thought you and your friend were spies. But when you told me you came to save a friend, well . . ."

"Well?"

She gulped. "I believed you. I do not think I have ever met a man who would wander into a viper's nest like this one to rescue a shipmate. Most men I've known would think only of their own lives."

"Maybe," Spider said. "There's not many who'd be worth the risk, but Hob is."

She stepped forward. "So I want to help you."

Spider lowered his own knife. "Do you know where Hob is?"

She shook her head. "I can tell you this much, though. I saw the men, Bonny's smugglers, when Jim and the boys brought them here. There was a young blond man with them!"

Spider's heart drummed. "Where is he now?"

"I do not know," Ruth answered. "I truly do not. But the captives were brought up here, like patients. I know that much. And I have heard no one tell of an escape. Jim would have raised hell over that."

"So Hob's in one of these rooms," Odin muttered, "or in one of those graves."

Spider headed toward the laboratory. "Oakes has a key, probably a master or he'd have a whole ring of them. I'm going to get it, and then we're going to find Hob!"

Spider entered the laboratory.

Fawkes was face down, bleeding badly from the back. But he was rolling over.

Half-Jim had three guns, Spider remembered. *Two on his chest, one on the crutch. And I can account for only two.*

Spider saw the pistol in Half-Jim's hand and dodged. Thunder cracked, flame fired, smoke and lead flew and steel flashed. The pistol's ball burrowed into the wall.

Spider's thrown knife burrowed into Half-Jim's neck.

Ruth and Odin sprang into the room, weapons ready. Spider shook his head. "I had no choice, Ruth."

She stared at Fawkes and swallowed hard. "Do not fret. I shall not miss him as you might suppose." But a tear clung to her cheek just the same. "I wasn't with him because I liked him."

She left the room quickly.

Fawkes stared, unseeing, as Spider retrieved his weapon. He wiped it on the shirt of Ambrose Oakes as he lifted the key from the man's pocket. Oakes lived, breathing shallowly. He had a horrid bruise on his head, but no blood loss.

"I ought to kill you," Spider whispered. "But I am trying to leave bloodshed behind. Lucky for you, you son of a bitch."

He started to leave, but a glance at dead Bram and the jar on the floor stopped him. Spider knelt by the jar, grasped the hose and sliced it with his knife. He looked at Bram. "Don't know if your soul is really in there, but if it is maybe it won't stay there." He glanced upward, wondered whether God or devil would wrestle for claim on this boy, then dashed into the hall.

"I have been trying to figure which room is Hob's, but they all look the same," Odin said.

"I know a way," Spider said. He filled his lungs, then shouted: "Hob!"

Odin spun, knife in hand, and Ruth raised her pistol and ran toward the window. She kicked dead Simon in the shoulder to topple him out of her way, then found a portion of the window that was not smeared with the man's blood. She peeked outside. "No one coming yet. Spider, that was a tad reckless, I think."

"I am done with sneaking around," Spider said. "We're pirates, goddamn it."

"Former pirates," Odin said. "Ha!"

"If anyone comes, just remember to say lamb, or wolf, or whatever it is. But if we must kill them, we kill them." Spider hoisted the key. "Hob!"

Ruth and Odin joined his cry.

Near the stairs, they heard a banging.

Someone was pounding on the other side of one of the doors.

"Hob? Hob!"

Spider rushed in that direction, the others behind him. A black shadow flew over Spider's head, and he dove.

Ben veered through the corridor.

"Fuck and bugger all goddamned birds and consign them to the lowest fucking hell!"

The others watched him rise from the floor.

"It was just a bird," Ruth said.

"They scare him," Odin said. "I don't know why."

Spider ignored all that and rushed toward the pounding noise. "Hob! Speak to me, son!"

Upon arriving, Spider nearly dropped the key in his haste. He had to try several times before the lock opened, while the hammering on the other side continued. When he finally got it unlocked, he did not find Hob.

He found Daphne, weeping.

"Guns and shouts, and me locked away! I saw none of it!"

The girl pushed past Spider and yelped with glee when she saw the corpses in the corridor.

"Peter! Simon! No more wet sheets for Daphne! And all the blood!"

She ran toward the bodies.

"Good lord," Ruth said.

"Aye," Spider replied, shuddering.

"We should bring her along," Odin said. "We might need the help. Can she shoot?"

"I'm not giving her a gun," Spider said. "Hell, I don't have a gun. And we waste time. Hob! Hob!"

They all raised the cry again, Daphne joining them but not quite seeming to understand why. They kept it up, all the while watching for signs of Jim's men rushing toward them.

Spider raised his hands. "Silence! Silence! I hear something!"

Odin and Ruth quieted themselves, but Daphne continued shouting Hob's name. Ruth clamped a hand over the girl's mouth. "Shhhh!"

Once it was quiet, they all heard it.

"Spider? Spider?"

"Hob!"

"Spider John!"

Spider ran toward the sound of Hob's voice. He leapt over Gold

Peter and nearly tripped over Simon as he rounded the corner and headed to the right.

"Hob! Hob, lad!"

"Spider!"

As he got closer, Spider realized the voice calling him was quite weak. "Can you pound on a wall, Hob? On your door? Where are you?"

Odin and the others followed him. "Daphne says there is a blond man in the last room to the right," Ruth called. "She says she's in love with him."

Spider rushed to that door and prayed the key would fit the lock.

It did.

He entered the room and saw Hob on a cot. The boy was frail, his head bandaged. A portion of the bandage was stained red, and all of it was damp with sweat.

But his eyes were open, and he was smiling.

"Spider John, I'll be damned." The voice was weak, and Hob fell back after an attempt to rise.

Spider knelt by the cot. "Hob, goddamn you, this is what you get for chasing Anne Bonny's tail across the Spanish Main, you fool!"

Hob smiled weakly. "You saw her tail, did you not?" He tried again to rise but failed.

Spider wiped away a tear. "There are plenty of women out there who won't get you killed."

Hob closed his eyes. "Name one."

34

The ship's bell behind the house clanged wildly, as though a gale blew through a bell tower.

Spider was carrying Hob over his shoulder, as Odin had carried him earlier. "Take a look, Odin."

Odin peeked out a window. "Missus Fitch, banging hard on the bell. No one else with her, just Missus Fitch."

Spider swore under his breath. "She heard all our goddamned noise."

"Everyone will come running," Ruth said.

Daphne clapped her hands and pointed at Odin's weapon. "Can I have that?"

Odin pulled the sickle away from her. "Fuck, I do not think so!"

"Come!" Spider headed toward the stairs, Hob on his shoulder.

"I can walk, Spider."

"No you can't, boy."

"I'm a man," Hob said.

"I know."

Odin kept pace with Spider, but he still limped. "I wish we had not shot all the guns."

"Ruth has one, and we've got knives. By the way, Hob, yours is in my belt."

"Really?" Spider felt the weapon being pulled free. "How did you possibly get this?"

"I'll tell you one day. Right now, it is tough to talk and carry you.

You've grown even more." Even as he said it, he worried. The lad felt lighter than he should.

"My shipmates," Hob said. "These bastards took us! Where are they?"

"Dead or locked up, Hob," Spider said.

"We have to free them!"

Ruth tapped Spider's arm. "Give me the key," she said.

"We have no time, Ruth."

She blew away a strand of hair. "There are other people locked behind other doors, and I don't like the notion of them starving to death after we've killed all their caretakers or chased them away."

"Give her the key, Spider," Hob said.

"Speed is our ally and that will slow us down," Spider said, but he stopped. He peeked at his wounded leg, and was relieved to notice it was not bleeding too badly.

"You are carrying a big tall lad and the old half-blind man limps," Ruth said. "I will catch up to you quite easily, Spider John."

"I think I dropped the key in Hob's room. Go! We are headed for the barn."

"I will meet you there." Ruth ran off and vanished around the corner before the others reached the stairs. Spider took a moment to prepare himself for the descent.

"Want me to help you carry him?"

"No, Odin. I want you ready to fight if you need to. And don't bother saying wolf."

"Or lamb," Odin said.

"Or lamb. Daphne, would you like to help us?"

"Yes! Give me a knife!"

"No. Nothing sharp for you. I do not think they will shoot you, so run ahead, and watch for anyone coming. If you see anyone, give us a shout. We'll go out through the kitchen. Go!"

Daphne kissed Hob on the head, then ran ahead, giggling.

"She says she loves you," Ruth said, breathing hard.

"That was quick," Spider said.

"Aye. I opened doors and told people to run like the devil chased them." Indeed, voices filled the corridor behind them. Spider glanced back and saw dazed people, a couple of them with tough skin weathered by sun, wind and salt, entering the hall.

Hob tried to lift his head. "The girl loves me? Is she pretty? My eyes are all blurry."

"Aye, she's pretty," Spider said. "Ruth is pretty, too."

"And you wasted time locked up," Odin said. "Ha!"

"I tried to escape. Gold Peter clubbed me with something. I think."

Spider took two deep breaths. "Let us go."

The damned bell continued to clang.

Odin led the way, and Ruth took up the rear. Between them, Spider headed down the steps, slowly, leaning against the handrail. The steps groaned beneath him. "This house needs so much work."

Odin scoffed. "I do not think you have the time, Spider."

"Aye."

The steps were agony, and Spider's back felt the strain of Hob's weight. But they made it all the way down and turned down the corridor toward the kitchen.

"We'll go out the kitchen door," Spider said. "Straight to the barn and into the wagon."

"The bell is out back, and that's where they'll gather," Ruth cautioned.

"They are scattered, with luck, so maybe we have a chance." Spider shifted Hob on his shoulder a bit. "We might get to the wagon in time, or we might have to slit some throats. But we will all ride out together. Missus Fitch, too."

"A plan!" Odin said. "And a ride, too!" He veered toward the sitting room.

"Odin, goddamn it! What are you doing?"

"I want that big gun on the wall!"

Good Lord. "Do you know where the fucking balls and powder are?"

"No."

"Then you waste time!" Spider headed toward the kitchen. "Come now or stay to die!"

Odin complied, but grumbled. "I wish we had that blunderbuss. And those exploding things, too, that they toss about."

"Are you limping, Odin?"

"My leg is fine, Hob."

"You limp."

"I know. My leg is fine."

The clanging suddenly stopped.

Spider swore. "Does that mean they are here?"

"Maybe," Ruth said, brandishing her gun.

They dashed through the corridor and into the kitchen. Daphne was holding the door open, and Mrs. Fitch stood beside her.

"Daphne says you saved some poor wretch and we're all to flee?"

"Aye," Spider said. "And you can come with us. Hurry!"

"Dear," she said, wringing her hands. "I'm sorry. I heard guns and I rang the bell and now all those horrible men are rushing . . ."

"We know! Go!" Spider sprang toward the door.

Hob snatched at a bottle on the large table. "Missed it!"

"Don't drink from any bottles here," Spider warned. "They are poisoned!"

Mrs. Fitch gasped. "Poisoned?"

"Aye," Spider said. "I'll explain later. Hurry!"

Mrs. Fitch swallowed hard and seemed to be searching for words.

Spider, Hob still on his shoulder, squeezed through the door and past Daphne and Mrs. Fitch. None of Fawkes' pirates were within sight, but he could hear shouts of confusion and they did not sound very far off. He headed toward the barn and thanked the Lord it was already open.

Chickens scattered, squawking madly. "Goddamned claws and beaks! Jesus!" Spider spun, using Hob as a shield, as the birds flapped all around him.

"Put me down, Spider!"

"Silence, Hob!"

"Poison?" Mrs. Fitch followed him, with Odin leading her by the arm. Ruth aimed her gun left, then right, then left again, ready to fire at anyone who rushed them.

"Later, Missus Fitch."

"You keep saying poison."

Spider sighed. "I drank a bit of that rum you have locked away, Missus Fitch, and then I got horrible sick. Rum doesn't do that to me."

"Poison? Who would do that?"

The shouts grew closer, and Spider expected hot lead to fly any moment. "Goddamn it, woman, I will explain later!"

Daphne smiled and trudged along beside him toward the barn.

Spider glanced at her. "You will come away with us, will you?"

She nodded. "I want to stay with Hob. I love him."

"Good," Spider muttered. *I still wonder about you, little girl.* "To the barn, quickly!"

They reached the door and found the giant Michael inside. Odin rushed toward him, sickle raised.

Mrs. Fitch shouted, "No! He isn't going to fight us! Are you Michael?"

The man halted, shook his head and raised his arms.

"Help us hitch up the horses, Michael," Mrs. Fitch said. "We are going to town. You can come, too."

Michael nodded and got to work.

35

Ruth stood guard by the barn door. "I see two men coming, I think. They are running hard. I hear shouts, too, so others are coming on their heels."

Even as she said it, a cutlass flashed at her arm. Someone had crept around the corner of the barn and snuck toward the door.

The blade caught the barrel of Ruth's gun. The weapon fired uselessly into the ground and fell from her hand. She grasped the swordsman's wrist and pulled him into the barn. She tripped him, and he toppled onto the dirt.

He rolled, started to rise—and Odin planted the sickle in his back.

Spider gritted his teeth. The dead man was Hugh, the Frenchman who'd served with Fawkes and who'd promised to share his wine.

You spoke true, Hugh. Fortune is a bitch.

"Get on the damned wagon!" Spider placed Hob into the back and exhaled heavily now that the lad's weight was off his shoulder. He climbed in behind Hob.

The wagon bed was covered by a frame and thin oak planks. "This will protect us somewhat from guns," he said. "I hope."

"Aye," Hob said.

Odin and Ruth helped Michael finish with the skittish horses as guns fired and balls thumped against the barn.

"Does anyone know how to run a team?"

Spider's question drew blank stares.

"I'll do it!" Odin tossed his bloodied sickle into the wagon bed, then ran forward. He started clambering up to the bench, but fell, grabbing his leg.

"Goddamn it!" Spider jumped out of the wagon.

"No!" Odin rose, and started climbing again. "I still have plenty of fight in me! And I won't drive the cart into the goddamned wall if a fucking chicken flaps at me!"

Goddamn it, old man. "Climb up, then!"

Odin climbed up to the bench and grabbed the reins and whip. He urged the team forward with a crack of the latter.

The horses bolted, and Spider lunged at the back of the wagon. Ruth and Michael lifted him in.

Spider noticed his own leg had resumed bleeding, but not badly. His thigh stung.

"This is exciting," Daphne said through gleaming clenched teeth. Her smiled widened. "Someone might die!"

"Heads down!" Spider yelled as more guns erupted.

Mrs. Fitch, Michael and Ruth joined Spider in ducking low as the wagon rolled out of the barn, Odin shouting like a madman. Daphne and Hob, however, kept looking out the back.

"Hob, goddamn it! Get down!"

"I saw someone come out of the house!" The boy lifted the knife that Spider had given him.

"I don't care! Death is flying all around us, you fool!" Spider tugged at Hob's shirt and Daphne's nightgown.

Hob pulled away. "I am not afraid, Spider!"

"That is the trouble," Spider said as he fell backward. Daphne rolled off him. "That is always the trouble!"

Spider rose again, trying to grab Hob and pull him down as three men came running. Then the wagon lurched crazily as Odin guided it around the house.

"I should have grabbed that big gun, Spider! Get down!"

Spider fell back, but not before seeing Ambrose Oakes standing near the kitchen door, raising the massive blunderbuss from his sitting room.

The man was dangerously close.

Spider gasped. *That big gun will rip the hell out of this thin wood.*

"Goddamn it, Hob!"

Spider grabbed at the lad.

Hob threw the knife. "Tallyho!"

The gun thundered.

Hob's knife flew uselessly into the rising smoke.

Oakes had aimed too high, though, and the balls flew over their heads. Wood splintered and flew apart as though it was made of eggshell. Oakes staggered and toppled as the gun's vicious recoil slammed him.

The wagon jolted its way down the road, past the graves and toward the gate at a speed Spider thought surely would send the whole damned thing toppling. He'd ridden rough seas many times, but this was wholly new to him.

Guns fired behind them, and swords glinted in the sun. Looking back, Spider saw a small gray object arc toward the wagon.

"Fuck and bugger! Duck!"

The ball hit the ground a few yards behind the wagon and exploded in a flash of green and orange. A sound like a cannon boom caused the horses to lurch.

Odin shouted, "We should have found some of those!"

They sped down the hill, rocking madly and praying. Another blast erupted in the road behind them, and Spider closed his eyes against the spray of dirt.

"Shit," Hob said. "I remember those!"

Odin cried out. "The fucking gate is closed!"

"Stop the horses!" That was Ruth.

"I can't!"

Spider cursed. "It's a horrible old gate! Ram it! It'll fall apart!"

Spider pictured the gate in his mind: A weak latch, rotted wood, and bad hinges. It should shatter, he thought, if the horses charge through it.

Please, God, let it fall apart.

"Hold on!"

He was still wondering if the team was frightened enough to tear the gate asunder or if it would try to halt when he heard the monstrous crack of wood and saw splintered boards flying in the air. Spider bit his tongue when the wagon turned into the road and swiped one of the stone pillars at the gate.

"Goddamn! Ha!" Odin shouted, "Hold on, all. We're Lymington-bound!"

36

The horses ran at a headlong pace, and Spider worried that a wheel might have been cracked at the gate. "Get the horses under control, Odin!"

"They are in command, Spider! Ha! Hope they know the way!"

"They'll tire soon," Ruth said. "I hope!"

Michael nodded.

"We should have had Michael hold the reins," Mrs. Fitch said.

Michael nodded again.

"Too late for that," Spider said.

The horses did slow down once they were beyond range of the gunfire and once Odin stopped cursing at them like a madman. Spider inhaled deeply, and all the passengers caught their breath as the wagon slowly came to a full stop.

Daphne held out her hand to him. It was streaked with blood. "I was shot."

"What? Jesus." Spider looked her over and saw a red smear on her gown, just at the left elbow. He ripped the fabric away.

"Will I die?" Daphne whispered. "Will I finally know?"

"No, you won't die," Spider said. "You got scraped. It's already stopped bleeding. You will be fine, lass."

He could not tell if she was disappointed or merely stunned.

"It was the blunderbuss," she said, quietly. "I always wondered what it would sound like, what it would feel like, to shoot it."

She peered behind her, where the lead had blown a large hole in the wagon bed's cover. "It might have done that to me."

"It might have done that to all of us," Spider said, "if he'd aimed just a bit lower."

"Well, he didn't," Hob gasped. "And we all shall live long happy lives, at least for a few days. How did you ever find me, Spider?"

Spider started to rub the lad's head, then stopped at the sight of the bloody bandage there. He clasped Hob's shoulder instead. "Little Bob Higgins killed a man with the knife I gave you. The knife you just threw away. That started us on the trail, though."

"Little Bob! I hate Little Bob! Where is he? I'll kill him!"

"He's dead, Hobgoblin. Throat cut."

"Good!"

Spider agreed. "No one will miss him."

"Little Bob is shit."

"Aye."

"I'll miss the knife, but I am glad I threw it," Hob said. "Oakes deserved it, locking us up that way. I am damned glad that fat bastard is dead, Spider John. Damned glad."

"He probably lives, Hob. You missed him by a yard, at least, you goddamned fool of a dandiprat! Did I teach you to throw a blade when you can't see beyond your own whore-sniffing nose?"

Hob tried to laugh. "Sorry, Spider. Blurry as he was, Oakes is fat as a whale. I thought I could not miss."

"Well, you did. And you lost a good knife." Spider shook his own head at a memory. Ezra, the best friend Spider had ever had in the piratical life and now gone to whatever afterlife pirates go to, had always admonished Spider about throwing a good weapon during a fight. "You might find you need it again quick and can't get it back," Ezra had told him.

Now, here he was, berating Hob for the same thing. He wiped away a sudden tear and wished he could bring his own son's face to mind.

Then he remembered his own knife, thrown over Little Bob's head in a Lymington alley, and laughed.

"We all misjudge, Hob. We'll get us some new knives."

He glanced over the low wall, but no pursuit was coming. "I guess we won't need the knife just now, anyway," he said, shaking his head at Hob.

Spider turned toward the rest. "Hob may be useless, but you have skills, Missus Fitch. I know a nice lady in Lymington, the Widow Bonnymeade, who might appreciate help running a tavern called the Crosskeys. You and Michael might fit in nicely there. And me and Odin need to stop in there, anyway, to tell that nice lady some news. Justice is done."

"Thank you," Mrs. Fitch said, looking confused. "I still don't quite know what all this is about!"

"I'll explain, as best I understand it," Spider said. He climbed out and hung his hat on a nearby elm branch. He peered at the others through the jagged hole left by the massive blunderbuss. "God damn, what that would have done if it had hit one of us!"

He muttered a brief prayer. *Thank you, Lord, for the luck I do not deserve.* Then he clutched Em's pendant.

"I am going to give this wheel and axle a look, but listen while I sort all this out," Spider said.

"Michael, see that the horses are not hurt," Mrs. Fitch suggested. The giant climbed out of the wagon bed to comply.

"There was a lot of death at Pryor Pond," Spider continued. "A lot of it, I say, and I was not convinced men were just getting sick. Sick one at a time? It did not seem likely, and Gold Peter and Simon and Oakes never seemed worried they'd catch it. I've seen men jump off a ship rather than stay close to sick men dying. It just did not make sense to me."

He took a look toward the gate. No one was coming after them.

"There were other odd things, too. It took me a good while to figure it all out. That might be because my head was full of bad rum. Poisoned rum, actually."

Mrs. Fitch gasped. "Poisoned?"

Spider stared at her, giving her time to worry and fret, waiting to see what she'd do.

But she simply stared back at him.

"Aye. I reckoned you were killing those patients, Missus Fitch."

"Me!"

"Aye," Spider said. "I thought you felt bad for them, stuck mad in this life, and so you were sending them on to the next."

"Why on earth would you suppose such a thing?"

"You had a bottle locked away, and I snuck me some and got sick drinking from it. And Oakes thought you had taken a, what did he call it, a sedative, from him. So I thought you stole poison from him and put it in the bottle."

"I should thrash you," she said.

"Aye," he answered. "Probably. Devil likely will do that for you one day. Were you killing men?"

"I was not."

Spider said. "You went on so about how miserable the patients were, and how death might be a mercy."

"Master Oakes gave me those bottles, he did, and he told me which patients could have some. As for mercy, I do not get to decide such things, Spider John."

"Aye," Spider said. "That is a task best left to the Lord."

Mrs. Fitch clasped her hands in prayer.

"Horses fine," Michael said, clambering back up into the wagon.

Spider crawled under the wagon. "Hold the horses steady, Odin."

"They do what they want, Spider."

"Do what you can, old man." Once underneath where he could examine the axle, he continued. "Not everyone died by poison, though, did they? There was that Wilson boy in the village, and Raldo, the Spaniard. They both died by violence, not poison."

Mrs. Fitch shouted. "For the Lord's sake, man, I never leave the grounds and that Raldo died in the fight!"

"Well," Spider said, climbing out from beneath the wagon. "I did not suppose you did. You could not have killed the Wilson lad. And Raldo died by knife and I doubt you could take him in a fight, Missus Fitch. No, someone stronger and faster killed them, whatever else was going on with the poison."

Ruth pointed at Michael. "He is big, and very strong."

The giant seemed bewildered.

"Michael?" Mrs. Fitch turned to the farmhand. "Not possible!"

"You told me Michael kept sneaking off, Missus Fitch. Remember? And I saw you, Michael, come across the wall one day, sneaking about. You are a right powerful bastard, you are. That Wilson lad, Odin told me he was mangled something terrible. You would be just the man for that."

Michael looked puzzled, while Mrs. Fitch glowered.

"I told you I thought he had a girl nearby!"

Michael lowered his head and blushed.

"Aye, you told me that. But I wondered if maybe you were just making excuses for him. Maybe you really thought he'd gone off killing. And maybe that was somehow tied to the poisonings—it just does not seem likely they were not tangled up together, somehow— and maybe you and Michael were working together."

Michael shook his head slowly. His lips formed the word "no," but without sound.

"No," Spider said. "You really did just have a girl, like Missus Fitch said, didn't you?"

The big man shrugged.

"So that left me wondering for some way to knot up the Wilson death with the poisonings, and I just could not see why you, Missus Fitch, would be connected to both. The Wilson boy was not killed to put him out of any misery, not that I heard. He was guarding his village because young men had vanished, and he paid with his life. I still reckoned that was connected to the patient deaths somehow, but I could not connect you to both. And I could not figure any way Michael might be tied to the patient deaths. So I had to look elsewhere for the killer."

"Or killers!" Hob's eyebrows arched. "Maybe there was more than one!"

"It occurred to me," Spider said.

Hob nodded. "You mentioned Raldo, too. I heard that name before. Was his death knotted up with the others, too?"

"Aye," Spider said. "Raldo. That death was not at the hands of Ambrose Oakes. Was it, Ruth Copper?"

"What?" She blinked.

"I found Raldo dead during the fight, but he was already cold and so I knew he'd been killed earlier. I supposed Half-Jim maybe killed him, because there was a bad feeling between those two. I noticed that more than once."

Spider reclaimed his hat, shook an errant leaf from it, and plopped it back on his head. "But then I thought it probably wasn't Half-Jim. Raldo got stabbed in the back of the head, a hard place for Jim to get to on his crutches and all and him being the type to come at a man head-on. But someone hugging Raldo, up close, might easily shove a knife up and into his brain, aye?"

Ruth stared. "I had nothing to do with Raldo."

"Not willingly, perhaps." Spider walked about as he thought out loud. "He was killed during the day, between the house and the south wall, where you normally patrol during the day watch. And he had a bit of blood around his mouth, and you have a bite or a cut on your lips that was not there when you tried to pull down my pants. Did Raldo kiss you, and maybe he got rough?"

"Lord," Mrs. Fitch muttered. "This is all too much."

"It is exciting!" Daphne leaned forward and clapped her hands, seeming to have forgotten her recent close call with death. Spider was happy to note the rapid movement did not cause the bleeding to start again. Daphne smiled broadly. "I have never had such a day as this! Never!"

Spider nodded. "Aye, we've made a full cargo of corpses in this place, for certain. Anyway, I am guessing Raldo came looking for you, Ruth, and tried to pay you more attention than you wanted."

"Spider John, I . . ."

"Jim mentioned the gentlemen sniffing after you and warned me off of doing the same," Spider said. "Raldo came looking for you, tried something you did not like, and you snuck a knife behind his head and killed him. Do I have it reckoned well enough?"

"Ooooooh," Daphne cooed.

"You are making wild guesses," Ruth said, coldly.

Spider reached into the brim of his hat and pulled free the scrap of cloth he'd tucked there after the skirmish with Anne Bonny's buccaneers. "You had a torn blouse after the night fight. This little scrap seems to be the same color and cloth," he said. "I pulled this from Raldo's dead hand."

She touched her shoulder, then blew out her breath. "There is no rip in my blouse."

"You wear a different garment now," Spider said. "But you did not remember that fact when you reached for your shoulder, did you? And I did not mention your shoulder just now, by and by, but that's exactly where I saw the rip when I was tied up in that damned laboratory."

Ruth's shoulders sagged.

"You only carry two knives now," Spider continued. "You used to carry three. I am betting you left one in Raldo's skull."

She squirmed. "You . . . you pulled cloth from a dead man's hand? And counted my knives?"

"He does things like that," Hob spoke up. "A great one for puzzles, is Spider John. They itch his brain, he says, and he has to figure them out."

"Aye," Spider said. "Raldo's death by knife, with the corpse left on the ground and all, did not fit in with the deaths from upstairs, or the death in the village. So I thought it a separate matter—matter, I say, not a crime. Maybe he deserved it. I am not a judge, for certain. But you killed Raldo, didn't you?"

She nodded, defiantly. "I choose my lovers, and I choose who to decline. Not him. I choose."

Spider nodded. "No one here is going to mourn for Raldo, I think."

Daphne clapped her hands and leaned toward Ruth. "What was it like? Stabbing him? While kissing him?"

Ruth looked disgusted. "What goes on in that mind of yours?"

"Oh, you all speak so casually of death and murder!" Mrs. Fitch covered her face. "It is all too much!"

"So, we'll call the mystery of Raldo's death solved," Spider mused.

"But we still have the others to ponder. One of them is this, Ruth. Were you trying to tell me something when I was on that goddamned table, with the goddamned bird ready to swoop onto me?"

"Only that Fawkes was aware someone was following him, and I knew it was Odin, so I thought I would tell you that your friend was in peril. But I had no chance."

"Aye," Spider said. "Thank you. Now, just what were you up to in the sitting room when . . ."

"I just wanted to know what you were up to," she said, though she averted her eyes. "I knew you had a secret, Spider John. You are always sneaking about and noticing things. I knew you had some motive for coming to Pryor Pond."

"You weren't spying for Fawkes?"

"No."

"Or for Oakes?"

"No. I had no reason or purpose for what I did, other than to learn what you were really trying to do."

Spider grinned. "How did you select that particular method?"

She smiled briefly. "Because it works. It certainly worked on you, Spider John."

Their gazes locked on one another for several heartbeats, and Spider felt a stirring

Forgive me, Em.

Hob paid particular attention to the whole exchange, Spider noticed, and the lad moved a little closer to Ruth.

"Aye, then," Spider said, "that little mystery solved, let's consider the big one. Who killed all the people in those graves? I think I have it sorted out."

"I was not involved, nor was Michael."

"Perhaps not, Missus Fitch," Spider replied. "I cannot prove so one way or another, anyway, but it does not matter, I reckon. As I said, I am not a judge. I still like to reckon it all out, though, if I can."

"So who killed them, then?" Hob rubbed his hands together. "Was it Fawkes? I did not like that son of a whore."

"It was not Fawkes," Spider said, "although he brought the poor bastards to the killer. The killer was Ambrose Oakes."

Mrs. Fitch was aghast. "The man who fought so to keep the patients alive? I've seen him stay up through the night, battling for them!"

"He fought to keep them alive long enough, you mean." Spider stopped pacing. "He wasn't trying to wave death angels away. He was showing them their prey."

Hob scrunched up his nose. "What do you mean?"

"I mean," Spider said, "that Ambrose Oakes needed to know right when his patients would die, so he could be there with them when they expired. And once they were in the throes, so to speak, he was willing to stay with them until that very final breath."

"What?" That came from Ruth.

"The master of Pryor Pond thought he could thwart the Lord's will." Spider held his hands out, palms upraised. "He called himself a delver into forbidden knowledge, or something like that."

Hob looked puzzled. "How?"

"The master convinced himself he could conquer death, by trapping a man's soul in a bottle at the last breath. Maybe he thought he could store the soul, heal the mangled body, and somehow put the soul back later. It was some plan like that."

Mrs. Fitch clasped her hands and closed her eyes in prayer. Ruth shook her head slowly. Michael stared at him.

"That is not possible," Ruth said. "Could he really catch souls? Could anyone?"

"I do not know," Spider said. "But Oakes sure to hell thought that he could, and he didn't care much how many times he had to try before he did. I saw the whole thing when he cut off that man's leg. He had hoses, jars, clamps, all set to trap that soul when it fled. He collected some blood, too, just in case the soul was in that. He told me all about it. Well, he did not admit to killing them, but he did kill them. I am certain of it."

"That is monstrous," Mrs. Fitch muttered.

"Aye." Spider scratched his chin. "But he could not force himself to wait for chance. You can't expect luck to hand you dying men at convenient times, not if you have to have a lot of gear rigged up and so on, so he took to killing young men. Slowly, so he could control it, like a cap'n being set for a change of wind."

"Lord," Ruth said. Daphne leaned forward, eyes widening along with her smile.

"So," Spider continued. "He took to killing men, young strong ones because he thought those souls might be best, might be strong enough to survive in a goddamned bottle. Do you remember, Odin, when we signed on? Oakes said he might have a use for me—the young one, he said—even if we were spies."

"Aye," Odin said.

"That's what he meant, that he might try to harvest my soul."

"Ha! He'd have to wrestle the devil for that!"

"Aye," Spider said. "So he killed men to grab their souls. But he's a fat coward and he needed to time things proper, so he used poison instead of a knife or a flintlock. That way, he could be standing ready when the poor bastards expired."

Mrs. Fitch shuddered. "So, he hired Fawkes and these brigands to go out and snatch other brigands so he could kill them?"

"Aye," Spider said.

"Why not just kill Fawkes and his men?"

"That would spark mutiny, and Oakes worried about that. You can't hire men and kill them one by one. They'll fight back. Little Bob and the rest of that lot who came swarming over the fence in the dark proved that, didn't they? Pirates, they will take care of their mates, they will, but you can pay them to go rough on some other bastards, and that is just business to them."

Spider resumed pacing. "I think Oakes sent his hired pirates to the village first, to grab young men there. I think that may be why he hired Half-Jim, to get him some subjects for this damnable business. He did not want to kill his patients, right? Families paid for their care. It would have been like tossing money overboard."

Spider sighed. "Capturing people in the night tends to cause a ruckus, though, so Oakes took another tack. Probably it was Jim's thinking on this, because Half-Jim knew the sweet trade and smuggling and all that. It would not have been too much trouble for him to find Tom Bonnymeade, who knew all the smugglers and all the merchants in Lymington, and arrange the ambush on your gents, Hob."

"I'll be damned," Hob said. "They hit us hard and fast, too. They were already hiding when we came ashore!"

"Aye," Spider said.

"Your Aggie said Tom was a fair dealer, too smart to turn against his blokes," Odin yelled from the wagon bench.

"He wasn't turning on his own people, remember." Spider shook road dust from his hands. "He was just turning on Bonny's crew. And she was off somewhere far away, but Half-Jim was right here close, with guns and knives. I do not think it would have taken much for Tom Bonnymeade to strike a bargain with a fellow as persuasive as Half-Jim Fawkes. Bonnymeade probably reckoned it was better to piss off a cap'n across the sea than an evil old salt right in front of him."

"Monsters," Mrs. Fitch muttered. "Monsters!"

"Aye," Spider said. "Anyway, they thought to find some smugglers and take them off-guard. They would be the perfect fellows for what Oakes had in mind. Aye? It wasn't the same as capturing men in town. No one was likely to notice some pirates who go missing."

Odin cackled. "Except their shipmates, by thunder!"

Spider nodded. "Pirates form strong bonds, sometimes. Little Bob and the rest thought to at least avenge their shipmates."

"All the shooting and yelling I heard," Hob said.

"Aye." Spider continued.

Spider felt the wooden wheel, trusting his fingers to confirm what his eyes told him. "I will be honest. I do not rightly know who in the house helped Oakes and knew what he was doing, and who didn't. I don't rightly care, either. I just wanted to find Hob."

"And you did," the lad said.

"We just went to where all the goddamned trouble was, and that is where you were. Ha!"

"Aye, Odin. It was a fine plan. Wheel and axle seem fine, don't know how. That was a mighty thump you gave us."

"The goddamned horses did it!" Odin yelled.

"My God. My God. My God."

"We'll get you away from all this, Missus Fitch," Spider assured her. "The wagon seems shipshape, which is a damned good thing because I haven't got any bloody tools, have I?"

Spider longed for a stiff drink and a full pipe. "Ruth, my friends and I plan to find a ship bound for the colonies. Do you want to sail with us?"

"You'll not tell the authorities about Raldo?"

"No," Spider said. "We have absolutely no intents to speak with no authorities."

"None at all," Hob said. "The sea for us!"

Spider gave Hob a stern look before returning his attention to Ruth. "Sail with us."

Sail with me, he meant.

She considered that. "Possibly, I may. You stand by your friends, Spider John, come what may, and it seems they stand by you. I am not accustomed to that. Maybe you and I can be friends, too."

Hob's eyebrows rose at that, and his gaze settled on Ruth. Spider reckoned the lad was trying to figure a way to get the weather gauge on her, and that theory was quickly confirmed. "Spider's got a woman, and a child, in Nantucket," Hob said. "He loves them both very much."

Aye, lad, Spider thought. *Woo her, if you will. I should not pay her too much attention. I'm going home to Em. If she is still there, waiting.*

"Well," Ruth said, without a hint of disappointment, "That is a fine thing. And I would not mind a voyage to the colonies. I have family in Virginia."

"It is settled, then," Spider said.

"Not many ships will take a woman, though, not as crew. And I have no means to pay for passage."

"Nor do we, but we might find a way," Spider said. "We learned a few tricks from the notorious Anne Bonny."

He walked up front. Odin was breathing hard and clutching at his knee.

"Are you hurt, Odin?"

"Leg hurts like hell, I was shoving my foot against the board trying not to fly off when we rolled down that fucking road! I hate horses! I hate them! They did not pay a damned bit of attention to any fucking thing I told them! And I don't know why I let you drag me all around after Hob. And you owe me three bottles of rum, Spider John! Hell, four bottles! And you owe me at least as much, Hob, goddamn you!"

"I owe you for coming to rescue me, certain," Hob yelled back. "And I pay my debts, Odin. You know that, so goddamn you, old man!"

Spider laughed. "Well, seems we are on familiar waters, snarling at each other and all that." He wandered back toward the rear of the wagon and peered through the blunderbuss hole. "All this rum talk, though, reminds me of a thing that just nags me. I have question for you, Miss Daphne."

She smiled. "I shall answer truly, sir! I no longer lie, though my family doubts that, I am sure. But I wish to be your friend, like Ruth, and I want to sail away with you, too, so ask me your question!"

Spider looked her directly in the eyes. "Girl, did you know there was poison in those special bottles of rum, the ones set aside for the patients?"

Daphne giggled. "It was our little secret, mine and the master's!"

Spider shook his head slowly. "Good lord, what in the bloody hell are we going to do with you?"

THE END

Historical Notes

While genuine pirates Anne Bonny and Ned Low figured strongly in the plot of this book's predecessor, *The Devil's Wind*, Half-Jim Fawkes and his crewmen are entirely fictional. So are Ambrose Oakes, Ruth Copper, the Bonnymeades, Daphne and all the rest.

Lymington, however, is a real English city that notes a real smuggling past.

Of the two chantey snippets presented in this novel, the one in Chapter 13 about sailing "beyond the lowering sun" is my own, but the one in Chapter 23 is a real song that was popular in colonial America. Variations are found with the titles "The Bold Soldier" and "The Valiant Soldier." There is a lot of gunplay and swordplay to be found in those old songs, by thunder. I first ran into this tune at Contemplator. com, where brief audio clips of very old songs can be enjoyed. The bouncy, lively tunes with lurid, violent lyrics pair well with bourbon or thick, dark beer.

Afterword

I hope you've enjoyed reading these Spider John stories as much as I've enjoyed writing them. It is hard for me to believe this is the third one already.

I still recall the day I looked at Deven Atkinson, singer for the garage band that puts up with my bass playing, and said, "I have an idea: Pirate murder mystery!" The look in his eyes told me I was, indeed, on to something.

It was a weird, untried idea, though, and I never would have brought it together without a great crew. There are many, many people I need to thank for helping me bring these stories of Spider John Rush and his piratical friends to life.

My agent, Evan Marshall, saw potential in these tales and decided to help me find a publisher. He also provides great editorial advice and helps me navigate the uncertain waters of the publishing business. Thank you, Evan.

Dan Mayer has the editorial helm at Seventh Street Books, and has saved me from one or two excesses in the course of writing these novels. I can get carried away, and Dan reins me in (but not *too* much). I am thankful for that, too. Thank you, Dan.

I need to thank many, many writers out there who have welcomed me into the fold and inspired me with their own works. There are too many of them to mention them all here, but a few have gone above and beyond in their support: Andrew Welsh-Huggins, Susan Spann, Lori Rader-Day, Nicholas Guild, and Mark Pryor (for whom Pryor Pond in this book is named, as I attempt to repay a debt. If you have not read his Hugo Marston novels, I really think you should.). I'll sail with any of you. Thank you.

Friends, too, have propped me up and listened to my thinking out loud. Tom Williams and Ty Johnston have provided inspiration, and I doubt these stories would have come to fruition had it not been for our many, many discussions of adventure fiction over the years. It is such a joy to know people who read the same kind of books you read. Thank you, gentlemen and comrades in arms.

My kid, Rowan, fills me with love and always appreciates a good adventure. Ro won't let me use the Xbox, but otherwise the kid is always in my corner and is quite proud of Dad. Thank you, Rowan.

Most of all, though, I thank Gere. My lovely bride puts up with much. She listens to my plot problems, reads my rough drafts, suggests improvements and makes sure I have time to write. More than that, she believed I could do this before I believed it myself. Thanks, beloved.

And thank you, readers, especially those of you who come to say hello at book events or send me kind words on social media. You make the tired eyes and hair-pulling and chair-sitting all worthwhile. I hope this latest adventure entices you to come along for the next one, and that we get to share many, many more.

About The Author

*S*teve Goble is the author of *The Bloody Black Flag* and *The Devil's Wind*, the first two Spider John mysteries. A former journalist, Goble now works for a cyber-security and digital investigations firm. He lives in rural Ohio.

Author photo by Jason J. Molyet